Martin Griffin is an exciting new voice in the crime genre. His debut novel, *The Second Stranger*, was published in 2023. Before turning his hand to writing, he was a deputy headteacher and a doomed singer who was once asked to support The Fall on tour, a gig he had to decline having only composed two good songs. Martin lives in Manchester with his wife and daughter.

GW00502635

Also by Martin Griffin

The Second Stranger

THE
LAST
VISITOR

MARTIN GRIFFIN

SPHERE

SPHERE

First published in Great Britain in 2024 by Sphere
This paperback edition published in 2024 by Sphere

1 3 5 7 9 10 8 6 4 2

Copyright © Martin Griffin 2024

A CIP catalogue record for this book
is available from the British Library.

ISBN 978-1-4087-2529-0

Typeset in Bembo by M Rules
Printed and bound in Great Britain by
Clays Ltd, Elcograf S.p.A.

Papers used by Sphere are from well-managed forests
and other responsible sources.

Sphere
An imprint of
Little, Brown Book Group
Carmelite House
50 Victoria Embankment
London EC4Y 0DZ

An Hachette UK Company
www.hachette.co.uk

www.littlebrown.co.uk

For Jo

Prologue

Your partner's out in the darkness filming, and she's left her phone in the car with you.

You're taking a break, resting your eyes and stretching your legs, when its light snags your attention. She skimmed it screen-down across the dashboard as she left, and you can see its edges glow as an alert arrives. Your laptop's on your knees, the heater's on and you've been checking over a recently finished sequence, headphones in as you assess your footage. But now, you set your equipment aside.

You've been concerned about her for weeks.

There's been nothing concrete, but the strengthening of unease into suspicion has been as real as an approaching cloudbank threatening rain. When you began making the documentary together a year ago, she'd been in awe of you – gaze studious and brow furrowed, she'd memorise every throwaway observation you'd made as if it were gospel. And she'd shared everything; rough cuts and rushes were passed back and forth, ideas were exchanged freely, trust was unconditional. That's why you know the passcode to her phone.

You lean across the driver's seat, flick the wipers on. With an arc of glittering raindrops swept aside, you can see the hire-car headlights illuminating the black ribbon of the lane and the chain-link security fence. The inkblot shadows of trees stand beyond. The silhouette of the abandoned terminal squats against the night sky. She's behind those fences somewhere. No sign of her emerging yet.

It'll only take a minute to check. You swipe her phone awake and key in the passcode.

There's a text message. It's from an unknown number, and it's only a few words long, but if ten years in investigative journalism have trained you for anything, it's knowing when you're being lied to. This – right here before your eyes – is confirmation of her betrayal. Fear stirs as the implications surface. She's done some sort of deal. Cut you out. Scalp tightening, you shut your laptop, bagging your stuff with trembling hands. *Drive away while there's still time.* You jink yourself awkwardly behind the steering wheel and grope for the ignition key in the dark.

It's missing.

She drove you out here, weaving along empty marshland tracks while you worked. She's still got the key. The fear within grows from fingers to fists, a pair of them gripping your gut. The nearest village is eight kilometres back. It's got to be ten minutes' drive to the nearest streetlight. You take a calming breath – in for four, hold, out for four – and just as you're beginning to wonder if you're over-reacting, a pair of headlights blink into life in the blackness ahead. No reason why anyone might be out here in the dead of night unless . . . a cold shaft opens in your stomach.

This is very bad.

You can't be caught sitting here. You slip out, knees weak, breath billowing, shoulder your bag and touch the car door shut as silently as you can. *Think*. The woodland beyond the fence would give you cover, but heading in the direction of the terminal takes you closer to her – and she's betrayed you. All around, there's nothing but flooded fields, the track you drove in on raised above dark drainage ditches. Your visitors are closing, headlights bobbing as the vehicle rides the rutted laneway. You'd bet anything there's three or four of them in there – tough guys like the ones you ran into in California.

Somewhere distant, you wonder if that's the sea you can hear, and a mad plan blazes into life. Slither through the sodden crops, cross the marsh to the coast, then follow the beach back to civilisation.

It's not great, but it's all you've got.

You back away, using the hire car as cover, and break into a run.

What have you done to me, Tess? you think as you flee. You don't know it yet – though you're beginning to suspect it as the lights draw closer – but these thoughts will be among your last. *Christ, Tess. What have you done to me?*

What have you done?

1

In my line of work, some jobs take a long time to secure. Other requests, though, appear out of nowhere. Here's what I've learnt after ten years in this business: speedy doesn't always mean good. Take the gig that falls into your lap from nowhere and it often means trouble.

These were the concerns I was pondering when I was approached by Seawild.

They were big fans of me – or so they said in their pitch – and wanted an immediate online meeting to discuss an exciting project. I'd set up my one-woman operation, Pocket Films, eight years ago, and worked out of a converted shipping container in Canning Town, the cheapest rental I could find. I had just enough room for a desk and laptop, a few framed stills on the walls and a collection of trinkets; reminders of the days when I'd won awards. Pocket Films had found its niche delivering nature docs; short films for charity websites, fundraisers for environmental non-profits and TV montage pieces, but it hadn't started out that way.

I'd once been the UK's most promising young film-maker. Acclaimed, even. But bad things had happened on that first, career-making project. After *Spill*, I couldn't pick up a camera for two years. When I finally did – and after much persuasion – I was nothing like the woman I'd been; instead, I found I'd become someone to avoid, a walking cautionary tale about the dangers of a star ascending too quickly. I didn't have the strength for investigative journalism any more. I had to put those days behind me.

On that level, at least, the Seawild job made total sense.

Their website told me they were a marine research foundation with contracts for protecting biodiversity and Pacific coral reefs. A landing-page banner celebrated their most recent success – *We are delighted to announce the acquisition of the management contract for the Ilhas Desertas!* A quick search told me the Desertas were four islands in the Atlantic; an isolated chain two hours off the coast of Madeira, uninhabited except for protected populations of monk seals. The website's '*work with us*' tab confirmed Seawild were indeed looking for a *creative, talented and experienced videographer with a proven track record of successful campaigns and documentary interviews.*

I fitted the bill. Nevertheless, it was odd they'd emailed me directly.

They must have had hundreds of applications. Maybe they'd already chosen their successful bid, only to have them drop out. Maybe they were casting about for a quick replacement and mine was one of a number of speculative emails they'd sent.

Or maybe, I told myself, they just worked quickly and knew exactly who they wanted.

There was only one way to find out.

The first face to appear on my laptop for the Zoom call next afternoon was one I recognised from Seawild's Directors and Trustees page. Leo Bodin was handsome; early-forties, wiry and energetic, a dark-haired Parisian sitting in a book-lined office, wearing a striped shirt and blazer.

He introduced himself, mechanically smoothing his tie. 'Director of Operations, Paris,' he said, his English lightly accented. 'Great to have a moment to sit down with you. In a second we'll be joined by Alex and we'll be able to ... ah, here she is.'

The second face was different; weather-beaten and sheened with sweat, it belonged to a woman with cropped blonde hair worn under a bandana. She froze on her elbows, steepled fingernails painted yellow, before her feed caught up and she waved at us. 'Hi! I'm Dr Alex Dahlberg. Hi Leo, how are you? And it's Tess, isn't it?'

'Tess Macfarlane,' I confirmed. 'Pocket Films.'

Leo began by talking me through Seawild's work. 'We're passionate about protecting the Ilhas Desertas, managing them properly,' he said. 'The Portuguese government wanted to open them up, have hundreds of people visiting a year.' He shook his head, disgusted. 'Crazy idea. During our handover, they had reported a colony of over forty seals,' he explained. 'But when we sent our first team out to study them it became clear there had been serious miscounting. We're estimating perhaps only twenty. It's Navigaceo that looks most promising.'

I'd done my research. 'Navigaceo,' I said. 'That's the last of the four islands. The furthest out.'

'Correct.' Leo counted them off on his fingers. 'Chao, Deserta Grande, Bugio, all in close proximity. Then a gap of ten kilometres, then Navigaceo.'

'And your website says no one's set foot on the last island for over fifty years?'

'Correct,' Alex put in, her accent a strange hybrid of London, Lisbon and Bergen. 'The permits out here are very strictly managed. Navigaceo hasn't been visited since its redesignation in nineteen seventy-one.' She grinned. 'We get to be the first!'

'Half a century untouched.' I smiled back.

'The film is my boss's idea,' Leo put in. 'He wants a full report covering the breeding grounds and population density of the monk seals and a mini-documentary for the website. Lots of visual evidence that supports our policy of continued closure,' he said. 'The island is special, the seal population fragile. We can't allow tourist boats.'

'Sounds like the kind of work I'm used to delivering,' I said. I shared my screen and took them through my showreel, my recent work for The Rivers Trust, and a piece I'd just finished for an Italian rewilding project. There were lots of smiles and a few follow-up questions.

'Some practicalities,' Leo said once I was finished. 'There's very limited internet coverage out on the islands, very little phone signal. And, as you know, Navigaceo is completely deserted, so there are challenges there.'

'I can cope.'

Leo made notes on a document out of shot then returned his gaze to me. 'Great. So, I know it's a quick turnaround, but if you're interested, we'd want you to fly out to Madeira tomorrow evening.'

The speed of the offer was unexpected, and a gentle pulse of unease stirred in me. They were unusually keen. I smiled politely, my nerves on edge, and tried some light-hearted comment that made the two of them laugh. Thing was, I needed the work.

An hour later I got the confirmation by email.

They were standing by, ready to send through tickets. The fee they were offering was twice what I'd have quoted, and the job advert, I noticed, had been pulled from the website. Though it was surely impossible to refuse now, I didn't answer immediately. Instead, I took the rest of the afternoon tidying my office, drawing up a packing list and locking up, all the while replaying the interview in my head, listening for alarm bells.

I'm pretty sure they were there, ringing distantly, but I couldn't find a reason to say no.

2

It was getting dark outside when I finally left the office, wharf-lights gleaming, the sky over the warehouses caught between apricot and blue.

I turned right along Orchard Place and headed for the bus stop outside Switch House. Just beyond the Whale Oil billboard, a thirties mural in peeling paint on industrial brickwork, there was a patch of waste ground home to a forest of head-height undergrowth and a rotting shipbuilder's warehouse. There was never anyone around, especially on a Friday night.

Except this time there was.

A middle-aged man in a windcheater with a thick grey beard photographed me.

Even above the grumble of the traffic on the East India Dock Road, I heard the click of the shutter as I passed. I looked back. He was examining the camera – a digital SLR – as if he didn't know how to use it. I turned again. He had the lens pointed at the street and was peering down the viewfinder like a novice. A Waitrose delivery van hissed past, bringing with it a sudden sense of normality.

I'd forgotten about him by the time I'd toiled over to the bus stop.

Except then I saw the man again, and this time he was on the bus with me.

He'd chosen a spot five or six rows behind. An aisle-seat next to a woman sleeping with her head tipped against the steamed-up window. Once more his attention was absorbed by his camera and I couldn't see his face beyond the beard. Making *Spill*, my partner Gretchen and I had spent a year investigating oil companies who considered tailing filmmakers standard practice. My senses had been so permanently heightened by the terrible experience that even now, ten years later, the man with the camera didn't feel like a coincidence. I decided to switch buses. I could jump off at Billingsgate Market, cross the road by the bridge and pick up the DLR at Poplar.

If he followed, I'd know for sure.

I waited until the last minute before rising from my seat. Outside I moved quickly. The road's impossible to cross – four lanes of traffic hemmed in by railings – but ahead, stairs rose to a covered walkway that took me over to the station. Pavement crowds heaved; bodies in autumn coats, swaying umbrellas, puddle-splashed office shoes and shopping bags. Safe in the surge, I made my way up the walkway stairs without looking back. I'd tuck myself into a nook on the station platform and check again then.

Crossing the glass tube of the bridge, my phone vibrated in my coat pocket.

I pulled it out, glad of the opportunity to talk. 'Hi. I'm afraid I'm away from the office at the moment. If you want to discuss a commission . . .'

'Am I speaking to Tess Macfarlane?'

'You are.'

'DCI Rafiq, Metropolitan Police.' The voice was female, the phrases rehearsed. 'I'm calling to arrange an interview. It's in relation to the Gretchen Harris case? I'm the new lead officer and we're re-examining events. We'd like to speak again with certain persons of interest.'

My stomach began a shuddering descent. Somehow, I forced myself to keep walking. 'I'm sorry?'

'We contacted those involved to say we'd be getting in touch. You did receive the letter?'

'I did.' It had come to the office two weeks ago. I'd skimmed it once then binned it. Ever since, I'd been engaging in that most tragic of magical thinking: total denial.

'I'd like to discuss a time that's good for you.'

'I'm about to go away,' I said, reaching the platform on shaking legs, snaking through the crowds onto the westbound side. 'Flying tomorrow evening. I've still got lots to arrange.'

'May I ask where and for how long?'

I steadied my voice, gave her the details and then said, 'Look. I went over everything with the officer in charge ten years ago. I'm not sure I'm going to be able to add anything helpful.'

'Actually, you'd be surprised,' DCI Rafiq said carefully. 'Repeat interviews often yield new and valuable insights. So, you're back in the UK late on the Thursday . . . ' I heard fingers skating keys. 'How about we put you in for the Friday morning at nine? Can you make your way to Brixton Police Station for that time?'

What could I do but agree? I ended the call, and put my phone away with trembling hands. Though I'd rehearsed endlessly a decade ago, I couldn't remember a word of the story I'd told. Would they ask me to retell it, then cross-check it against my previous account? Surely if they tried that they'd expect two vastly differing versions; no one can remember precise details for years at a time, even for traumatic events. I ran a hand across my brow. A lock of hair was plastered to my forehead so I tucked it back behand an ear, calming myself. Maybe this whole thing was just routine and I'd be in-and-out in an hour.

I managed to refocus, found a bench with a view of the crowds, and watched people pass. No sign of the guy with the camera. Except – a thought flared with bright certainty, its truth almost physical – the man following me and Rafiq's phone call could be connected. What if my pursuer had been a police officer, plain-clothed and disguised, keeping an eye on my movements? I studied the throng, feeling a sudden, sharp note of envy for the blameless lives of those around me.

Get home, I told myself. Say yes to Seawild, pack your bags and catch your plane. Leave everything behind, if only for a week. Concentrate on the project – the beauty of those tropical island landscapes, the stories of the re-search team, the seal colony.

I worked my way into the crowd again, jumped on the next train. I'd ride as far as Limehouse, then have a re-think. Standing room only as usual. With the doors safely shut behind me, I released a breath. We pulled out of the station.

One of the last things I saw as the platform spooled away was the bearded man with the camera, scanning the crowds.

The next evening, my flight out to Funchal was delayed by fog.

Cradling my equipment, still jittery about my stalker, I spent my Saturday night trying to sleep on the chairs in Heathrow's departure lounge. Though I'd dreamt about Gretchen Harris regularly in the months after our time together on *Spill*, I hadn't for over a year. The call from DCI Rafiq must have primed my subconscious, though – during a rare spell of sleep, my old mentor put in a disturbing appearance.

At first, I thought I'd woken.

My neck ached as I swung my legs to the floor, my feet felt hot in my trainers. Gretchen was sitting opposite me, her back to a vending machine, wearing heeled boots and jeans under a belted raincoat. Her sunglasses were up on her head, as usual. When she spoke, her voice was sticky and distant, filtered through the silt of years. She said, 'You were calling but I couldn't reach my phone.'

I felt the working of my throat as I tried to reply but my tongue was fused to the back of my teeth.

Gretchen was dark and blurry but I could make out her eyes – she always had such a piercing gaze – and those loose curls framing her face. 'I saw you from the ditch,' she said. 'You were up on the road.'

My second attempt at speech was as breathless as my first.

'You were calling,' Gretchen said. 'But I couldn't reach my phone.'

I coughed some obstruction clear and managed to make my voice work. 'Let's talk about something else.'

'You were up on the road in the rain.'

'Gretchen,' I said. 'Let's talk about something else.'

She pouted, twisting her fingers together. By some curious dream-logic, her hands were now wet. Clothes too. Her face collapsed and I thought she might cry.

'Hey,' I said gently. 'Let's talk about something else. How have you been?'

She mastered herself, her expression losing its vulnerability. I watched her cool, then harden. 'Oh, you know,' she said, and pointed at her legs. 'The usual.'

3

The following day, Madeira's arrivals lounge was heaving. I helped an elderly Portuguese woman with her suitcase, waited with her until she'd located her husband, then headed for the exit.

In passport control, a woman with acrylic fingernails nodded at my documents, and outside, a queue of drivers held up tablets with typed names. Mine turned out to be a young guy wearing a Ramones t-shirt and open-toed sandals. He led me out into a wall of boiling air and opened the boot of a lemon-yellow Mercedes queued up beneath a row of palm trees.

'Funchal, yes?' he asked as I climbed in. I gave him the name of the hostel and he nodded through the rear-view as we queued to the exit barriers. 'Holiday?'

'No, working. I'm making a film.'

I watched landscaped lawns punctuated by palm trees and cacti; outcrops of volcanic rock, a whirl of gulls. The sky was a strong pale blue and cloudless. A shiver of excitement passed through me. There'd be very little in the way of luxury out on the Ilhas Desertas – it'd be tents and camping rolls, tinned food and long days – but at least it meant I could ignore what waited for me back in the UK.

'Casablanca, nine hundred kilometres that way,' my driver was telling me. 'Gran Canaria, that's five hundred in that direction.' A thumb over his shoulder as he pulled out to overtake a truck on the ER101, Madeira's only motorway. The steep green inland hills to our right were studded with houses. Impressions of the island blurred past: billboards outside a town called Santa Cruz; a fountain throwing rainbows of spray. We bridged a steep-sided canyon that made my stomach lurch, then plunged into a tunnel. 'And Lisbon a thousand this way. You are filming the festival in Funchal? Sugar cane festival? Cakes, wine.'

'No. I'm going out to the Desertas.' I couldn't see the distant archipelago just yet, but they were a permanent smudge on the horizon, the guidebook said.

There was a prolonged pause, and he raised his eyebrows. 'Ilhas Desertas? You're crazy.'

I met his gaze in the rear-view. 'Why?'

'Lonely places, haunted places,' he said as he drove. 'Out there is nothing. Like a row of knives, yes? Just rocks and a lighthouse, that's it. Many bad things happen to the men who stay there ... '

'Sounds great,' I said, deadpan.

'But you film the seals, yes?' he asked, brightening. 'Beautiful creatures. Here we say *lobo do mar.* Wolf of the sea.' And he grinned, howling in demonstration as we drove over a white-winged suspension bridge, Funchal tumbling down to the water's edge below us.

Outside the bus station, the seafront festooned with festival bunting, my driver lifted my rucksack from the boot and pinned me with a stern, paternal gaze. 'It's not a holiday out there,' he said. 'Difficult water. A long way from safety. And in festival week, harder for people to come and get you. You be careful.'

'Don't worry,' I said with a smile. 'It'll be fine. I'm with an experienced team.'

I found my hostel, showered, changed my clothes, then took the camera out to collect some footage of the city.

I shot the cable-car station on the seafront, its swinging cabins rattling as they began the long climb over the rooftops to a mountain garden; I got tourist tuk-tuks weaving through traffic, food vans serving churros, skateboarders vaping in the shade of palm trees. When Alex messaged early evening to suggest I meet the team in a bar in the old town, I texted my agreement and followed her dropped pin to Revolucion, a two-storey cocktails-and-tapas place.

The sun was low over Funchal's harbour by the time I arrived. The busy backstreets were still warm and the bar's packed tables spilled out onto the cobbles. The place smelled of garlic and grilled sardines. Serving staff carried salt-rimmed cocktail glasses and bowls of olives.

I spotted Alex waving me over.

'Tess! So nice to meet in real life!' Her cropped hair was streaked with early grey; her glasses gold circles. She indicated a tumbler of juice. 'I got you a Poncha. Rum, raw sugar, honey and oranges. Classic drink of Madeira, a bit of a tradition when we work out here. And grab a sweatshirt!' She waved a hand towards a pile. Mine was the last one folded.

I held it up against me. *Seawild* across the front, a wave design in white, a dolphin leaping above the water. I smiled at her companions. 'Tess Macfarlane,' I told them. 'I'll be filming.'

'It suits you,' said the man closest to me, a black guy a few years younger than I was, thirty or so, a neatly bearded Londoner. 'Mike Woods-Hughes, Seawild. Good to meet you.' He leaned in and adjusted his shirt cuffs beneath his linen jacket, eyes flashing with excitement. 'You made *Spill*, right? Amazing film. Should've won a BAFTA, you were robbed. That sequence in those oilfields? The photography is beautiful. You're a superstar.'

'Thanks. That's kind of you.'

A middle-aged man, wearing a trucker's cap over shoulder-length hair and a slack-necked jumper, introduced himself. 'Vincento Perriera.' He had chapped olive skin, and when he smiled, crow's feet sprung at his restless eyes. 'Looking forward to the trip?'

'Very much.'

Alex opened her arms to the three of us in a gesture of maternal pride. 'We're together in real life at last. To the Ilhas Desertas.' We tapped glasses across the table. Mike gave a good-humoured cheer and Alex smiled. 'I'm very lucky to have you along. What a fantastic little team! I'm excited to get started.' I wondered if we were seeing a deliberate amplification of her enthusiasm but her smile seemed charged with honest energy. 'Thanks so much for dedicating your time to our project. Cheers!'

We toasted a second time. Alex ordered tapas and more drinks.

Vincento leaned across to me as we ate. 'Looking forward to seeing the seals?'

'Absolutely. Leo's very keen to keep the island protected, ensure there's no expansion of tourism.'

Vincento swallowed beer and wiped his mouth. 'Agree with that. Careful management is key now. The numbers, they are growing slowly but well.' He waved a waiter over and a minute later was eagerly pouring us all glasses of a dark wine. 'Try this,' he commanded the table.

Mike laughed. 'Oh, God. Vinny's going to give us another lecture.'

We raised our glasses and sipped. The stuff tasted like sugared coffee and cigar smoke.

'This is Bual,' Vinny said. 'Sweeter than Verdejo. Barrel aged . . . ' he had to stop, grinning as Mike jeered at him, before persisting. 'Great colour, depth of flavour. A beautiful wine, no?' I took another sip. Vinny caught my eye. 'Smoke?' He waved a packet of Chesterfields. I shook my head. 'Good answer,' he said, rising with a grunt. 'Expensive habit. I'm down to one a day. I promised myself I'd quit before the wedding.'

'Wedding.' I raised a glass his way. 'Congratulations.'

He took a bow of thanks. 'Love of my life,' he said,

holding up the plain band on his finger for inspection before adding, 'again.'

I smiled as I watched him weave his way through the crowd, clap a fellow customer on the shoulder and exchange noisy laughter. He was surely fifteen years older than me. Still hope, then. After *Spill*, I'd become a ghost in my own industry, the kind of person whose proximity seemed to stop conversations. It wasn't a quality that made dating easy. Those months working with Gretchen Harris had left me guarded and guilty, and rebuilding my career had taken years of attention. Over the last decade, I'd spent an awful lot of my Saturday nights home alone, swiping left. At least Vincento's engagement ring told a more optimistic story.

With our glasses topped up, Alex passed her phone round and we looked at pictures of Navigaceo.

'Northern tip is where the seal population gathers,' she said, holding up her screen as Mike and I leaned in. 'Southern point, the lighthouse. It's an island of two faces,' she explained. 'To the west, sheer rock. But on its other face, a more gradual decline made by old landslides.' She showed us shots of the accessible coast; a spit of rust-red rock dominated by a mountain, its lower creases dressed in thick forest.

We chatted, ate, and for the first time since the man with the camera, I actually relaxed. With another bottle of Vinny's Bual on the table, I made the three of them pull their sweatshirts on and panned the camcorder, checking the thumbnail image as my new colleagues, fully branded-up, waved into the lens.

The food was good, the company easy, the music got louder, and gradually the thought of Brixton Police Station became nothing more than a background ache like the beginning of a hangover; a distant threat that was easy to ignore.

At ten-thirty, we exchanged hugs. I'd been such a late addition it hadn't been possible to book me in at the team's hotel, so as the three of them accompanied each other in one direction, I set off in the other, heading unsteadily for my hostel. A bar played fado music. Outside a tattoo parlour, a group of friends exchanged boisterous jokes. Above my head, the *teleférico* had stopped for the night, the cable cars static spots above the rooftops.

The streets quietened and, like the flicking of a switch, I was alone once more.

As I began my uncertain navigation, a blurry phone map for a guide, I suddenly felt as if I were at the edge of the world; that if I walked too far in any one direction I might fall off and never be seen again.

FIRST DAY

4

I woke at eight, my head broiling and my laptop open on the bed beside me.

It took me a moment to remember what I'd been doing. I stared at the dead screen until eventually a memory swam into focus; I'd been digging around on the Seawild website.

I switched on again. That's right – I'd found an unexpected picture of Alex, standing in the doorway of a research station, breezeblock walls topped with a corrugated tin roof, set against a backdrop of exposed rock. I restudied it. The picture was captioned *Team Leader Dr Alex Dahlberg on Deserta Grande*. Grande was the second of the four islands of the Ilhas Desertas. So Seawild had sent a team out there before. Funny she hadn't mentioned it. And there was something else that had struck me last night – the text beneath the picture. *Photo credit: Lukas Larsen*.

Wildlife documentary-making is a pretty small world. I knew Lukas.

The memories returned in a rush. Late last night I'd got in touch with him. Lukas Larsen was a brilliant filmmaker; I expected Seawild would have asked him back to work on this project again. There were any number of reasons he might have declined, but it certainly wasn't the money. Lukas turning them down would at least explain the speed at which I'd been brought on. I found his number and sent a quick text: call me when you've got a min before I realised I wasn't as memorable as he was, and added a second message: Tess Macfarlane, remember? Then I'd typed a hello via the contact form on his website. He owed me a favour or two, and he could give me the lowdown on what to expect, working with Seawild. There'd been no immediate answer last night and there was still nothing now, but knowing Lukas as I did, that made perfect sense. I'd first met him at the Berlinale five years ago. A freelance videographer, he was an off-grid guy with elaborate tattoos; always in combat gear, always making films about smallholders in woodland cabins or tracking migrating caribou alone for months. Most documentary-makers' websites were carefully curated showcases of pitch tapes and testimonials, but Lukas was different. Strident in his opinions, he'd reserved his blog posts for hotly argued takedowns of multinationals and government ministers.

I sat up in bed and went through his website again. My attention snagged on his most recent post. It was a couple of years old, but warranted a closer read. Seawild weren't named directly but Lukas hadn't been circumspect in his use of dates and locations. '*Guess what,*' he fumed, '*working for another one of those plastic charitable status organisations in it for the tax breaks.*' It had been written just after the photo of Alex Dahlberg was posted on the Seawild website. He was surely referring to them. '*Feel sorry for the folks who find themselves slaving for these companies,*' he continued. '*Enough to drive good ecologists mad, which btw, it clearly has done.*' The team members were cruelly skewered as well: '*I hear them argue loudly. One drinks a LOT, the other's a fake. One will have a nervous breakdown before the year's out. Atmosphere weird and angry.*' And he finished, '*a gig I'll be very glad to leave behind.*'

Good old Lukas, I thought, reading it again with a more sober eye. Never one to mince words. I wondered whether he was referring to Mike, Vincento and Alex. My Seawild team members had seemed all right last night, but even so, it was concerning. If they turned out the way Lukas described them, I was in for a very difficult trip indeed.

I felt my situation announce itself vividly.

I'd run away from London so I could pretend I wasn't part of a police inquiry. Three days ago, a man had followed me from my place of work and I'd been lucky to shake him off. Now here I was on an island more than a thousand kilometres from Africa, working with a potentially toxic team. I found myself wishing, not for the first time, that I'd ignored the encouragement of my lecturers back at Westminster, that I'd never made *Spill*, and never met Gretchen Harris.

I could still remember my bemused response when one of my university tutors had pulled me aside to tell me how much he'd enjoyed my end-of-first-year submission.

I'd known I wasn't entirely in control of my material, and that I'd arrived at something good almost by accident. But chance or not, over the next two years I'd continued to excel. I won an award for a monologue, a cash prize for a competition submission, and made numerous national shortlists. Everything I'd turned in was a hit, and I hadn't had to labour like my peers. When they'd shared stories of creative crises, missing footage and disasters on location I'd commiserated, of course, but I had to make up problems in order to contribute. That had soon changed, though. Final-year undergrads had to produce a fifteen-minute piece for the degree show, and it had loomed large over those last semesters. It had been all any of us could talk about – talent scouts and TV people would be crowding the auditorium and our work would become our calling card. The stakes had felt huge. So I'd spent nine months working on *Spill*, and had learned for the first time what it was to become obsessed. The object of my fixation? Chase Industries, a UK-based oil company engaged in a programme of greenwashing, financed by fraudulent use of government money. I'd unpeeled layer after layer of misinformation and lies, buried deep beneath the surface of the glossy brochures and press conferences. The story had swallowed me up. I'd driven myself close to breakdown, prey to an instinct I couldn't control.

By the time the end-of-year show arrived, I'd stopped sleeping.

Commissioning editors had crowded the auditorium that night. Where others had enjoyed the relative safety of anonymity, I'd felt as if all eyes were on me. My tutors had each come over to wish me luck. Fellow students, judgey and envious, had stayed away and I didn't blame them; many were as good as me and some were better – I couldn't come close to explaining why I'd been the one drawing a crowd. The night had been awkward and uncomfortable. By the end, though, I had a verbal offer from Channel 4. The department staff were delighted; even my peers had offered grudging nods of congratulation.

I wondered what they all thought now, my fellow students from those Westminster days. I sometimes imagined the kind of discussions they might have at reunions; my early promise, the girl who went to work with Gretchen Harris and how it quickly flamed out; a rueful where-is-she-now discussion to finish. How simple life might have been if I'd had the success my work likely deserved, rather than what it got. If I'd never made the fifteen-minute short, never caught the attention of the commissioning editor, never been paired with Gretchen ... and never ended up in those Kern County oilfields.

I drank two cups of coffee, each with a *pastel de nata*, then returned to my room and packed my bags before checking out and heading towards the seafront.

A guy in chef's whites swept the square outside the hostel. Festival organisers were stringing bunting and setting up stalls, and above, the mirrored windows of the cable cars, trapped on their endless loop, glinted as they moved through the morning sky. I took a different route to the harbour this time, passing the shops and bars by the bus station, recognising the spot my taxi driver had dropped me off. *Difficult water,* he'd said. *Long way from safety, you be careful.*

Following the cobbled backstreets towards the market, the ocean still a little way off to my left, I began to feel a preparatory tightening inside. As remote as Madeira was, it had colour, vibrance and life. I was about to travel a further two hours out across the water. Once there, we'd be the first to set foot on a particular rock for half a century, and we'd be alone for four days of research.

Waiting at a pedestrian crossing by the river, I happened to swing my gaze across the café tables outside the market. A queue for *gelato*, a van driver unloading trays of green bananas; wide-brimmed sunhats and loud shirts. My attention roved, snagged, then returned in response to one of those moments when two strangers make accidental eye contact.

The man who'd looked at me had already glanced away. He was studying one of the festival maps volunteers were handing out.

I watched him for a second or two, certainty flickering into alarm. Was that the guy I'd seen carrying a camera back in London? It couldn't be. And yet the beard was the same. And something about his demeanour, about the careful attention needed to deliberately avoid my gaze, made the hairs rise on the back of my neck. In Canning Town he'd been in urban utility gear; here, he was in chinos and a pressed pale-blue shirt. It was a different man, surely – the Met wouldn't send a cop more than a thousand kilometres to Madeira to keep an eye on a person of interest. Unless they were more than that: a suspect. Despite the warm air, my skin puckered.

Then the pedestrian lights changed and the crowd bore me away.

I stumbled as I glanced back. The man never looked up from his tourist map.

The *Auk* was moored at Funchal harbour, its silver hull gleaming in the morning sunshine. An offshore breeze had the bay masts singing. Gulls circled in broken haloes. In the streets beyond the seafront, a band was playing as the festival began. I was certain no one had followed me down to the water, but I must have looked harried because Alex, brisk and cheerful, asked if I was feeling all right. I nodded as firmly as I could, forcing a smile.

'Great. Our transport,' she announced as we all descended a ladder to the floating dock, our bags at our feet. 'I love the Auk. We've used her before.'

The boat was bigger than any of the bow riders I'd filmed in the past. I estimated about fifteen metres top to tail, sizeable enough for a winch and drum on the rear deck, a small cargo crane, a six-man rib lashed to the upper deck and a separate dinghy suspended above the water at the bow.

Safe amongst my colleagues, I felt myself relax a little. Soon we'd be off, heading southeast out across the water, forty kilometres from anywhere.

And whoever I'd seen back at the café on the square would be staying here.

5

A balding man in denim cut-offs and bare feet had emerged from the steps at the rear, carrying a box of equipment. 'Hello!' he shouted, his Portuguese accent thick.

'Arnaldo!' Alex called back. 'Good to see you!' She turned to me. 'Arnaldo will be taking us out to the islands and dropping us off, then we've got four days to attach tracking devices, check the feeds, gather data . . . before he comes back around to pick us up again on Thursday.'

'We're nearly ready to cast off,' he said, making a lazy leap to the dock and approaching; a fifty-something veteran of the sea complete with missing front tooth. 'Come aboard – we're just completing some final checks.'

We clambered onto the rear deck and dumped our luggage. I squinted back at Funchal harbour. The heat was rising now, the shallow bay-water Caribbean blue.

'Easy journey,' Arnaldo told us. 'A little cloud, some

swell but mostly calm. I finished loading up your equipment. There's a lot!'

'Satellite communications,' Alex said. 'There should be a PVC too, and a powerbox. Tents, supplies. It's all here. Looks like we're ready to go.'

As we motored out across the bay, Funchal softened to a white-walled tumble of buildings dwarfed by the mountain. Distant beachgoers dwindled to dots beyond the foam-line, cars on the motorway bridges became winking jewels. I wondered if, somewhere along the seawall back there, the bearded man with the camera was looking for me. No, I'd imagined it. The investigation may have been re-opened, but there was no way a plain-clothed officer would cross the Atlantic just to check on me. Which meant I'd been jumpy, that's all, scanning for dangers that didn't exist.

The smaller Madeira became, the better I felt. With the cool ocean air relieving me of my troubles, I promised myself I'd forget everything. There was nothing to be gained by fretting about Friday morning at Brixton Police Station, or some imaginary pursuer.

I spent half an hour at the rail, stomach heaving as we churned through the water. The *Auk*'s engine puttered as we motored up the flanks of each grey wave, crested, then dropped into a trench before labouring up the next. I heard the unmistakable sound of seasickness and turned to see Vinny leaning over the side.

He wiped his mouth with the back of an unsteady

hand. 'Oh my God,' he said as he saw me, pale, dark-eyed and, despite the falling temperatures, sweating. 'This never seems to get any easier.'

'Always takes a day at least.'

Vinny laughed grimly. 'And the ground will sway for a day after that.'

I nodded, taking deep breaths against the shuddering of my stomach, fixing my gaze on the horizon. The cliffsides of Chao, the first island in the chain, were growing slowly.

Mike emerged from below decks and moved across to us, arms wide like a tightrope walker. 'It's going to be incredible,' he said, leaning on the rail alongside us, 'being the first to set foot on Navigaceo since – what, nineteen seventy-one?'

'I'll make sure I get some good shots of you all making landfall,' I told him.

'One small step for man ...' Mike said, laughing. Struck by a thought, he opened his roll-top backpack. 'You might be interested in this.'

'What is it?'

'Seal tracker.'

He handed it over. Its size and weight reminded me of my first digital camera, except it was of hard-wearing clear plastic. Inside, its connected components were visible; a battery; a transmitter. 'What's this bit?'

'Wet-dry sensor,' Mike said, pointing a delicate finger. 'It tells you if they're in water so you can study haul-out patterns. Where they pull themselves ashore, how long they stay for.'

He handed me the tracker. 'Check it out,' he said. 'Clever machine.'

I took it, examining the smooth plastic. Back in London, it felt as if I'd had a tracker attached, one I might never shrug off.

Out here, I was going to have four days of freedom.

First on my shooting list; footage of the islands approaching, shot from the stern.

I was glad I'd read the in-house guide Seawild had sent through; I recognised each of the islands as they towered over our tiny vessel, focusing first on Chao. The sight of our destination had brought the team to the port deck. Alex and Mike paused their work organising camping equipment, and we stood together at the rail as we drew alongside Deserta Grande, the second island of the four. In full sun, Grande would have glowed a burnished orange. Right now, it was brown and brooding with its tumbling shelves of scrub-covered rock. It was the easiest of the four to land on and, watching the shore, I saw how. A stone tongue jutted out, giving access to a flatter expanse on which nestled the research station beneath a funnel of whirling gulls.

It was unmistakably the building in the photograph I'd found last night. So Alex had definitely been out this far last time, presumably with a team. Odd she hadn't mentioned it.

Soon it was Bugio's turn to loom, another inhospitable blade, this one long and curving. Then the three fell away behind us as we motored slowly across the ten-kilometre gap to Navigaceo.

We drew level as the clouds passed and the sun returned. This was another red-headed rock but, unlike its cousins, it was dusted green with woodland. This place was to be our home for the next four days. I couldn't have chosen a more remote spot if I'd tried. There was a single sign of previous habitation: the white tip of the lighthouse on its farthest cliff, tucked in against the wind. I could film from up there if the access route was still passable, and found myself imagining the crews over a century ago unloading construction supplies and hauling them up the sides of the mountain by packhorse. It was hard to picture a more back-breaking task.

Vinny tightrope-walked his way over. 'Amazing landscape,' he said.

'Feeling better?'

'A little. Can't wait to get on dry land.'

'Doesn't look like it's going to be easy,' I said, filming.

Skirts of scree marked much of the shoreline. Like Grande, there was a flatter open section – the local name for it was a *faja* – where the rock levelled out and hardy shrubs sprouted, but the route ashore wasn't yet apparent. The place struck me as the kind of spot that might resist intrusion, working slowly to thwart any attempt at colonisation. I understood the relief that the last lighthouse men – they were surely men back then – must have felt as they turned their backs on the mountain at the end of their shift and headed down towards the shore to their boat.

Vinny pointed. 'There's a place to land over there.'

I felt the *Auk* begin to slow; heard the engine change key. Soon we were treading water. With forward momentum gone, the push of the ocean returned. Our boat heaved and fell in big, slow pulses. My head felt foggy with nausea.

Arnaldo emerged from the helm. 'As close as we're allowed!'

He descended, crossed the deck barefoot and dropped anchor as Alex and Vinny busied themselves unlashing our boat. The sun had passed its peak now, and bounced lines of gaudy brightness off the water as we gathered at the ladder.

'OK, are we all feeling good?' Alex asked, eyes eager. Mike descended first, positioning himself in the centre of our little vessel. We lowered our equipment down to him; food first, then rucksacks and electronics. Beneath its hull the ocean glittered coldly like cut diamond, clear and deep. I was the last aboard.

Arnaldo, working from the deck of the *Auk*, helped steady us before we cast off. 'Be safe,' he said with a wave.

Alex gunned the outboard engine, Mike and Vinny pushed us clear, and that was it. We were a crew of four, alone on the ocean.

We motored across the short span of water. Alex slowed and we drifted closer.

From here, Navigaceo was a spine of bare cliff above tangled woods. As we approached, I could see the red ground rising up through the water. Ahead, the shoreline was all slick, steeply angled plates. Water gulped and slapped against an imposing metal sign. Still prominent at the top were the words: *Anuncio. Propriedade Privada: Prohibido, Secretaria Municipal de Conservação*, then something the salt had scrubbed away, followed by *Autorizado Em Dezembro 1971.*

For over fifty summers and fifty stormy winters, the sign's fading message had faced this lonely stretch of water, warning away those who wished to land. Perhaps we were the first to come near enough to read it in all that time.

We motored closer and swayed in the glassy limbo between one world and the other.

Alex threw a coil of rope forwards. Mike was first to it, attaching it to a cleat and unspooling a section in his hands. 'Want me to go?' he called back, rising to a low crouch.

'Absolutely,' Alex said. 'I'll hold her steady.'

I moved to the stern, camera rolling. We brushed the rock, Alex cut the engine and Mike made his move, leaping for the shore. He came close; one boot finding a foothold, the other plunging into the shallows. He was quickly out of the water, scampering up and circling the mooring post with the rope, checking it for sturdiness and tying off.

We cheered. 'First on Navigaceo!' I called, making sure I had a good shot. 'How does it feel?'

Mike raised his arms in a victorious prize-fighter pose, laughing. Then he was back down to the water's edge, holding out a palm to Vinny.

I waved Alex forwards. 'I'll film you.'

She grinned. 'You sure?' Her eyes were wet; from the salt spray perhaps, but at the time, I fancied it was an emotional moment for her.

Later I'd come to question that assessment.

6

How to describe the shape and feel of that place once they'd hauled me up?

Desolation was the word that most quickly sprang to mind: a land of tilting rock-slabs smashed together like giant terracotta tiles. The sea sucked its way beneath those closest to the water, snaking through inlets. Further in, the cracks between planes were grit-filled and harboured colonies of plants. Beyond that was the woodland and above us, dominating the skyline, the mountain rising swiftly to serrated peaks, its flanks directing a brawling wind down at us, so that it snagged our clothes and laced our hair with salt.

As we turned to face north, the shoreline beneath the peak extended for a kilometre or so, descending gradually towards a series of caves at the base of the mountain. Seals at the north, lighthouse at the south, Alex had told us. Up north, white-tops broiled, each pulse of tide charging into the caves before retreating again.

'My God,' Mike said above the wind. 'What a place! Untouched!'

To our left, the *Auk* began to move, turning slowly and motoring back the way we'd come. I raised a hand to wave. I couldn't see Arnaldo, but imagined him waving back as he returned to Funchal. Between us and the distant emerald glow of Madeira, we could see the rest of the Ilhas. They seemed a long way away.

'Just us now,' Alex said as she watched the *Auk* retreat. She laughed. 'You lot better behave yourselves.'

I kept shooting, gathering the team together as they unzipped waterproofs to expose their Seawild sweatshirts. With the rushing ocean their backdrop, I captured my camaraderie footage, the team giving an enthusiastic thumbs up as I filmed.

Alex gathered us all together to distribute GPS devices. 'Now,' she said, 'once we've shifted the gear, we'll look for a good place to set up camp and get our first look at the seal population. Nothing higher up for now, those mountain paths could be eroded. For today, we stay where we can all see each other. Understood?'

Our first job was the equipment. It took half an hour as a human chain, Mike passing boxes up from the shore, before we had a jumble of gear assembled. Once that was done, we gathered either side of the boat like funeral pallbearers, and lifted our little vessel as best we could, drawing it up and away from the water. 'Don't want a storm stealing it,' Vinny said, 'or we're stranded.'

'Let's leave everything here for now,' Alex said as

we tipped it upside down, 'until we've decided on a campsite.'

We moved along the shoreline in a loose excited group, heading north towards the seals. Out of the wind and salt, a springy coating had formed on the rocks; a young soil of gravel and moss. Clumps of grass had established and rotted wood bloomed with life.

Alex kicked at the ground with the toe of a boot. 'This looks good stuff,' she said. 'Deep enough for tent pegs.'

Walking was easier on the softer surface inland, and Vinny, alongside Mike, had opened up a gap ahead of us. I hadn't noticed until they called. Vinny waved from the edge of the woods ahead. 'Come and look!' The two of them were examining something on the ground, hands on their hips, as we joined them.

'What do you make of this?' Mike asked.

They were standing over a depression in the rock, a dip that held maybe a trowel's worth of ash. Alternate sun and rain had dried it, washed it flat and baked it black. It looked like someone, at some point, had built a fire here. In any other context it would been beneath notice but out here it was freighted with strange significance. I crouched for a closer look at the blackened soil around the dip. If there'd been kindling or logs, they were long gone, but some tiny fragments remained: fingernails of burnt wood, the blackened twists of tougher roots.

'They seem a bit out of place here,' Alex said, turning to assess the island as if expecting an explanation in the emptiness of the afternoon.

'Well, it's a decent spot for a blaze,' Mike said with a grin. 'Anyone bring marshmallows?'

'Good point actually,' Alex said, stamping her boots against the soil. 'Relatively flat, not too exposed.' She was right. Whoever had constructed the fire – and however many years ago – had chosen its position well. Though there was something unspeakably bleak about it too, this small evidence of human existence against the wilderness.

It's always interesting how quickly a hastily erected ring of tents can transform a place.

Pretty soon we had a base, a neatly edged border where wilderness ended and our tiny civilisation began. We laid out groundsheets in a circle around the old fire, the pegs went in easily and soon Alex was onto the supply tent, a home for our waterproofs, powerbox and laptops. Mike and Vinny swapped their attention to the satellite transceiver, laying out the components, and I pitched in, unpacking the antenna while they worked on the solar panel. We unspooled coax cable and attached laptops.

Vinny checked the power. 'Enough in the battery for a quick call with Leo,' he said to Alex, switching it on.

Mike got the fire started, then decanted soup into a saucepan and heated it over a portable gas burner. I spent some time in my tent cleaning and lining up my lenses before returning to the fire's edge for an early-evening cup of wine. I was about to drink when Alex waved me over. 'The boss wants a word!'

Inside our newly erected supply tent, a laptop sat on an empty packing crate, taped-down cables snaking out to the transceiver. A tangle of phones charged at the powerbox.

'Great to see you again,' Leo said as I settled myself. He was a touch greyer than I remembered, with the chiselled face of a long-distance runner. 'I'm so sorry I can't be out there with you but . . .' he shrugged, adjusted his tie and indicated his office. A stream of streetlight – city-inflected; dusty, carrying with it the sound of traffic – illuminated the high-ceilinged space lined with bookshelves. My imagination populated the room out of shot; there'd be a coffee machine, I guessed, an easy chair and table for reading, parquet flooring. 'I'm stuck here in Paris,' he said, 'but delighted to have you on the project. I know I've said by email, but I just want to repeat, I'm a huge fan of *Spill*. Such an accomplished film, so powerful.'

It seemed any discussion of my work was doomed to operate within a sentence or two of that project. I was momentarily disturbed by my phone screen glowing with alerts as it connected briefly with our transceiver's internet; a fleeting reminder of the outside world. 'Thank you,' I replied, ignoring my phone and changing the conversation. 'Tomorrow I'm covering the seal-tagging. Later I'll explore the mountain, try to get some height up over the bay.'

'You have our information pack?' I nodded in answer. 'Well, you'll note what it says about routes up the mountain,' Leo said. 'Those paths haven't been used for a century and there have been landslides. It's a dangerous place. If you must risk it, be sensible, travel in pairs. Use rope.'

'Will do.'

'OK. Speak tomorrow,' he said, gaze already elsewhere. 'Good luck.'

I switched off, looked at myself in the dark mirror of the screen. Paris was gone and I was out here in the middle of the ocean again, one of only four people on a chain of empty islands.

'I'm powering down!' I heard Vinny call. 'Are we all done?'

Outside, the air had cooled further and the stars were beginning to bloom. I stood by my tent, craning my neck to watch a thousand brittle lights awaken. I'd gone hours without thinking about the police, I realised. It was a good feeling.

'Beautiful evening,' Vinny said as he positioned the solar panel for tomorrow's sun and joined me. Gazing upwards, hand cupped beneath his chin, the point of his cigarette illuminated his face. I watched as he made a tight O with his lips and produced a perfect smoke ring. He grinned, pulled his cap off and ran a hand through his hair, tucking it behind his ears.

'Fancy stuff,' I said. 'You don't learn that on a one-a-day habit.'

'True. It used to be way more.' He picked tobacco from the tip of his tongue. 'But then I met Sofia. She's from Madeira originally. And she's always wanted to come back. You know, family, friends. The scenery.' He indicated our canopy of strengthening stars.

I fake-shrugged and said, 'Well, it's OK I guess.'

He laughed, extinguished his cigarette against the heel of his hiking boot and cradled the butt to dump it in the double-bagged trash.

I smiled at him as he returned to the fire.

A redemption story, I thought. I'd also known someone good like Sofia once. Reece and I had been together for two years at Westminster. We made a great team; while I became consumed by projects, he provided a calm and humorous sense of perspective. I can see now the way my relentless focus must have exhausted him. Hindsight made his gentle patience appear all the more impressive, a healthy counterpoint to my obsession. It was *Spill* that broke us in the end.

No surprise there. *Spill* broke everything.

7

We ate around the fire, darkness thickening at our backs. The soup was good. We dipped crackerbread, then spooned the rest straight from the pan. After we'd eaten, Mike unpacked four squat candles and handed them out.

'Mosquito repellent,' he said.

We each lit ours and Mike stretched his legs. 'So what's with the lighthouse?' he asked. 'Vinny, you're the local. You know this stuff.'

Vinny finished his soup and ran the back of his hand across his mouth. 'Well,' he said, examining the mountain as if trying to spot the building in the darkness, 'it was abandoned in the seventies. There used to be a trading route out to the States.' He raised his plastic cup. 'Lots of Madeiran wine going directly to America back then, but nowadays they ship it to Portugal first. Big tankers going from Sines, much cheaper.'

'So it hasn't been used since?' Alex asked.

Vinny shook his head. 'It was never automated, so it cost a lot to have people out here. Also, difficult weather, isolation. And the place had a bad reputation.' He sipped his wine, eyes glittering over the rim of his cup in the firelight.

I got the distinct feeling he'd told this tale before. I took the bait, remembering the words of my cab driver. 'So, did something happen?'

Vinny nodded, pensive. 'The isolation was too much for the men. It made them crazy. There's a famous story about the last group here.'

Alex ooh-ed. 'Is it scary, Vinny?'

He grinned. 'Of course! I'm telling it around a camp-fire, yes?'

I wondered if I should get my camera. This could be tough in the light, but fun to film. The fire was warm, though, the wine had me glowing and I'd clocked off, I decided; I could always capture this some other time.

'Go on, Vinny,' I said, sipping my drink. 'Let's hear it.'

And so he leaned forwards.

Sadly, it was a story that circumstance ensured we'd only ever hear once.

'The lighthouse keepers did long shifts out here back then,' Vinny began, face craggy in the firelight. 'They'd drop them with their supplies about where we are now and it would be three or four months before they were picked up again.'

Mike mock-shuddered. 'Imagine that long out here.'

'Bliss,' Alex said with a grin.

'Back in seventy-one there were three men on Navigaceo. I still remember the names I think.' Vinny closed his eyes, conjuring memories. 'Reveles,

Carras – who was the third guy? Montalvo, that's it. So these three guys are dropped off. Reveles, Carras, Montalvo. Experienced men, family men, good Catholics, popular on the island.'

'I like the sound of them,' Mike said, probing the edge of the fire with a stick.

'Don't get too attached,' Vinny said, suddenly sombre.

'Here we go.' Alex winked at me.

'So they've been out for a long time already,' Vinny continued, settling into a rhythm. 'A month or two. One night, it's in March, a thick fog descends. Fog comes suddenly round the islands because of the height, the climate, the sea currents bringing colder air, right? The lighthouse is important for passing ships, so Carras and Montalvo make sure the lights are strong up there, and Reveles, he takes torches to the shoreline.'

I thought about wreckers in those old Cornish tales you often hear.

'So anyway,' Vinny continued, 'Carras and Montalvo work the lights as long as they can, Reveles on the shore, but the fog stays all night,' he said. 'And all three are exhausted, working in shifts, patrolling the water. It's not clear what happens, whose fault, but by the morning ... ' here he paused dramatically, 'there's a boat against the rocks. The *Bernadina*. The story goes it's a small trading ship from Port Elizabeth, South Africa, using the Western Cape Brandy route, but it's got lost at sea. Miles off course. And here's the strange thing; there's no crew on board.'

'Classic,' Mike said, rubbing his hands. 'I love a *Mary Celeste* story.'

Vinny shook his head. 'The *Mary Celeste* was a big brigantine, a hundred-footer. The *Bernadina*'s only small. But still, the whole ship's been cleared out, so it's likely pirates killed the crew and stole the cargo. The lighthousemen investigate. Reveles is first out to the wreck and he searches. There's nothing left.'

I sipped my drink, enjoying its warmth. 'So what happens next?'

'No one is sure. Except after the men find the boat, things start to go wrong.'

'What things?' From Mike.

'You hear different stories depending on who tells it. Some say they all go mad. Maybe they fight over something they found on the *Bernadina*. Or they try and kill each other in a drunken brawl ... the main thing is, when the boat from the mainland comes to pick them up, only Carras is waiting. Reveles and Montalvo are gone.'

'They swam to America,' Mike quipped.

We laughed, but I felt something pull at me; an undercurrent of discomfort stirring between the four of us until we couldn't quite meet each other's eyes. In the pause that followed, the bottle went round again. Night sounds in the darkness beyond the scope of the firelight: rollers against the rocks, the wind tugging at the tent-flaps. Orange faces, flushed with wine, reflected flame. I should've had my camera running.

'So what does he say?' Alex asked. 'The man who's left?'

Vinny talked softly. 'You know how these things go. He never spoke a word of it ever again, even to his family. There was some sort of investigation, but no bodies were ever recovered. They closed the island after that, and Carras, he died a few years ago.' He shrugged. 'Nobody knows the truth of what happened.' More brittle silence, until our storyteller, tipping the last of the bottle against his glass said, 'Disaster, friends. The wine is gone.'

Whatever spell we'd been under was suddenly broken. Mike laughed and led a little round of applause against the dark.

'Well,' Alex said, hands on her knees as she made to rise, 'it's probably a good thing. Clear heads needed for tomorrow.'

And so our little party broke up. I waved the others off and zipped myself into my tent, settling on my camping mat. I was peeling off my jeans when I realised I'd forgotten to leave my phone charging at the powerbox in the supply tent. I hooked it out of my pocket.

It was registering a new email.

Of course; the glow of the screen earlier during our brief window of internet connection. I scanned my inbox, saw the sender; felt a shiver of anxiety. Confirmation of DCI Rafiq's request to speak to me. I forced myself to read it, wincing at the blunt emotionless phrases; *confirming your attendance at interview . . . vital role in assisting us . . .*

My throat prickled uncomfortably, and I wiped my eyes.

Ten years ago, my interrogation had been over in a couple of hours and, though the police suggested we might need to speak again, the call never came. Gradually the tension began to fade. A year after that interview, I remember thinking it was over. Another year and I'd started Pocket Films, moved on with my life. Clearly I'd been wrong to consider it done. Maybe things like this were never done. *Report to reception at Brixton Police Station at 9 a.m. . . . we request you arrive promptly . . . ongoing inquiries . . . Gretchen Harris . . .*

I swiped my inbox shut. That night it took me a long time to find sleep.

While I lay awake, I thought about Gretchen.

8

As a Film and Television student at Westminster, I'd passed the sculpture outside the Channel 4 buildings many times going to and from classes. But standing before it as a budding documentary filmmaker in the summer of 2011, twenty-one years old and frothing with fear and excitement, it felt as if I were about to cross a threshold; to step behind the curtain.

Inside, in a minimally decorated street-facing office, Patrick Hannah introduced himself. The man who'd orchestrated the commissioning of *Spill* was compact and energetic with a tidy upright posture. We sipped iced water and began by discussing, as everyone did all that summer, the riots. That was the August a twenty-four-year-old man had been shot by police in Tottenham. The protests began peacefully but swiftly snowballed and the looting started, spreading to Walthamstow and Brixton. A day later it was Bristol, Manchester, Liverpool.

Once we'd skated the surface of the topic, Patrick

placed his glass down and interlaced his fingers. 'Exciting news,' he announced. 'We've got a collaborator in mind for *Spill*.' He'd emailed to tell me about the channel's pedigree in unearthing new talent, explaining how I'd work with an already-established filmmaker to complete a guided re-shoot of the entire film, fleshing out my footage into a full hour. 'She's busy at the moment, working on a piece about the riots actually, along with another project. But we've managed to secure you some time with her early next year. We're delighted with this one.' He paused for emphasis. 'You'll be working with Gretchen Harris.'

I felt a curious lightness, as if I were dissolving. 'Oh my God,' I spluttered. '*The* Gretchen Harris? *Shortie, Hoodie and Mr Average*?'

For the last five years, since my mid-teens, I'd reserved for Gretchen Harris the kind of burning admiration that only came from being struck at that impressionable age. I was seventeen when *Shortie, Hoodie and Mr Average* was released. It was a ninety-minute doc telling the true story of a gang of thieves – each had disguised their identities with nicknames, hence the title – who'd stolen millions of pounds in cash from a security depot back in 2006. Teenage me, and I flinch to recall this, actually emailed her production company to freak out about how good it was. When the BFI shortlisted it in the cinematic non-fiction category but it didn't win, I was so incandescent I couldn't sleep. Her follow-up, *Twenty-Five*, investigated the rise of far-right parties in an English by-election. Even now, people talk about that film as an overlooked masterpiece; a snapshot of a society pre-social media, experiencing the growing divisions that would dominate the culture in the decades that followed.

I'd borrowed and copied Gretchen's style shamelessly in all my early efforts: choppy, grainy footage, fast cuts, natural light. 'So has she actually seen *Spill*?' I asked, anxious she might find it derivative.

He gave a firm nod. 'Loves it. Has some really exciting ideas for how you might develop it, too. I've arranged to get the two of you together.'

And so, I ended up sitting in a café in Camden Market in late November of that year.

I was half an hour early, having spent the whole morning agonising over everything from what to wear and how to tie my hair back, to what my opening line might be. I don't remember how I chose to dress in the end, though I'd worn the same second-hand leather jacket every day through university so it was probably that and jeans; what I do recall is that I'd brought along notes about my influences just in case Gretchen asked me searching questions.

I split my attention between checking them over and watching the door, jumpy from too much caffeine. I waited nearly an hour before Gretchen Harris finally arrived.

There she was.

She headed for the counter, tall in heeled boots, wearing a blazer and pleated skirt and scanning the room with a sharp-featured watchfulness. A quick word with the barista whilst texting and then she turned and leant her elbows on the counter, picking at the buttons of her coat, an oversized bag on her shoulder and aviators up on her head. At first, I thought she might be surveying the crowds for me and I raised a hand like a nervous student. Thankfully she didn't notice; instead, she continued to study the market stalls through the windows with a thoughtful intensity that made me check to see what I was missing. All I saw were regular crowds weaving along regular pavements.

She was seeing the world with a master filmmaker's eye.

She collected her coffee — takeaway cup, I noticed — before catching my repeat wave. And then it all became real: the actual Gretchen Harris was sitting before me. I don't remember what I said. The rush of that first conversation only comes back in snatches. What stays with me was how nice she almost was.

'I'm so glad Pat brought me in on this,' she began. When she talked, I discovered, she dipped her head forwards conspiratorially, her long hair swaying and her eyes piercing. I caught the warm glow of her perfume. 'I adored *Spill*. Really strong work.'

'Thanks so much,' I said, spellbound. It wasn't until later I'd consider her use of strong might have somehow implied weak. But what did I know? I was still a kid, a first-timer who'd struck lucky. And Gretchen had watched *Spill* numerous times; she heaped praise on the scenes she most liked, patiently returning me to them every time I tried steering the conversation to her own stuff.

I remember we had to keep stopping as she took calls, clearly as busy as Patrick had said. 'You've got a bright future,' she told me at one point. I squirmed in my seat, thrilled. 'I'm a little further down the line now,' she said – she'd just passed thirty – 'but I remember all the challenges that came with starting out. That's why I'm here, OK? To give you the kind of guidance you don't get at film school. Some things you have to learn out in the real world.'

'Absolutely,' I replied. I had no idea what that might eventually entail for me, my safety and my life.

'Now,' Gretchen continued. 'One of the things that really strikes me, is how your investigation is steering you towards those Californian oilfields. I was expecting some footage, but there isn't any. I ended up feeling you'd pulled your punch.'

She was referring to Chase Industries, the British oil company I'd been investigating, and she was right.

Every oil company had a disastrous environmental record, but not all of them worked as hard as Chase to give the impression of benevolence. They claimed carbon dioxide produced during oil extraction could be treated and stored underground – carbon capture storage, it was called – good for the environment, they claimed, and good for profits. Except to make it work, you needed big treatment chambers and a vast underground storage capacity. Chase had attracted huge amounts of UK government funding for their California pilot project. But my investigation suggested it was all fiction; nothing was happening and the money was simply getting banked or invested.

California was the next link in the chain, but I hadn't followed it up for a very simple reason. I tried to brush it off, laughing. 'Have you seen the price of flights to Los Angeles?'

Gretchen frowned. 'No more than a few hundred, surely. Anyway, that's where we need to be regardless of the cost. Pat will pick up the tab.'

'Really? What about accommodation? Food?'

Gretchen laughed. 'That'll be covered too. And if you need any new gear, we'll bill him for that as well.'

It was only later I found out I had to pay for it all first, invoice, then wait months for reimbursement. I'd maxed out my credit cards getting *Spill* that far – just submitting your stuff to pitch events is five hundred a time – and I ended up having to borrow money from my dad.

It was to be a mistake with repercussions.

I tortured myself replaying it until I finally slept.

SECOND DAY

9

Outside, the sun had risen and the sky promised heat. By the fire, Vinny was eating. Mike had posted himself on a rock nearer the water, watching the wind whip up white-tops.

He turned and gave me a wave, zipped his jacket neatly. 'Sleep all right?' He was kneeling next to a sketch pad, a fan of fine-nibbed pens on the rocks before him. 'Getting too old for roll-mats,' he said as I approached, setting aside a drawing pad and rotating a shoulder. 'I'm requesting a fold-out bed next time.'

I poked fun. 'Vinny seems to manage.'

The older man grinned. 'In your forties you wake up aching even in a good bed.'

'Let me pack this stuff away,' Mike said, pulling together sheaves of pen-and-ink drawings.

'Yours? They're good.' They were landscapes: rocks against the sea, a black-feathered bird perched on an outcrop, island shapes.

He shrugged. 'I try. When you travel as much as I do,

photographs don't cut it. I like trying to capture things differently.'

'Lovely picture,' I said, indicating a sketch of a woman and child. 'Is it your daughter?'

He plucked the picture up and smiled at it. 'Yeah, Ella. She's seven. Not a great drawing but a great kid. I'll get these put away.'

'I don't want to disturb . . . '

'No problem.' He folded them into the leaves of his sketchbook. No wedding ring, I noticed. 'I miss her on these trips,' he said fondly. 'Always bring her something back, of course. She's got this thing about shells at the moment, so I'll be on the lookout. Shells and strawberry laces.'

'I'll keep an eye,' I said. 'For shells, I mean.'

'Superstar.'

'Folks!' Alex called. Mike and I drifted back to camp and Vinny returned from setting up the transceiver's solar panels. 'A reminder,' our leader said as we gathered, 'that we're on tagging this morning, then lunch.' She was referring to a time-blocked plan she had in her notebook. 'Mike, you've got the Mid?'

'All ready. Midazolam,' he explained to me. 'Easy to deliver, straight into the bulk of the muscle tissue. Keeps them quiet while we tag them.'

'A sedative, not a tranquiliser,' Alex explained. 'Night Nurse for seals. We want them recovering as quickly as possible. Tess, you're with us all morning to film?'

I nodded. Trapping seals in big nets might not play well, I thought, but the process of attaching trackers and releasing animals back into the wild would look good. 'I thought I'd do some establishing shots from the lighthouse tomorrow,' I reminded her.

'Right.' She double-checked her plan, made a scribbled note. 'Another round of tagging this afternoon so that we've got two, maybe three tagged by the end of the day. I've set aside a couple of hours to check the data later on, once we've got some back – Vinny, are we set up for that?'

'Yes. We should get our first packet early evening when they surface. I'll switch us on for an hour or so once the battery's good.'

'OK. Let's get started.'

The four of us zipped up and headed off.

Alex led, Mike and Vinny followed, and the three of them moved towards the pack, nets at the ready. I filmed them as they discussed their plans. They were looking for a post-adolescent, I gathered; an animal that would range widely and best reveal hunting patterns, but also one small enough to quickly sedate. The seals sunbathed in contented packs, barking and braying, pebble-coloured pelts beaded with water. As we drew near, the animals sensed danger, the ones closest rearing up and beginning to roll. Others followed, bellowing a warning, until the whole haul-out was pulsing for the water, an ungainly crowd pursued by three researchers with raised nets.

Vinny missed, but Alex dropped hers expertly over the nose of a rearing animal, and suddenly it was a squirming fish between them. As the escapees turned the ocean white with the foam of re-entry, I watched the three scientists administer the drug with a swift stab and push of the needle. Once the animal settled, I followed them over. Out in the shallows, inquisitive heads bobbed, watching as I approached.

The seal was subdued and compliant, a big soft bullet with wet black eyes and marbled fur. Gloved and kneeling, Alex and Vinny handled it with gentle care. I filmed as Mike applied the epoxy resin with what looked like a decorator's sealant gun.

'Talk me through this,' I said, capturing the animal as it slept placidly beneath Alex's gentle strokes. 'Remember – look at me, not the camera.'

'He's doing fine,' Alex said. 'This process doesn't take long, and in a few moments he'll shake off the sedative and make his way to the water to join his family.' She wasn't as warm and natural on camera as her colleagues; a little stiff and earnest in comparison, but edited properly, I thought this would play really well. I gave them the thumbs up as they continued.

'Just finishing mixing here,' Mike said, pumping a thick layer of the syrup on the fur behind the seal's head. Alex and Vinny oriented the tracker and held it down while the glue hardened.

'The data we'll get will tell us so much,' Mike continued. 'Where he hunts and for how long, the water temperature, the depth, haul-out points . . . '

A moment later, Alex released the animal. It stirred and we backed away. Slowly at first, and with effortful awkwardness, the seal flippered its way free and within moments was plunging into the water.

Alex and Vinny were huddled together, checking a

read-out on a laptop. I plugged my earbuds in and re-watched my footage.

'Happy?' Mike asked, approaching.

'You're a natural.'

He pretended to blush and fidget. 'Aw shucks,' he said.

I indicated the caves. 'I'm heading over. Leo wanted some film from inside.'

'Can I come with? Ally and Vin will be ages with the readouts.'

'Sure,' I said. 'Why not?'

The caves opened at the base of the cliffs where the rock became ash-coloured sand.

The arched entrances were strangely ecclesiastical, a gothic accident carved by wind and water. I stopped filming in the shadow of the cliff face, wondering what kind of lighting I'd need to shoot seals rolling through these sandy chambers as the sea crashed over their beached bodies. The tide, such as it was on a small island, was out, and we made our way into the empty interiors without too much of a soaking. The cave roof soon dropped, forming a lower space furred vivid green by moss. Exposed rock faces threw angular shadows over seeping kelp beds.

'Good luck filming in here!' Mike said, his laughter echoing as he planted his boots in the softening sand. I pulled a face in reply. 'Think you'll be OK?'

'I'll figure something out with a GoPro.'

Mike wandered deeper, hands on hips as he examined the darkness. Considering a longer exposure, I was thinking I'd need my tripod. But its legs were going to sink in the soft sand if I wasn't careful, so a firmer surface would be necessary. I began looking for low rocks where I might set up. The ocean had wormed out a honeycomb of passages.

'Careful!' Mike called. 'I bet this can be dangerous when the water rises.'

'Some of these tunnels are endless.'

I set up my mini-tripod where the passage wall shelved, then attached my GoPro to its mount, activated the battery-powered light module, and set up the motion-sensor. I'd be leaving it for a couple of nights if I was to get enough footage, so a shot every thirty seconds should do it. I checked the sensor, passing my hand across the lens, and watched the camera blink into life and take its first shot. Ready to go.

'Hey, there's light further in,' Mike said, turning. 'Look.'

He was right. The undulating features of the passage wall were picked out faintly. 'Let's check it out.'

We left my GoPro and headed inward, following the space as it curved right around the headland. The air was cold and wet against my skin but, ahead, the light was strengthening, and pools of trapped water at our feet suggested the tide chased its way in here regularly. The light was increasingly warm on the wet rock as we neared the exit. We sloshed through slippery pools clotted with fine-leaved weed.

Pretty soon we were forced to squint again; I held a hand over my eyes against the hot blue of the sky.

We were standing on a black sand beach on the far side of the headland. Glassy water sucked and brawled, the waves foaming in over shelves of volcanic rock.

They were just the kind, I realised, that might wreck unwary boats.

10

A company of seabirds broke upwards, white wingbeats scattering. I watched them circling against the green foothills, but Mike's attention was drawn ahead. I heard his breath hitch.

'That looks old,' he said. 'Really old.'

In the shallows was a shape. The upturned ribcage of a shipwreck. Tipped on its side, the remains were twenty metres out from the beach, anchored by accretions of gravel.

I drew alongside him. 'Wow. I bet you're thinking what I'm thinking.'

He turned and grinned. 'It's the boat from Vinny's story.' We both laughed. 'We're all doomed!'

We splashed out to study the boat from closer. We'd found the remains of a forty-footer. Its wooden bones glistened with seaweed. When the water withdrew, I could see its central spine carpeted in rich green algae; the remains of the hull-boards, grey with lichen, crushed against exposed rocks. There was even the collapsed remnants of a deck. The wreck was angled towards us so I could see items buried around it; an old cargo hatch, the exposed tip of a submerged anchor.

'You want to get nearer?' Mike asked.

The water was shallow enough for us to wade within a couple of metres of the port side. 'Absolutely,' I said.

I shouldered my camera and began shooting.

The wreck was a glittering treasure trove, its contents glossed and distorted by mirrored water. I filmed crabs, lifted and dropped by the rushing water, spinning and scuttling at our feet. In a more intact section, a cargo hatch opened onto a pocket of trapped water that had become a swaying forest of seaweed. I could detect shapes in there; a clay pot blooming with growth, buried flotsam crowding the corners, fish darting against the surface of an old lockbox. I was conscious of a goofy smile fused permanently to my face as I filmed.

'Amazing,' Mike said above the sound of the sea. 'Like a museum. Let's get the others!'

We sloshed back the way we'd come. On shore I felt the welcome warmth of the sun begin to dry my t-shirt and shorts while Mike made his way across the black sand towards the caves.

'Come and look!' I heard him call to his colleagues.

Pretty soon, the rest of them emerged into the sunshine to share our discovery.

'Must have been here for decades,' Alex breathed as she arrived. 'Let's be careful. There could be sharp rocks, broken glass. I'm not sure our insurance covers exploring shipwrecks.'

'We've already been right up to it,' I said. 'It's safe enough. And beautiful.'

'Ringing any bells?' Mike asked us all, a playful smile dancing.

We turned to Vinny. He removed his cap and fanned himself. 'What, the *Bernadina*? From the story?' He laughed. 'Who knows?' Beneath the relaxed exterior, I got the sense he was examining it greedily as if it were a repository for untold tales. 'Anything interesting inside the remains?'

I told him about the sand-and-rock-choked interior.

'Let's just examine it from a distance for now,' Alex said. 'I don't want to have to call out an air ambulance because someone's broken an ankle. This thing looks like it pre-dates the island's last visitors.'

'It's the *Bernadina*,' Mike said, laughing. 'Has to be.'

Vinny began tugging his boots off. 'I'm going to wade out.'

Alex checked the time and, chewing her bottom lip, referred to her notebook. 'Vinny.'

'Oh, come on. I'll be careful.' Boots kicked aside, he held a hand out to her. 'Just forget the itinerary for a minute. Come and look with me.'

Alex smiled tightly and relented. 'All right,' she said. 'A quick explore.'

Mike and I opted to stay and watch from the waterline. The collective excitement of the group was palpable. I watched Alex and Vinny, wading out like pioneers charged with the energy of a new discovery; watched them talk with animation, moving eagerly, laughter and conversation drifting towards me while, thigh deep, they pointed out the ship's faded features, exchanging observations, dipping arms into the water to sift its contents.

I had the same liberating feeling as yesterday; that Brixton Police Station was a long, long way away. I was hundreds of kilometres and countless hours from having to face the distress of that interview room. I could have been stuck in South London watering my pot plants, kicking around the streets below my first-floor two-bed. Instead, I was out here, watching a pair of marine ecologists explore an old shipwreck. I thought about Lukas Larsen's blogpost, briefly scanning what I remembered of the text. *They argued. One drank too much, one was a fake. It was tense and angry.*

Well, I concluded, watching them explore the remains, I certainly wasn't feeling any of that.

11

Vinny, who'd been leaning into the water and digging at the intestines of the hull, suddenly reared upwards. Arms straining, water pouring, he straightened. He'd managed to excavate the lockbox I'd seen earlier, bringing it into the light for the first time in decades.

I made my way back across the rocks to meet him as he returned to shore.

We gathered around the item. Semi-corroded metal, with reinforced joints, it struck me as twentieth century, possibly military. Vinny worked his fingers through salt-tangled hair. 'Finders keepers,' he grinned, then stooped to work the rusted catches. 'Maybe I can make some money at Século Passado.'

He opened the lid. Inside was a long shaft of metal, rifle-like, with a handle and trigger at one end. Its steel tube was mottled but the sealed lid had kept away much of the water. Halfway along the item's length was a second hand-hold, but it was the barbed steel arrow that protruded from its tip, and the loose length of rubber used to pull it back, that identified it.

'Some sort of speargun,' I said. 'So the ship was a fishing vessel?'

Vinny shrugged, lifted the gun and studied it. 'Maybe for dog sharks. There are lookout posts for big fish up and down these islands, apparently. I guess you pull this back ... ' he was running a cupped palm across the thick rubber, examining how it worked. Towards the back of the shaft near the trigger was a hook. Vinny experimented, stretching the thick rubber band. 'Like a catapult,' he said. 'You attach it to this hook here. Then fire.'

Alex was immediately alert. 'Don't point that thing. It still has the spear in.'

'Don't worry.' Vinny grinned, soothing her. 'I'm not even sure the rubber's strong enough.'

Alex stood, clapped sand from her palms. 'Come on, everyone, let's get back to it. Vinny, if you really want to keep it, that thing needs to live in the supply tent, packed away and safe.' She checked her watch. 'Time for the haul-out count.'

We worked our way back through the caves, Vinny bearing his new discovery, and returned to the seals sunning themselves on wet rocks, the noise and spray assaulting our senses as we emerged.

'I'm going to leave you all to it,' I explained as we gathered, raising my voice above the hoarse calls. 'I want to get some establishing shots of the island.'

'OK. But remember what Leo told us,' Alex said as

the others busied themselves. 'No mountain paths today, OK? Don't go off the beaten track. Seriously.'

'I'll stick to the foothills,' I told her.

I wasn't entirely sure I was being truthful.

I knew I wouldn't have to go far to get the kind of elevation that would deliver crisp wide shots. The plan was to stay away from the mountain routes and be back before I was missed.

Turning inland, I began to climb, the going easier as I reached the scrubland of the foothills. I was the first person to pick my way across here, moving from rock to rock, for half a century.

Pausing to catch my breath, I shielded my eyes and assessed the view. All around, the Atlantic sang and shifted, vast and glittering. The light was good. I could get some pictures from a little further up, I decided. Use foliage to frame the shots, foreground the twisted branches of shrubs, their dry leaves baking, roots working through red gravel, a nest of lice processing along cracked bark.

As I set off once more, I noticed something unexpected. Here was a path worn and weaving between outcrops. Maybe this had been made by our lighthousemen in the seventies. Or Portuguese naval officers during the Second World War. I followed as it steepened, sometimes clear and beckoning, sometimes lost until I gained the vantage point of a flat-backed rock and took a rest. I shrugged off my camera bag, my t-shirt sticking to me, and took a long drink of water. Just a little higher, I told myself, despite Alex's warning.

Pretty soon I could shoot the whole archipelago; moss-green Bugio in the foreground just a few kilometres across the water, Deserta Grande behind, and further back, Chao.

I'd be back down on the shoreline before they knew it.

I tucked my bottle away and set up my camera, attaching and adjusting the monitor and cleaning the lens, then plugging in my headphones. I made some experimental sweeps of the landscape and watched them back. Just a little higher. Soon, I crested a rise and found myself at the edge of a copse of trees.

I approached. A little deeper in, I saw an unexpected thing. Collapsed after years of neglect, overgrown by tall grasses and tree saplings, was a fence. Once composed of sturdy posts, many now leaned, and the wooden cross-rails had fallen in.

Beyond the fence, the ground fell away.

There'd been some sort of slip here. I approached, and was rewarded with stunning views of the sea from between the trees. The drop was steep, a tumble of rocks and exposed roots. There was an irresistible pathway clinging to the steep sides of the hill. I remembered Alex's warning, but the views exerted their siren call.

I didn't know it at the time, of course, but I was minutes away from everything going to hell.

12

I lowered myself onto the path and worked my way carefully down, leaning into the hillside, right hand pressed against the rocks. I was looking east rather than west, so somewhere a week's slow sail beyond that shifting blue was the coast of Morocco. Considered this way, Navigaceo's isolation felt so intense it was suffocating.

The path steepened, rocks becoming the kind of slippery scree that gathered in the cuffs of walking boots and sent up clouds of dust that stuck to sweat on skin. The sun stirred the blood, the smell of seed-heads and salt on the wind felt cleansing. The path became a series of stepped rocks that dropped to a cove.

Seawater eeled its way into my boots. I rounded an outcrop, the sun a hot band across the back of my neck, and saw the extent of my discovery. Twenty metres across, a strip of sand backed by a spidery tangle of undergrowth clinging to the steepness above.

And everywhere, plastic. A bodyboard with a faded logo, a diver's mask, water bottles pregnant with silt; a supermarket bag patrolling the shallows in jellyfish undulations. The current must pull southwards along the archipelago, dragging the shorelines of the other islands.

I panned across a background of smashed seashells – nothing worth taking home for Mike's daughter Ella – then made my way towards the back of the cove, and saw the strangest thing. My first response was to smile, bemused.

Someone's abandoned clothes were here, tangled amongst the undergrowth.

I approached. There was a pair of waterproof trousers beneath a cage of branches. And was that a pair of walking boots? Inside a cat's cradle of shrub growth, a hoodie was also visible, its zip still glistening. And a heavy-duty torch with a cracked lens. I framed the strange sight and zoomed in. There was no way this was left here in the seventies. I examined the boots sitting beneath the trousers. Thick soles, yellow laces, technical fabric; weather-worn as they were, it was easy to see they were twenty-first century.

I almost never watch that footage back now, but on the rare occasions I have to, I'm still surprised by what I hear. I laugh at this point, a curious, amazed sound. The sound of blithe ignorance, of someone seeing what they expect to see. I reach for the boot – my hand appears in shot – and then comes the realisation. That sharp intake of breath is painful to hear. My voice, ragged and dry, says 'Jesus Christ' and then the camera stops.

I couldn't pick up the boot. There was a fibrous resistance. The shoes, the trousers, the hoodie open over a toast-rack of exposed ribs, they were all linked, held to each other by the connective tissue of dried flesh. I was looking at a dead person. There was a head in there against the trunk of a low-growing shrub, the face a tight mask. Lipless grin and a fuzz of hair. I fell back, shouting, and boot-heeled the beach until I'd pushed myself clear.

Time slackened. My heart hammered in the super-charged stillness.

Eventually the world returned – rollers lapped the sand behind me, soaking the seat of my shorts. Stirred by the chill, I managed to move, forcing myself to look again at the thing in the bushes. A slick sense of the uncanny moved in me.

Nature was acting slowly, day by day, on the components of the scene. Seasons spent outside in storm and sunshine had warped the leather of the boots, salt-scoured the fabric of the top; layered grime over everything. But I could still see the open sockets of the face, a snarl of grey teeth, skeletal fingers fused into fists.

I recovered my camera. Filming steadied my pulse. I might be capturing something years old, I realised, but I was first on the scene since this beaching had occurred. I pushed in as close as I dared; shot the teeth, the salt-preserved skin, tough and black as jerky. Animals had removed most of the soft tissue. The body was hollowed out and stiffened; bugs and worms had devoured the soft rot and the salty wind had preserved the rest.

Here I was, a thousand kilometres from the nearest significant land mass, shooting a body on a beach.

A body that logic said couldn't be here.

I'd only be at the scene for the first time once. I'd need to capture and offload as much footage as I could, but I had a good-sized hard drive back in my tent.

An old instinct, dormant for a decade, stirred.

Without thinking, I began to speak aloud. The sound of my own voice – disembodied and distant, as if it belonged to Gretchen – came as a surprise. I'm not sure I was entirely in control of my own actions as I began to narrate; I was channelling a version of myself I thought I'd left behind. A version that was all instinct, hunger and muscle memory. 'The dead person has been washed up,' I narrated. 'The currents here are relentless; always southwards, so the body came from the north,' I pointed the lens towards the green shoulders of Bugio.

Then I faltered, a current of fear sparking in me as a possibility surfaced.

There could be something to this. A real story. If I gathered all the footage now, shot it properly and investigated when I got back to London, there was the possibility of a film. A proper one, for the first time in ten years.

I might have abandoned that life, but I saw the whole project unfurl in that moment: an account of the discovery, the subsequent pursuit of the truth. I might get interest from production companies, secure funding, keep creative control. I shook myself. This road, I knew, led to obsession. I'd have to travel carefully, watching for signs. If I lost my way like I did before, God knows who I might become.

'Looks like a storm washed them up here,' I narrated. 'Although there's a chance that they managed somehow to pull themselves from the water, hauling backwards up onto the rock.'

If so, they hadn't made it very far. I turned my attention to the objects in the immediate surroundings. A pair of glasses folded as if carefully set aside, the plastic strap of a watch, the curled snake of a bootlace. 'There's a torch. Big, with a strong beam, I'd guess. Did this person arrive at night, drag themselves upwards in the darkness?' I approached as close as my revulsion allowed, until I was capturing the grime accreted on the soles of the boots and folds of the trousers. 'Modern, technical clothing for outdoor work but little signs of wear and tear. Maybe bought specifically for this journey?'

I moved up the body and it was only then I saw the hoodie properly. Faded lettering under a patina of leaf-mould and dirt. Holding my breath, I reached forwards into the branches – there was my hand in shot again, scratched by thorns and trembling – and picked aside a little of the vegetation. 'Oh my God,' I breathed, withdrawing.

It was a Seawild-branded top.

An exact match for the one I was wearing.

13

I waited until my lungs began to cooperate, turned the camera on myself and got ready.

When my voice returned it was husky. 'Seawild,' I said, indicating the logo on my own top. 'But that makes no sense.' When I turned the camera back, the shot juddered like found footage. 'It's been in a state of decay for some time,' I managed. 'Need to identify the body. Track down a wallet or passport.'

I pulled out, my narration faltering as I spotted what I'd missed. Something in the pocket, I could tell. In the right-hand side, a soft, compact shape.

The development gave me a decision to make. Sometimes telling a good story means inserting yourself into it even if, by doing so, you alter its direction. Buried instincts surfaced again, strong and sharp. I mastered my fear and reached down through the net of branches, pushing my fingers into the pocket opening. Out came a wallet in technical fabric with a zip-pouch and a Velcro snap. It held a handful of coins, a wad of paper and a single card.

I went for the card first, pulling it from its slot, my hands jagging. It was an ID with a magnetic strip; the kind that swung from corporate lanyards and, held against card readers, unlocked doors. Time in the water had polished its surface almost featureless; there was one readable word, *Staff*, across the top, but the name beneath was a ghost in smoke. Tipping the card this way and that, I found an angle where it offered up some of its secrets; an initial, possibly W, and a surname that began with P. Was it p-e-n? I squinted. An 'r' near the end, and the final letter possibly 'o' in the manner of Italian surnames. WP.

I turned my attention to the paper. Once carefully folded, it was now a glued-up wad, soaked then stiffened with salt. I tried unpicking it, and found I could tease apart the edges and reveal the inside. Printed on the paper was a diagram of a car. An inspection form from a rental company.

I knew I should leave the scene as close to how I found it as I could, but something made me take the ID card. I had threads to work with here. *And a project. A story.* The possibilities made me burn. Everything would depend on where the clues took me; who WP was and how they got here. I backed away, assessing the emptiness of the beach.

This wasn't the first time I'd seen a dead body.

The circumstances might be different but the parallels brought memories rushing back in streams.

Ten years ago, I'd filmed another. I'd been with Gretchen Harris making *Spill*.

★

The spring following my first meeting with Gretchen, we flew out to Los Angeles.

Once through immigration we drove north cutting through flat landscapes punctuated by boulders and sandbanks. Driving was easy. On Gretchen's insistence, we'd rented a sleek Chevrolet, an automatic whose leather seats would've burned our thighs if it weren't for the powerful air-con.

The first hour, north from LAX through the cool, tree-lined streets of Santa Clarita, felt familiarly Mediterranean. We'd stopped for coffee, found a hardware place to buy wire cutters, and were quickly back on the 33. Through Lebec and Wheeler Ridge the hills were clad in clouds of green, but once we'd picked up the Maricopa highway, the land became baked dust. Because the roads out there were concrete plates, the heartbeat of that journey became the pulse of our tyres against the seams. Both sides of the route were lined with telegraph poles, and the swooping tracery of passing wires hypnotised. Now and again, we'd pass a pickup or dump truck, maybe an SUV, but that was it. There was so little traffic, I could watch the hazy hills of the Sequoia National Park shift slowly in the distance as I drove.

We'd booked a motel in a place called McKittrick, but our first stop was a blink-and-you'll-miss-it desert town called Dustin Acres. It was here we were meeting our contact.

We'd tracked down a local journalist – a columnist for Kern County's local paper, *The Bakersfield* – who was already orbiting the Chase Industries story. Leland

Redfern had years of experience. Heavyset with thick-rimmed glasses propped on a bulbous nose, he looked as if he'd consumed liquid lunches for much of his career. A lead was a lead though, and Redfern's columns had proved useful. His remit was environment – agricultural pollution in the Kern River, extreme weather events and storm damage clean-ups plus a couple of speculative columns about the Midway-Sunset Oilfields which hinted at Chase malpractice.

This was a man I reckoned we needed to speak to. Gretchen, juggling other projects as she was, had felt otherwise. 'I've worked with guys like this before,' she'd said. 'They can be useful when they're young and hungry, but have you seen this one? He's spent a career in local news in the middle of nowhere; he's hardly a hotshot. And he looks like he's a year away from his pension. He won't put that at risk.' My old obsession, the one that had devoured me in my final year at university, was burning again. I couldn't let it go. Redfern might be a way in, I persisted, until eventually I pushed Gretchen into a reluctant shrug. 'It's your film, Tess,' she'd said, one eye on her inbox.

Redfern was pretty clear he had information to share but he wasn't keen on meeting at the newspaper's offices in Bakersfield. Instead, he wanted our discussion to be discreet and on his own turf. His address had him on the southern edge of Dustin Acres. The properties were spaced well apart out there, the single-storey wooden buildings set back from the road, each fenced into its own half-acre of sequestered desert. Opposite was a vast plain of cropless soil ploughed ridge and furrow. We pulled up and got out, swapping the cool air of the car for shimmering afternoon heat.

Gretchen assessed the scrubland through aviators. 'No car out front,' she noted. 'Let's hope this isn't a waste of time.'

I crossed the road to the house but she called me back. 'Phone.'

I sighed. Gretchen's other project – a story about a phone-tapping scandal – had heightened her paranoia. I'd already had her lecture about big-tech snooping, satellite-tracking, voicemails and memos being recorded. Ever since, when we shot sensitive footage, we began with the ritual of leaving our devices in the car.

I returned, handed the phone over.

There was no answer at Redfern's door.

'Come on,' Gretchen said. 'He's bailed out. Let's get back on the road.'

But I could already see the footage we might get. I was imagining myself framing Redfern on his sofa, a clutter of personal objects about him: folded newspapers, books, a laptop. I could see the insight he might provide as a local man on his own patch and couldn't let it go so easily. 'Let's check around the back.'

Redfern had marked-out a modest bed with a circle of stones and planted three sad shrubs. The rest of his yard was an empty allotment of hardened soil.

His car was parked there, a sandblasted cruiser that reflected sun. I tried the back door of the house, thankful for the shade of the porch. Again, no response.

'Tess,' Gretchen said, over by Redfern's car, leaning in at the driver's side door. 'This damage is recent.'

I joined her. Someone had banged up the door in a barrage of blows. The metal was a mess of dents, and Gretchen was right – the paint had come away under the force, and a puddle of flakes drifted through the sand at our feet. The attack was new, and had occurred here. Holding a palm out against the glass-reflected light, I peered into the vehicle.

A dead man looked back at me.

I pulled away. 'Jesus!'

Gretchen checked and recoiled. 'Oh my God,' she said, retreating to join me. 'That's him.'

It was. I only had the briefest of glances, but the driver was Leland Redfern. He was older than his picture and heavier too; mouth open and fat tongue grey, stubbled jowls, shirt unbuttoned to reveal a distended belly pushed against the steering wheel. Sightless eyes stared out at us.

Coursing with adrenaline, I took a step towards him. 'What's he doing out in his car?'

'Do not touch anything,' Gretchen said. She was thinking swiftly, passing a finger across her lips. 'We need to go. But first we need footage. Get the camera.'

I ran around the side of the house, checked the road-way in both directions. No sign of another vehicle. The next house along was a couple of hundred metres away and looked empty. Across the fields a distant farm build-ing flexed in a heat haze.

I grabbed the camera from the back seat and returned to Gretchen. She'd improvised a brush using a tangle of hardened weed and was sweeping away our boot prints. 'Looks like he had a heart attack,' she said. 'Open shirt, hand pressed against his left arm. Maybe someone frightened him to death.'

I popped the lens cap, powered up, checked the viewfinder and started filming, circling poor Redfern's car, making sure to capture the damage, heart pistoning hard enough to make my hands shake.

'We'll need to edit carefully,' Gretchen said, thinking aloud. 'Imply his presence, glimpses only. Got enough? We need to go.'

I had a couple of minutes of film. We retreated out front, Gretchen sweeping away evidence of our visit as we returned to the roadside. We hurried across, climbed in. No sign of movement at the house next door, no one on the fields . . . 'Shit.'

A vehicle in the rear-view. I didn't have time to clock what it was, just saw the sunlight flare from its windscreen.

'Take it slowly,' Gretchen said as I three-point turned, hands slippery on the wheel. 'We're just two gals taking a drive.'

I pulled away, heading for the highway, passed the truck – that's what had been approaching, a big flat-bed with windscreen stickers – and kept driving, pressing the accelerator hard, bulleting us back to highway 33.

Our eyes were glued to the rear-view all the way.

14

I'd fled that first scene a decade ago, but there was no-where to go this time – I had two more days on this island whether I wanted it or not.

I couldn't keep this secret. I'd need to speak to the team about it. Alex had been out here before, maybe the others too. Their memories of the previous trip might be crucial, and I could jigsaw the story together as I went. The possibility felt frightening and wild.

I ran across the sand and worked my way up the hillside, sweating and blowing, until I emerged at the clifftop, then followed the flattened ferns back the way I'd come, calling for my colleagues.

They were down at the camp, three dots of colour. I waved my arms above my head as I descended, hoping they might read the urgency in the semaphore. They did. Alex led, the others followed, and we met at the edge of the forest.

'What happened to staying on the *faja*, Tess?' Alex

called as we drew closer. 'Do you know how hard it is to get insurance for trips like this?'

I held up a palm, acknowledging my guilt. 'There's a body on the beach.'

Mike, hands on hips, a bib of sweat on his branded hoodie, inhaled sharply. 'A what?'

'My God,' Vinny said, breathing hard from the climb. He ran a hand across his jaw, the stubble bristling against his calloused palm.

'You need to come and see.'

Alex shook her head with a distasteful grimace. 'Absolutely not. What are you thinking?'

'There's something you have to see.'

'Tess. This will be a police matter.' She placed her hands on her hips, eyes scanning the glittering sea. 'Shit. I'll need to speak to Leo, we shouldn't be going near it.'

Too late for that. 'It has a Seawild hoodie on.'

'Jesus,' from Vinny.

Alex stared at me, open-mouthed. 'What?'

I told her again. 'Same branding,' I explained. In the silence that followed, the sea beat a steady rhythm. I watched Alex and Vinny exchange a furtive glance I couldn't read. Mike looked lost. Alex traced her hairline with the fingers of one hand, a smoothing motion, her gaze glassy.

Vinny checked with her and, getting no guidance, began, 'I don't think it could be . . . '

'No,' Alex said. 'I don't think so.'

A realisation struck me then. Lukas Larsen had been right. 'What happened last time you were out here?' I asked, something slow and cold moving through me. 'Alex?'

'Listen,' she said, then faltered and reconsidered, before speaking again. 'I think you might be right. We'd better take a look.'

We descended to the cove in a silent line. Down by the water, my companions moved with trepidation. Alex didn't want to follow me. It took Vinny, leaning towards her, a gentle hand on her arm, to lead her like a spooked horse. We drew up with some distance to go. It took them a little while to look properly; brief glances becoming stronger gazes as they adjusted.

'So,' I said eventually, 'it's hard to identify who this might be, but ... do you think you know them?'

Mike said, 'A trawlerman? Surfer?'

A warning glance from Alex. Vinny saw it too. 'We may as well talk this through,' she said, with a hopeless gesture of the hands. 'This must be Steven.'

Vinny stiffened, then nodded.

'Steven?' That didn't fit with the card in the pocket. WP.

Alex gnawed at a fingernail. 'Two years ago,' she said shakily, 'the three of us were working on Deserta Grande. Just a week during the autumn. We had another colleague with us. And he went missing.' She took a breath. 'He was never found.'

'Steven Clay,' Vinny said. 'This is him.'

'OK,' I said carefully. 'Well, I found something else.' I held out the ID card, and, clearing my throat, prepared a slight adjustment to the truth. 'It was lying just next to him. Except it's got a different name on it.'

Alex, already shell-shocked, managed, 'What?'

'It was just there. It's difficult to read but I'm pretty sure it doesn't say Steven Clay.' Alex and Mike leaned in. Vinny, his face drawn and his eyes empty, stared over Alex's shoulder as I turned it against the light. Brows furrowed and faces pale, the three of them looked bereft. 'Any ideas?' I prompted.

Vinny's voice came out at a whisper. 'This is mine.' He cleared his throat. 'It's my card. I lost it on the last trip.'

Everyone turned to Vinny. There was a pause that nobody seemed able to break, and I saw Mike's eyes momentarily narrow.

The card read VP, I realised, not WP. Vincento Perriera.

'I remember now. They had to issue you a new one,' Alex said. 'What's it doing out here?'

'I've never been anywhere near this island before,' Vinny said. I couldn't help but note an edge to his voice.

Mike examined the beach. 'There's loads of stuff here. The current deposits everything.'

Except only I knew that Vinny's card had been in the wallet of the dead man. 'So this is someone called Steven Clay,' I said. 'But with Vinny's card? What exactly happened?'

'God. It was a tragedy.' Alex lifted her glasses to pinch the bridge of her nose. 'One morning we woke up and Steven was gone. His stuff was still in his room, but one of our rowboats was missing.'

'He must have taken it in the night so as not to wake us,' Mike explained.

'And that was it. He never came back,' Alex said, her voice a dry tremble. 'No sign of the boat, no sign of Steven.'

'The police came afterwards to search,' Mike said, 'but didn't find anything.'

'They recorded death by misadventure because of the currents,' Alex finished, pressing an open palm against her chest.

I swung my gaze across the three of them, assessing the extent to which this neatly wrapped story might be unpacked. All eyes were on the sand. They weren't telling me everything.

'Steven was a good man,' Alex said. 'Principled, passionate. Great ecologist. Always reading, arguing ...' she faltered, her voice wavering, her eyes wet.

Vinny touched her arm. 'Great guy.'

The four of us, gathered on a strip of churned black sand in a half-circle, examined Steven Clay's remains. Above us, a crew of gulls rode an updraught, calling back and forth.

Alex cleared her throat and began, 'Maybe Vinny's card ...' then furrowed her brow, baffled by its presence. 'Steven took your ID?'

Vinny gave a helpless shrug. 'Or I leant it to him, I can't remember.'

'And it was washed up here?' Mike asked.

'Guess so,' Vinny said. 'The rips are strong.' He turned to Alex. 'We got a long lesson about using the boat last time, remember?' We each studied the high-water line. Vinny shrugged. 'A storm must have spat him out.'

A cloudy sense of fear shifted beneath my ribs. Had

94

the dead man stolen Vinny's ID card, then drowned? Had a storm deposited his corpse in the undergrowth? There were other possibilities; the man might have tipped his boat, made it here and pulled himself from the ocean.

I looked out to sea, trying to imagine it. The absolute isolation. Our cove was a pocket ringed by rocks. Bugio dominated the northward view, and tucked in behind it further back, the tip of Deserta Grande was still visible. Out of sight between the two islands were kilometres of deep and shifting currents. With the push-and-pull the way it was ... I tried to picture a clothed man in the ocean, each stroke a fight against the water.

'Do you mind me asking,' I said carefully, 'about Steven's state of mind before he went missing?'

Alex dabbed tears from her eyes with the back of a hand. 'The police thought the same. Was something troubling him? Did he behave strangely? That sort of thing.'

Vinny was the first of us to move towards the corpse. 'This is no way to die,' he said, indicating the sad scattering of washed-up objects. 'His stuff all pulled around like this. Poor Steven.'

The invisible barrier was broken and the group drew closer. I waited, curious to watch this sympathetic urge to gather together his things.

'No one deserves this,' Alex said bitterly.

Mike's eyebrows raised in surprise. Unaware of my gaze, and under his breath, he mouthed a single word. 'Debatable.'

I felt the obsession strengthen. These responses were telling a story. Vinny, crouching to recover a beanie hat and carrying it to Clay like an offering, seemed guilty.

'Perhaps we shouldn't move things about,' I suggested.

Distracted, Alex joined her colleague, probing the low brush. 'Left alone here,' she said. 'Exposed to the elements, everything pulled apart by birds ... ' She recovered a glove, returned it carefully to its owner.

This attempt to dignify Clay's resting place was surely the product of guilt. 'Come on,' I said. 'It's not your fault, Alex.'

She registered me and nodded slowly. 'I'm sorry. I don't want him left like this.'

Vinny took her arm. 'There was nothing we could have done.' He drew Alex closer and they stood, heads bowed, no doubt recalling the past, looking for errors of judgement.

Mike adjusted his feet, hands clasped before him like a funeral mourner. 'So what now?'

'We'll need to call the PSP,' Alex said, distracted. 'They'll have to launch an investigation. I'll get in touch with Leo. We'll take it from there.'

We began to move away. Vinny remained.

'You OK?' I tried.

'I thought I might take a moment,' Vinny said to the group. 'If you don't mind.'

I deferred to Alex. She wiped her eyes then gave a nod. 'We'll wait for you at the top.'

It's funny how memory works. Like footage, it's in the re-playing that we often notice significance. Vinny's request didn't seem important in the moment, but by the time he joined us, just a matter of minutes later, I was reviewing everyone's responses and considering how I might draw more from each of them. Vinny's need to take a moment alone was interesting. Did it suggest a greater closeness with Steven Clay, a greater degree of guilt, or neither? And what did the presence of his ID card contribute to the picture? It certainly felt incriminating, and there was a suppressed panic in Vinny's movements that felt suspicious. But I was at a disadvantage: these were crew members who'd worked together before. They knew each other well, and had perhaps known Steven even better. I was a stranger without context.

We returned to camp in a silent line, downcast, each of us seeking a trustworthy path through the undergrowth.

15

Alex's call with Leo was a long one.

For half an hour, Mike, Vinny and I sat in silence around the ashes of last night's fire. The previous evening's wine and laughter, its leaping light and shipwreck stories, felt awkward in the hard brightness of the afternoon. The three of us stared north along the *faja*, listening to the low murmur of Alex's voice and watching the distant seal pack wallow.

Eventually, our leader emerged from the supply tent. 'Thanks for your patience,' she said solemnly, joining us. 'These things are never easy. So, Leo's been in touch with the island's police. We have a case number, an investigating officer assigned, a team being put together.' She took a breath, wiped her eyes. 'Unfortunately, what we haven't got is anyone here in the next three days.'

'What?' Mike spluttered. 'We'll be gone by then.'

'The force is small. There's territorial command, but they're just coastal monitoring. It looks like the PSP are all we have at the moment. And since this is technically a cold case, they're prioritising the festival,' Alex said.

'Small force,' Vinny said. 'So we're just . . . stuck here with Steven?'

'I'm afraid so. For now.' We nodded our silent assent, shattered by the news. 'OK . . . ' Alex turned to me ' . . . Tess, Leo's with the CEO. He wants to talk to you next. We've left the call running.' I hovered, not quite believing it, until she tipped her head in the direction of the supply tent. 'You were first on the scene. He's concerned for you, that's all. Go on.'

I crossed to the tent. I guess the feeling the others were watching me was nothing but paranoia. Inside, the laptop was open. I stepped over the snaking ethernet cable and sat cross-legged. Leo wasn't yet back. I was looking at the Paris office through his laptop camera. During the pandemic, we'd all got used to assessing each other's spaces through cameras like these. They spoke a rudimentary language all of their own. Leo's told me he hadn't upgraded his computer for a couple of years – the desk lamp, switched on despite the time of day, meant he needed additional light. His space was an interesting reflection of his personality. The potted plant in the left-hand corner of shot was well cared for and glossy-leaved, the pile of papers on the desk spoke of someone who still dealt in hard copies. The background bookcase was an unhelpful blur, but looked like it held lever-arch files and document wallets.

Leo appeared, pulling his chair up to his desk. His

troubled gaze was directed elsewhere; I imagined an aide out of shot. He gave a nod in response to something, then turned his attention to me. I could see the tightness in his jaw and read the tension in his eyes.

'Tess,' he said. 'Sorry about that. As you can imagine, Alex's news has us somewhat at a loss. I'm trying to . . . ' he paused, attention once more drawn away. Another nod – some decision clearly made – and then he was loosening his tie. 'OK, so I just wanted to check in with you in particular. I hear you were the one who found Steven's body. It must have come as a terrible shock.'

'It did. It's hard for everyone. Did you know him well?'

'We worked together on a few projects, yes. He was helping us deliver on a research piece in Gran Canaria. He was an impressive guy, a very gifted ecologist. We were lucky to hire him.'

Vinny had said something similar. Clay had been a popular, respected colleague. 'I guess he must have drowned,' I said. 'Vinny mentioned that the currents are strong around here.' I watched Leo's face closely.

He nodded. 'Strong and cold. They can bring water up from the deep, it's one of the reasons the islands are temperate. He took a boat if I recall, though no one knows why. Alex was saying you found a number of items around him?'

'A torch, gloves and a hat. We found Vinny's old ID card there too.'

This was news to Leo. His gaze snapped back to me. 'Really? Vinny Perriera? Alex didn't mention it.'

'She's shocked,' I said. 'So much has happened it's easy to forget details.'

'He had Vinny's ID card . . . '

'Yes, along with some hire-car documentation. That was it, really.'

Leo leaned forwards on his elbows. 'Tess, I need to be frank. This is a delicate and very sad business. I've contacted the PSP but, as Alex will explain, they can't attend the scene immediately.' Eyebrows raised in stern emphasis, he continued. 'In the meantime, I need you to carry on with the important work you're doing out there and focus on that alone. This is a tragedy we'll need to handle with professionalism and dignity. Needless to say, no one will be communicating anything about this until the police release a statement. That includes you too.' Something about the hard silence that followed made me shift position, uncomfortable. Leo cleared his throat. 'I need you to say it.'

Christ, I thought. He's recording this as evidence. Seawild's main concern seemed to be covering themselves. Leo had been explicit about mountain paths yesterday, Alex had been equally dogmatic about the scope and extent of our wanderings. I guessed with lives at stake and insurance policies that swallowed up huge proportions of annual budgets, organisations like Seawild needed clear protocols. It wasn't something I'd come across before. Even the well-funded, super-efficient expeditions had never been quite this prescriptive. 'Understood,' I said.

Leo gave a quick nod. 'Thank you, Tess. You're sure you're OK?'

'I'm coping. We all are, don't worry.'

He dabbed at his forehead with a handkerchief, composing a response before once again becoming distracted by some development out of shot. I watched him give a nod into the space beyond the screen, add some indistinct gesture, then return his gaze my way. 'OK. Right. A final word with Alex, if I could.'

I rose, legs aching, and waved her over.

Vinny and Mike were waiting for me.

'What did Leo say?'

I offered them a shrug. 'They're working hard to arrange things. He seems distracted and stressed. The police will be out in the next few days.'

Mike drew his knees up and hugged them. 'This is insane.'

'Listen. I want to be clear about something.' Vinny was worrying at his thumbnail. 'I don't understand why Steven had my card. I just want you to know I have no idea what it's doing here. It's a crazy feeling, seeing something that belongs to you on a beach a thousand kilometres from anywhere . . .'

I nodded, thinking about the weight of water between here and Funchal; the miles of empty swell that divided us from civilisation.

Mike put a hand on Vinny's knee, patted gently. 'Don't worry, buddy,' he said. 'There'll be some logical explanation.' Their shared tactility came easily; they seemed close.

A few minutes later, Alex made her way around the

firepit to join us. I guessed Leo had given her explicit instructions about procedure because checklist-Alex was back, calm, professional and insistent. 'OK, folks,' she said, 'I know this is a tragic and difficult situation. Uncomfortable for everyone. But there's nothing we can do about it at the moment.' Her face was a moving landscape of pain and regret. 'It's been a horrible shock. But we have two days to complete the work we came here for.'

There was a slow silence. Mike drew shapes in last night's ash. Vinny said, 'Sure.'

'Though I don't know if we're in the right state of mind for work,' Alex added. 'Perhaps we all need a little time to process this.'

I couldn't face an afternoon of introspection. 'I'm going along to the colony,' I said. 'To get some more shots.'

Mike rose from his chair. 'I'll come with you,' he said. 'The movement will do me good.'

I celebrated inwardly at this. A plan was developing. There'd been enough furtive glances back at the cove to convince me there was more to the Clay story than anyone was ready to tell. If I could get each member of the team alone, I might tease out whatever secrets they were hiding.

'Great.' I smiled, making a pretence of checking my camera equipment. I usually gather audio as I film to make synching easier, but on this occasion, I decided, I'd leave just the mic on, carrying the camera between us as we walked.

Mike would never know I was recording him.

16

'You OK?' he asked as we set off.

'It's been a shock,' I said, but I was thinking of Mike's *debatable* back at the beach. 'How well did you know Steven Clay?'

He shook his head. 'Vinny and Alex knew him well, they'd worked together before. I met him for the first time on the last expedition.'

Strange. That meant he'd come to his conclusion about Clay's character over the course of a few days. I wondered what the signs had been, and why the others didn't seem to hold the same opinion. 'I guess there was an internal investigation after the last trip,' I said. 'It must have been tough.'

Mike nodded and we proceeded in silence. Ahead, I could see the haul-out was smaller now; the shoreline dominated by older creatures – a couple of huge bulls bellowed – while younger colony members went out hunting or exploring.

Hoping the background noise wouldn't interfere with

my audio, I began probing for more. 'So what do you make of Vinny's ID card being there?'

Mike was busy watching his footing on the rocks – or searching for shells – hands tucked neatly into his trouser pockets, so I couldn't read his expression. I did see him work his lower lip between his teeth. 'The currents could be washing it from one island to the next but it doesn't feel likely, does it?' I made a non-committal noise and waited for him to continue. 'I've borrowed ID cards before,' he said. 'You shouldn't do it, you can get into trouble, but people get casual.'

'Why borrow someone else's?'

'Doors,' Mike explained. 'Sometimes if you've left your ID in the office, you might arrange to use someone else's to swipe into the labs. You need certain colours to get places. Mine's purple, next to useless – offices, conference facilities, strictly admin.' He laughed. 'No one would want mine.'

I smiled. 'So what colour was Vinny's?'

'Oh, he's senior, he has a yellow pass. For labs, you know. Samples need to be kept contaminant-free, data's sensitive, that sort of thing. Nothing major, it's not hazmat suits and retinal scans, but still.'

We skirted the colony, all braying and rolling as the waves crashed in. Beyond the shoreline, the flanks of Bugio glowed in the afternoon light.

Two scenarios began to crystallise for me. One: Vinny had given Clay his pass as part of some mutually agreed access to spaces or information. The other was that

Vinny had been there the night Clay died, and that the presence of his pass was a damning piece of evidence he'd need removed.

The second possibility chilled me.

We crossed to the shoreline. I gave credence to my cover story by gathering some shots of the colony, then joined Mike scanning for shells. The afternoon was past its hottest point and the ocean rolled and glittered, each low breaker depositing little cargoes: semi-translucent crabs no bigger than coins, tiny pebbles rolled as smooth as marbles, the suspended shrapnel of smashed seashells. There weren't many big or interesting enough to delight a child, I reckoned, sifting the crevices with my eyes as we walked.

'Poor Alex,' Mike said. I turned to him, positioning the camera mic as best I could and waiting for a further observation. He shrugged. 'I just mean she's been unlucky.'

I steered him away from the sound of the water. 'Losing Steven on her last trip,' I said.

'And finding him again on this one,' he finished. 'She doesn't deserve this.'

'It must have been so difficult to cope with.'

Mike squatted to study the rock crevices. 'She went through a bad time afterwards, I know that much. During the inquiry.'

'That's rough. It doesn't sound like it was remotely her fault.'

'Nothing she could have done but they hauled her over the coals anyway. As far as they were concerned, it was Alex's expedition so she was held to account. They were covering their backs.'

The fact she hadn't shared anything of the previous expedition had bothered me when I'd first seen Alex's picture on the Seawild website. Now it made sense. Who would want to revisit such a difficult time? 'It's brave of her to return at all.'

Mike nodded. 'She's been given another chance, so that's positive; before this she'd been out in the cold for a while. But she's a great ecologist, and I think she wants to prove she can move on, put it behind her. That's why I volunteered to come along. I wanted to help her complete that process.' It seemed like Mike was everyone's friend. He smiled grimly. 'Things haven't gone quite to plan though.'

'She's been pretty impressive. Stayed calm, dealt with a difficult situation, called it in. We just have to get on with things now.'

'Particularly since the cops won't be here for three days. It's going to be a bit bloody weird, isn't it, carrying on as if nothing has happened.'

He was right there. 'Did you try that last time too? Carrying on as normal?'

Mike's gaze loosened. He stirred a finger absently against the rocks, returning to the past. 'There was nothing normal about that trip, right from the start.'

I stiffened, felt the hairs on my arms rise. Now we were getting closer. 'In what way?'

Mike took a breath, eyebrows knit, and for a moment I thought he might share. Instead, he seemed to remember himself just in time and, aware of my curiosity, he grew guarded. 'Oh, just the usual professional gripes.' He grinned. 'Bad food, crappy equipment.'

He returned to his search. I was pretty sure there was something to pull on, but needed to appear casual; blithely unconcerned. I scanned for shells and struck lucky. 'How about this one?' I said, my eye caught. I lifted a lovely cowrie from the water, as smooth as polished granite, unzipped by teeth along its ventral face. Inside its lipless grin was a tiny cargo of black sand.

Mike laughed at its perfection. 'Superstar,' he said.

Back at camp, Alex gave me a wave. 'It's Leo, for you.'

Again? As I crossed to the supply tent, I gave Alex a quizzical look but she didn't respond. Inside I squatted before the screen, wondering what Leo might want from me. This time, he was somewhere beyond the Seawild offices and was video-calling on a smartphone. Even with the smaller portrait-oriented image, I had the impression of space around him; indoor and high-ceilinged, with strip lighting and movement. He'd called me from a train-station fast-food joint, I guessed, on his way home from the office.

'Tess. I'll be uploading some documents to the network,' he said, 'and I'll need you to take a look at them. We've had them drawn up specifically for you. I know this will sound unusual, and it's not intended that way, I promise, but we need a quick response from you on this.'

I took a breath, assessing this turn of events. 'OK. What are they?'

'We just need your signature at the bottom of each page. You just click the box and it'll drop your name in. Very easy.'

'What sort of document?'

'It's an agreement about how your footage is used, that's all.'

After my conversation with Mike, I knew what was coming. The fact that this was being mentioned now – late in the working day and hurriedly arranged – surely meant it was a response to this afternoon's discovery. 'Leo,' I said, 'are you asking me to sign an NDA?'

He laughed, gave an off-hand gesture. 'Not quite that. Here's the thing. The police aren't in a position to begin their investigation yet, and they've asked me to ensure information is contained for now. Once they're on the island, they'll need to gather evidence in the right way ...' he smiled, rolled his eyes, 'who knows exactly how they operate, the mysteries of foreign police departments, eh? But the document means I can assure them that we won't be sharing any images or information during the course of their investigation.'

It sounded like an NDA to me. 'I'm sorry,' I said, aware I was staring wordlessly at his face. 'I've had to be careful around documents like these in the past.'

'I understand.' He was on the move now, distancing himself from overhead speakers as a tannoy announcement began in distorted French – *porte d'embarquement vingt-six* – I saw a blur of white background; a glimpse of plush travel-lounge seating that suggested Leo commuted business-class. 'I'm sure you've signed plenty before,' he said, resettling himself. 'It will have no effect on the film, I assure you. That will go ahead as planned.'

But what about the film Seawild didn't know I was making? 'So it covers the period of time before the police investigation goes public?' I asked, searching for a loophole.

'That's right.'

It made sense. My hands wouldn't be tied for too long. If I collected footage and audio here, then smuggled it out, I'd still be able to use it back in the UK. Eventually. I took a slow breath, in for four, hold, release for four, an old trick Gretchen taught me for controlling anxiety. 'OK,' I said. 'I'll look it over now.'

'Great.' He smiled at me. 'Don't forget – we need a signature too. It's very quick. Could you get Alex over, please?'

Outside, I summoned Alex and we swapped places. I unzipped my tent and sat in its entrance with the flap cloaking my sunburnt shoulders, levering off my hiking boots and rubbing the arches of my feet. I'd have to check the document carefully to ensure it reflected what Leo had told me. It might specify the confiscation of existing footage. The film I'd captured of Clay's body might end up stored in some solicitor's office in a sealed box, the dead man's story untold.

I'd back the stuff up immediately, I decided. That way, even if our internet wasn't strong enough to get it off the island, I'd have it stashed somewhere secret. I worked quickly, hooking my camcorder up and transferring the day's footage to my detachable SSD, watching the transfer-bar slowly fill. I double-checked the data was safely shuttled across and, once that was done, headed outside to help prepare the evening meal.

Leo's NDA was waiting for my signature somewhere on the platform, but I wasn't about to look at it now.

Like so many other things I was dreading, I decided it could wait.

17

Around the fire we decanted three tins of cooked pasta into an elderly cookpot, stirred in a bottle of tomato sauce and unwrapped bread. I added salt, pepper, dried herbs, and went through our supplies until I found some vacuum-packed chorizo, bottled water, crackers. Alex returned and the four of us consumed a solemn meal, appetites robbed by the sadness of the day; heads down, spoons clattering against metal bowls.

Vinny finished first and went searching for a bottle of wine. I helped him line up plastic cups, and we poured a few centimetres into each. Mike positioned last night's mosquito candles. Yesterday's geometry was gone and, instead, four glutinous shapes remained, the wicks sitting in bullet-holes. Something about the translucent wax suggested dead skin. He lit each one, passed them round, and we pulled our chairs up around the fire.

The sky was the rich blue of early evening. Bats flitted across the face of the forest. Seabirds, still on the wing even at the close of day, circled drowsily.

'To Steven,' Alex said, raising her cup.

We answered in kind, sipped at our drinks. The wine was sweet and dark. In the silence that followed, I thought about the body on the beach and examined my colleagues. Alex, head bowed, cropped hair tucked back with a tie-dyed headband, beads of sweat visible on her forehead. She was rotating her cup in her hands, her painted fingernails chipped and grubby. Next to her was Mike, his dark top tucked into fitted chinos. If it wasn't for his loose gaze and the unease etched on his face, he'd look like he'd just emerged from an air-conditioned office. Vinny, by contrast, seemed shattered by events. He'd placed his wine on the circle of bricks and lowered his head against steepled fingers. I watched his hands tremble, his long hair falling tangled over the upturned collar of his shirt. Candles wobbled and the fire puttered and spat.

I reached for my phone and, keeping my movements light and casual, opened my voice memo and hit record, tucking the device screen-down against my thigh, its mic facing outwards. No one noticed.

'I wonder if it might be helpful to talk about all this,' I said carefully.

Alex blinked, looked around the circle. 'Sure. Yes.' She exhaled, her brow furrowed. 'Vinny and I knew Steven pretty well.' She checked in with her colleague but he didn't look up so she continued haltingly. 'He was a principled guy, different from others.'

'I always imagine you ecologists are all principled,' I said.

Alex shrugged. 'For some it's just a pay cheque. Not for Steven. He came to us from a project clearing ocean debris in Kenya, I think.'

Vinny raised his head at this. 'Mombasa,' he said. 'Years of work.'

We lapsed back into silence. Beyond our little camp, the treetops sang in the wind and the waves rolled, restless and relentless. Mike topped up our glasses while I toed the dirt with my boot, surreptitiously double-checking the position of my phone.

'He didn't have any family of his own.' Alex sipped her drink. 'I think his parents died when he was in his twenties. His work was everything to him.' A silence again. I'd wondered how a missing man might go un-searched for, but this explained it; an absence of grieving relatives pushing police teams for answers.

'He had these incredible contacts across loads of African projects.' Vinny ran the back of his hand across his mouth. 'Worked in Mali. And Tunisia after that.'

'An experienced guy,' I said.

'Hadn't become cynical either,' Alex said. 'Still calling out corporate malpractice, still fighting.'

'Fighting is right,' Vinny said with a raised eyebrow. Alex laughed.

I made sure not to lean forward in my eagerness. 'He could be opinionated?'

'It was a strength if you channelled it properly,' Alex offered.

Vinny rolled his eyes. 'And how often did that happen?'

'Give him a break, Vin.' Alex stared ruefully at the flames then explained. 'When he first came to us, he was excited because he'd never had proper funding before. A lot of projects don't have the impact they could because they run out of money, and he'd had enough of that, wanted somewhere well resourced. At Seawild, he got it. But he could be – I don't know – too ambitious, that's all.' Alex sipped her wine and over the rim of her cup I saw her expression darken. I guessed she was remembering everything that came after the last trip; the investigation and its criticisms, her period out in the cold, as Mike had called it. *Too ambitious* was an interesting phrase. I found myself recalling Lukas Larsen's blogpost. The prose had been pure Lukas, the kind of unrestrained criticism that would sink anyone else's career, but amongst the foaming-at-the-mouth outrage, there'd been those memorable phrases. *Atmosphere weird and angry* had been one, alongside *enough to drive good ecologists mad*. I wondered about that. Last time out here, had someone – Steven? Vinny? – been difficult to manage? Maybe Alex had lost her temper with one of them. Lukas had summed up much of the team in two brutal sentences: *One drinks a LOT, the other's a fake. One will have a nervous breakdown before the year's out.* So, which were which? I tried attaching names to descriptions but didn't get past the obvious one – Vinny was the drinker.

It was odd no one had yet mentioned Lukas' presence last time out. He had a personality capable of disturbing any established equilibrium. I had no idea how long he'd stayed on the project, but I knew him as someone who took up space. Given that, my companions' silence felt like some sort of conscious omission.

I flicked a glance down at my phone. 'So it was just the four of you?'

'Just us,' replied Alex. I waited, wondering if this was a case of poor recollection. It felt more likely a lie.

'There was a videographer as well, for a short while,' Mike put in. 'Remember him? Miserable bastard.'

'Of course', Alex said absently. 'Lukas someone. It's easy to forget he was there. He barely came out of his room. Wasn't very well. And found the whole thing boring, I think.' His blog indicated otherwise, but nobody challenged Alex's reading. There was more to this, but instinct told me now wasn't the time to push.

'You must have enjoyed working with Steven,' I said, 'last time you were out here. What was it like on Deserta Grande?'

'All about the petrels there,' Vinny said, avoiding the implied question. 'They colonise remote islands, stay out at sea. We were tagging them, looking at nesting grounds.'

I sipped my drink and tried again. 'And did Steven enjoy the work? It sounds less dramatic than his African stuff – those ocean clean-ups.' There was a short silence and I watched my companions. Micro-changes in expression sometimes told stories.

'He loved it,' Alex said.

It was the kind of endorsement that was rather too ringing to be true. Maybe there was something here; the heart of the tension and conflict. I wondered whether it was too soon, but risked it. 'Do you remember much of what happened the night he went missing?'

We listened to the breakers beat.

'Little bits,' Mike sighed. 'We played cards every night, the four of us, remember? I went to bed early, I think. These guys stayed up bickering as usual.' He offered the others a smile.

It was interesting to see it go unreturned. When it became clear no one else wanted to continue, I raised my cup again. The others followed suit.

'I need a moment,' Vinny said, after we'd drunk. 'Why don't I switch on the transceiver. We'll have a decent amount of charge now, if anyone wants half an hour's internet.'

Our impromptu meeting broke up, leaving me wondering. Mike's contribution had been innocent enough; it was the response of the other two that had my interest piqued. What exactly had happened the night Clay went missing? I watched Vinny walk along the *faja*, the sunset blazing across the water in rose-coloured trails. He would be the one to interview more closely, I reckoned – he'd stayed behind on the beach earlier, and there was a fragility in his manner that implied something I couldn't yet read. I knew this much: they'd been closer than just colleagues, and the discovery of Steven had hit him hard.

I watched the sky darkening, trying to arrange my mind, and felt a sudden rush of longing.

More than anything, I wanted to be spending the

night in the comfort and safety of my hostel room in Funchal. To be sleeping under cotton sheets, listening to the sounds of the festival drifting up to my street-facing window.

18

My tent seemed suddenly fragile, its thin walls nothing more than symbolic. The hostel back in Funchal had a sturdy dependability, but out here, if the Atlantic decided to brew a storm, it could shear my little space to rags. My thoughts, hazy and directionless, somehow landed on my taxi driver's words, or something like them: *it's not a holiday out there. Be careful.*

Outside, Vinny called confirmation we were online. I brought up the Seawild website again. Back when I'd been scoping them out, deciding whether to take the gig or not, I'd mostly dug through the 'About' and 'Projects' tabs so I knew the basics, and re-scrolled my way through board members, Leo included, smiling in his statement glasses; double-checked the projects section; then selected 'Blog' and scrolled recent posts, each a picture and a couple of paragraphs.

Searching further back, there were project announcements, pictures of contracts being signed in wood-panelled boardrooms and the usual charity-donation shots. Five pages deep, I eventually tracked down the short piece about the previous expedition to the Ilhas Desertas. No mention of Steven Clay, I noticed; zero acknowledgement of any tragedy. This felt like a project that had been quickly buried. I even wondered whether the flurry of entries that followed were designed solely to push it deeper into the archives. That raised an ugly possibility: was my presence here a PR exercise, my film commissioned to occlude Seawild's first visit to their newly acquired island chain?

It was a thought that felt too close to paranoia for comfort, but I turned it over nevertheless, recalling the process that had brought me here. The hastily organised online interview took on a fresh complexion, particularly the speed with which I'd been chosen and announced. Perhaps I hadn't been impressive at all – perhaps I was a commission selected to perpetrate a little commercial gaslighting. I closed my eyes against the emotional torture that thought could inflict and, instead, redirected my attention to the website piece about the last trip, looking again at Lukas Larsen's photographs. I checked the one of Alex in recognisable uniform – denim dungarees over a bright-pink tee, blonde hair tucked under a cycling cap – then scrolled down. There was another picture; one I'd ignored before. There'd been nothing eye-catching about the three male figures arrayed on the island's black-sand shoreline when I was scrolling back in my hostel, but here in my tent, the image took on new significance. Knowing my companions as I now did, recognising them was easy. Mike was neatly turned out in the bright-yellow oilskin I'd seen him wear on the *Auk*. Next to him was Vinny, who'd clearly lost weight since the last expedition. I wondered whether he'd put himself on a pre-wedding diet. The final man I didn't know. This must be Steven Clay. I pored over the picture. Any zooming resulted in instant pixelation, but I could map Mike and Vinny onto those distant, indistinct faces. Clay, on the other hand, remained homogeneous and unreadable: a stranger.

I stared at his blurred features, doing what I could to pick out a personality. Sandy hair flecked forty-something grey, a muscular man in glasses and a khaki Seawild t-shirt, cargo shorts and hiking boots. His posture, shoulders thrown back, chin raised, broad smile, felt self-assured and confident. It was strange to think he was dead now, his body on a beach less than a kilometre away. And he'd had Vinny's ID card in his pocket.

'Switching off now,' Vinny called from outside. I could hear him padding around the firepit, close enough that I could smell his cigarette smoke over the salt of the ocean. 'Powering down, folks.'

'Just one second,' I called. I'd become so absorbed I hadn't had time to transfer the audio of Mike, or try and send my footage off-island. I brought up my e-transfer provider and attached a file. Hit send. 'Hang on, Vinny. One minute.' I watched the send-bar slowly travel the width of my screen. Twice it hung, seeming to stop. At fifteen per cent, I gave up.

I'd need to chop the files up, which meant rewatching the film from earlier and trimming it into send-able sections. I attached the SSD to my laptop – I couldn't use the thumbnail on the camera, a bigger screen was essential – and took a moment to cue it up.

As anyone who's ever tried shooting a sunset on their smartphone will know, there's a twilight period at the edge of each day where the eye sees colours the camera fails to catch. But the opposite circumstances more often exist; those times when the camera sees more than the eye. And my film of Clay's body on the beach was an example. Watching it back that night, I was struck by the detail I'd missed in the moment. The sea had buffed clean the waterline plastic but the treads of the dead man's boots were thick with sand. I paused my playback and peered. They'd surely been clogged as he'd moved up the beach, hadn't they? So did that make Clay alive as he'd reached the shore, or had the stuff gathered post-mortem? I rewound, watching the beach in reverse. It didn't seem likely that someone had pulled him clear of the water, though when I steeled myself to study the close-ups of the body itself, there was something else I'd missed.

The dead man's clothing was loose; misshapen and stretched over his shoulders.

An undertow could do that, I persuaded myself, but so could a strong pair of hands pulling at the material. Then there were the tendrils that had worked their way into his clothes. Could their growth give me a sense of how long he'd been there? Perhaps he'd pushed himself into the undergrowth in a bid to hide.

I watched a little more. Then, a flash of something against the sunlight.

I paused, rewound. What had I just seen? I moved forwards frame by frame. The zip of the hoodie perhaps, or light reflecting off the belt clip. I paused. There it was again, and it was neither of those things. It came from the man's navel: a flare of light from the cavity beneath the ribs.

I might have been losing my mind – but it looked an awful lot like there was something metal inside him.

I put my laptop aside, crawled to my tent flap and assessed the evening sky. If I took a torch, I'd be able to get to the beach and back in time.

I could hear Alex and Vinny talking. I reckoned my camera would provide some cover, so I gathered it up and wriggled my way out. Alex had the laptop set up in the equipment tent and was sitting cross-legged, her back to the door, the tent flap open, looking as if she too was finishing up her work for the evening. Vinny was charging his phone at the powerbox.

'Hey,' I called. 'I'm going to follow the path up here for a little way, try and get some shots of the sunset on the water.'

Alex turned at this, stiffening. 'Can you please be careful?'

'I will.'

'We need to stay as close to the shore as possible,' she said. 'Higher paths can be dangerous even in full sun-shine. Don't go up the mountain. And don't be long, OK? Find Mike and take him with you.'

I nodded and, ignoring her instruction, made my way out of camp alone, crossing to the path that skirted the woods. Alex's care about safety and procedure had been a feature yesterday, but this afternoon's discovery and the call with Leo had triggered a change towards neuroticism. I wondered what it must be like leading a team through tragedy once, only to find it haunt you a second time. For Alex, these islands must feel cursed. I wondered whether she'd be able to hold it together, wondered also why she'd come back at all. Lukas had said one was a drinker, the other a fake, but he'd also written something about a third member: *one will have a nervous breakdown before the year's out.* I wouldn't be surprised if that was a reference to Alex; in fact, a flat refusal to revisit the islands would have been entirely understandable for her. I couldn't see her being forced to do anything against her will by her employer. That made me think of the Seawild blog and consider again the possibility that this visit had been organised to erase the first. If so, it had inadvertently done the exact opposite. And if this second visit ended up being disavowed and buried, my film – like Lukas Larsen's – might not find its way out at all.

Another reason to chase the Clay story.

The lack of path during the day had been a challenge. In the twilight, it was almost enough to make me reconsider. The tough-leaved understorey clawed at my bare legs. I thought about changing my shorts for a pair of jeans; almost turned back, then pushed on, putting up with the scratches. A cloud of gnats pursued me, dancing specks in the torchlight. The underlit canopies threw camo-patterned shadows.

I followed the sound of the sea, wary at my prospects

of descending to the cove safely. Luckily, the path was still partially illuminated and my torch helped. Not as treacherous as I'd feared. I shouldered my camera bag and worked my way down at a crouch. The water glowed beneath a sky banded royal blue and a breathtaking, supernatural tangerine. The rocks were warm from the day's sun and the wind lifted veils of grit.

Down at the water's edge, that cove felt sorry and forgotten, a trash-clogged pocket. My torch painted the plastics moonlight-pale as I made my way across the sand. Crabs scattered before my advancing steps.

I made a final check of the mountains and, satisfied I was alone, approached the body alone for a second time.

19

In the gloom, the dead man looked like the loneliest thing in the world.

I had to swallow back hopelessness at the sight of him. This was everyone's fate, after all: abandoned bones. Though being worm food with an ocean view was surely preferable to rotting in a cemetery trench. I leaned in, passing the torchlight across his ribs. What exactly had I seen earlier? A cage of shadows flexed against the toughened grey inside him. Salt and seaweed were the dominant scents; whatever rot had thickened the air as he'd decayed was long gone now.

There it was, the glint in his interior.

A feeling stirred and tingled. An old friend, dormant for many years, was surely waking in me. It was the beginning of a fever; the same one that had driven me through *Spill* all those years ago, a burning that had filled me with obsessive focus, robbing me of sleep. I had to be careful. If I didn't remain vigilant, the illness might swallow me whole. I knew what that would mean.

I leaned forwards. It was entirely possible to push a hand beneath the poor man's sternum and pull the object from the salt-dried gut within. My hand hovered.

I could see what the thing was now, and I wanted it.

I drew in a breath, held it tight and darted my fingers inside to pluck it free.

Fists on my knees, prize in my palm, I steadied my nerves. Another moment to gather composure, then I unfurled my fist and looked. I was holding a key. It looked older than the man it had been inside; small, with a cylindrical stem, a hollow end and an old-fashioned bit.

The sea inhaled stones, breathed them out on the beach beneath my boots. My feet were wet again but I barely felt the discomfort. I swung my bag down and pulled out my camera, still not quite believing what I was seeing.

Clay had swallowed a key before he died.

A clatter of rubble disturbed my filming. I looked up towards the mountain path, my skin puckered and senses sharp. There was movement up there.

'Tess!'

It sounded like Mike, though I struggled to locate his position in the gathering gloom. He called again and I pinpointed him, a dark shape amongst evening shadows. I wondered briefly how long he'd been there.

Arms above his head, he shouted again. 'Tess!'

I waved. 'Wait there,' I called, bagging my camera. 'I'll come up to you.'

Together we toiled back to the summit, the effort

preventing any discussion. The key in my pocket buzzed with a heat that was impossible to ignore. Once we'd got our breath back, cooling ourselves in the evening breeze, Mike spoke. 'Alex said you'd gone to shoot sunsets. I was meant to come along.'

'Sorry,' I improvised, turning to look out across the water. 'It was stunning up here, it couldn't wait. You should've seen it half an hour ago.'

He gathered his breath. 'Yeah, listen. She's not happy. You understand why, right? After everything that happened two years ago, she doesn't want another accident.'

'I get it.'

'Then why were you down there with Steven? She'd lose her mind if she knew.'

'I was just exploring.'

He pulled a face. 'Come on. We need to steer clear of that whole area, you know that. It was tough enough for Alex to keep us all in line on the last trip – she doesn't need a repeat of it.'

I felt my attention sharpen but managed a casual smile, choosing my next words carefully. 'She had a team of mavericks last time out, eh?'

Mike sighed. 'Something like that. That videographer was a law unto himself. Vinny's not always easy to manage. And Steven . . . '

I thought of something Alex had said around the fire; something about Clay's energy and ambition being a strength if you channelled it properly. 'He was principled,' I said, fishing, 'so I guess that made him pretty angry at the greed he saw in the world around him.'

'Partly. Thing with Steven was, he didn't like management. He'd got used to running small projects himself, but Seawild's a different ballgame. Big budgets come with accountability. And Steven had a suspicion of anyone trying to hold him to account. Alex had to take him to task . . . ' Mike faltered, swung his torch.

'Take him to task?'

'Well, they fell out.' Mike's expression wasn't easy to read in the dark, but I heard his sigh clearly enough. 'Must have been the night before he disappeared. Alex did most of the talking. Voices were raised, it was impossible not to hear them, even from my room.'

This was a thread. I contemplated reaching for my phone to record, frustrated I hadn't acted sooner. 'Any idea what they argued about?'

We began walking back down the mountain path, Mike leading, his torchlight throwing distorted shapes across the grey-green blanket of undergrowth. 'I don't remember,' he said. 'But she was shaken up the day after. Which is why we need to toe the line now, OK? I'm saying this for Alex – life's difficult enough for her without us making things worse.'

'I get it,' I said. 'I'll apologise.'

'Good. Thanks, Tess.' He turned and slowed, his curiosity piqued. 'So did you . . . find anything interesting down there?'

I knew answering too quickly might indicate guilt. I took a breath. 'Nothing much,' I said. 'I was looking at all the washed-up rubbish and thinking about the currents.' At least Mike couldn't see me wince at how lame it sounded.

My thoughts spun back to my find in the silence that followed. Why would anyone swallow a key? It was an uncomfortable, not to mention unpleasant, way to secrete something. Swiping at mosquitoes, I examined the metal stem glinting in the moonlight. I tried imagining the process of ingesting it; the feeling of it scraping the throat or working its way painfully down the oesophagus. Surely something to avoid unless it was a last resort. Which suggested some desperate act of concealment. That possibility conjured images of prisoners hiding objects during full-body searches, which couldn't be the case here. Smugglers might ingest objects for similar reasons, I guessed. Whatever Clay had done it for, the strange presence of a key in his stomach didn't suggest anything good. Could it be linked to his argument with Alex? Despite the lateness of the hour, new energy coursed through my muscles. *A swallowed key.* There was no debate now – I was in possession of a story with sufficient power to set a fever burning.

We scrambled back down the bank, scrubby plants tearing at our ankles, Mike's torch strafing as he slithered. Ahead, I could see Alex and Vinny together in the firelight, their drained faces lowered in contemplation or exhaustion. I wondered what might have passed between them while I'd been away. Perhaps they'd been sharing warm memories of their dead colleague. Maybe there'd been a cloying sense of shared guilt, or barbed recriminations traded back and forth as they relived events they were yet to share with us.

Alex wasn't going to be happy with me, that much was certain.

I lowered myself into a chair, relieved to feel the warmth of the fire on my bare knees.

Mike settled himself next to me and reached for the bottle, tipping it. 'Found her,' he said as he poured. He flicked a glance at me and added, 'shooting the sunset up there.'

His shielding me came as a surprise and a relief. 'I'm sorry, Alex,' I said. 'I know you said to wait.'

Alex removed her glasses and pinched the bridge of her nose, her eyes dark and tired. 'Those paths can be dangerous. I can't lose another team member.'

'It was time sensitive,' I said. I wiped my forehead, suddenly as drained as my colleagues. 'The colours were great, I just needed to get up there. I was careful.' I couldn't help glancing at Mike as I finished. He was covering for me for Alex's sake. The less she knew of my indiscretion, the less she might worry.

'Our insurance arrangements are complicated and expensive,' Alex said. 'Listen, everyone. Just for a second, I want to be clear. We're covered for most activities on the island as long as we take professional precautions.' She checked we were all focused on her before continuing. 'Tess is taking a trip to the lighthouse tomorrow but that will be the only time we use the mountain paths. She has her sunset footage now, so there's no reason for any further exploration, particularly in low light. *Faja* only. OK?'

We all nodded.

'Right,' Alex said, weary again, 'today has been a shock and I'm tired. Let's just try and—' she faltered, then redoubled her determined effort. 'I guess we just carry on. There's a job to be done here and we have to get on and do it. Then we leave everything exactly as we found it for the police.'

Vinny nodded. Alex checked in with Mike, eyeing him until he agreed. Then she swung her gaze my way. 'Are we all clear?'

'Of course,' I said.

Alex gave a final, firm dip of the head. 'Come on,' she said. 'We should all try and get some sleep.'

I watched her move back to her tent, then helped Mike break the remains of the fire apart. 'Thanks,' I said. 'I appreciate you helping me out there.'

He shifted the remaining wood with the point of a burnt stick, raked the embers so they bled heat. 'Just protecting Alex,' he said, before leaning forwards, his face serious. 'Listen,' he said. 'I can't do that again, OK? You need to stay out of trouble.'

20

I zipped myself into my tent and spent some time listening to low voices and movement; someone washing at the water bucket, someone cleaning their teeth. Beyond our little encampment the ceaseless ocean rolled.

I unlaced my boots and rubbed my lower back. I had a lot to process. Clay's body, Vinny's ID card, the impending arrival of the police, the swallowed key – together they tangled and spun, each triggering new possibilities until a kaleidoscope of images and ideas competed for my attention. I knew I wouldn't be sleeping anytime soon. I lay on my bedroll, hands behind my head, body still glowing from the heat of the day, and tried to untangle the threads of the story one at a time. Back when I filmed *Spill*, the leads were complex too, and priorities often competed. Gretchen, a woman used to working multiple investigations at once, would be at her most helpful when I was struggling to decide next steps.

I wondered how she might deal with this particular

story, and found myself transported back to California again, remembering those days we spent together ten years ago, driving the Kern County highways.

★

In the passenger seat, Gretchen worked on a laptop, editing together footage while I drove.

I hadn't anticipated *Spill* being her sole focus – she was documentary-making royalty, after all – but I didn't expect to find myself third-in-line behind two other gigs. That's how it was on that trip though. The piece on the previous year's riots might have been in post but there was now the phone-tapping scandal to explore. We didn't know it then, but a major national newspaper was on the verge of being brought down in disgrace, its final edition only months away. The project was at a delicate stage but, though it occupied much of her time and attention, Gretchen couldn't discuss it in any detail. That, and the shock of finding the body of Leland Redfern in his car, made for a lot of long silences.

We were closing in on McKittrick, the horrors of Dustin Acres behind us, when I saw my first pumpjacks.

We'd reached the southern edge of the Midway-Sunset Oilfields. Chase Industries land. This was just a tiny proportion of the operation we were here to investigate and there they were – a dozen pumpjacks, the machines slowly labouring to extract oil from the ground, secure behind Chase-branded chain-link fencing in shafts of afternoon sun. Gretchen was driving, so I dropped the passenger window to film. Eventually she complained about the heat and dust so I contented myself with watching them, camera on my lap, and it struck me how much they resembled a congregation at prayer; perpetually rising and kneeling, rising and kneeling.

The edge of the oilfields meant we were less than an hour from the company's pilot carbon-capture build. The Chase website prominently championed the project's green credentials, and their blueprints suggested three large carbon-treatment chambers should be under construction just a few kilometres up the road. I was pretty certain their promises bore no relation to reality, and I was about to prove it. The prospect sent a kinetic thrill through me.

'Whoa,' Gretchen said, slowing. 'Look at this.'

Her attention was across the road, where a break in the fencing served as a meeting point. Three SUVs, once black, now wearing dusty desert coats, were parked. They had big, dirt-baked tyres and grubby grilles. A crew of guys in security gear were gathered around the backs of the vehicles near a guard's cabin serving as a checkpoint. I noticed the pipes, too; an intestinal tangle of them running along the road edge inside the fencing.

Gretchen slowed further. 'One second,' she said. 'Put the camera under your seat. And if they say anything, just be nice, OK?'

With a jolt of alarm, I realised she was going to stop. I hurriedly pushed my camera out of sight. Gretchen rolled the window down as we pulled up in front of their SUVs. 'Hey guys!'

All of them looked up. I counted seven in total. Not one of them smiled. The man closest to the road checked his colleagues then, volunteering himself as spokesperson, passed between the black trucks towards us. Eight-hole boots with ridged soles, black cargo pants, a black gilet over a grubby t-shirt and – I felt an electric thud as I saw it – some sort of machine gun across his chest.

'Ladies,' he said, Latino heritage evident in his voice. Sweat beaded his brow and he armed it away. 'What can I do for you?'

'We got a little lost,' Gretchen said. 'Looking for McKittrick. Are we on the right track?'

We were so close to the little town by this point, the deception felt risky. The man clearly thought similar. He leaned in slightly, got a good view of us both, and chewed his gum until he was satisfied his silence had created a sufficient level of discomfort. I squirmed, my internal alarm beginning to blare. 'Not from around here,' he observed.

His eyes seemed very empty to me. I tried smiling politely. Gretchen said, 'Over from the UK on a driving tour.'

'That so.' He turned to face his black-clad pals, all of whom were watching. I couldn't see his face, but I saw the response in the expressions of his colleagues; wolfish smiles I guessed matched his own. When he returned his attention to us, his expression was neutral. 'You're on the wrong road.'

Even Gretchen seemed taken aback. 'For McKittrick? I could've sworn . . .'

'McKittrick's just up there. As I think you know.' He licked his lips. 'You're on the wrong road for a driving vacation. You people all pick the 101 up to Salinas. Or the coast road. Beau-tiful out there, right?' He said it like just that, extending the word until it sounded the opposite. 'Very beau-tiful. Not here, though. All we got here is dust and oil. You ladies, you're on the wrong road.' He turned to his compadres and, laughing, said, 'They on the wrong road, right?'

The group laughed back. One man spat an arc of dark liquid. 'Way wrong,' another agreed.

I realised I was cowering and shifted in my seat, trying to appear casual. Gretchen, by contrast, held the man's gaze, her head tipped slightly, both hands firmly on the wheel. She had years more experience than me, and made it count. Blessed with a self-belief that worked like armour, she said, 'No need to be an asshole about it.'

Then she pulled away quickly, hissing a haze of dust in our wake.

'Jesus Christ,' I said as we accelerated. 'Are you crazy?'

Gretchen watched the rear-view, her lips a tight line. I bent to study the man's response in my wing mirror. Watching us go, he strode from the road's edge out across the concrete until his boots were planted either side of the centre line. As the dust cleared about him, he raised his gun, pushing the butt against his shoulder.

I managed a breathless expletive as he lifted his shades, tipped his head, and settled the scope into the socket of his left eye.

My every burning reflex failed in that moment. Senses jamming, I found I couldn't cover my head, couldn't even shrink behind my seat. Instead, I was fused into fatal stillness, watching as the man's finger tightened on the trigger.

Then he simply lifted the barrel – moving from coiled to casual in a heartbeat – and fired into the sky. I flinched so suddenly the movement shook tears from my eyes.

Gretchen shrank against the wheel, features drawn, as the sound of the shot rolled out across the desert. 'Oh my God,' she said.

I wiped my eyes, checking the wing mirror again. The man stayed right there in the middle of the road, gun raised, and watched us through the scope until we'd dwindled to a dot. The shocked silence that followed was profound. I thought about Leland Redfern's heart attack. Imagined him retreating to his car, shutting himself in and scrabbling for the ignition key. Pictured an armed man in black combats hammering at the locked door of the vehicle with the butt of a loaded gun. The terror. The growing tightness in the chest.

Eventually, I managed to shape a few cracked words. 'Were those guys Chase security?'

Gretchen watched the road, and didn't answer.

Ten minutes later we reached the edge of town.

As we pulled up, my partner lifted her hands from the wheel. 'It's OK, Tess.' She'd had time to think, and her confidence was returning. 'They're all front.' I tried to interject but found myself waiting dutifully at her raised finger, in thrall to that persuasive self-confidence. 'What happened back there tells us something,' Gretchen said. 'Those guys might have all the kit, but they're easily riled. Which means they're ill-disciplined. They're going to get sloppy. They'll still be in bed when we film tomorrow. Trust me, OK?'

I nodded, drawing my camera from beneath my seat. We climbed out. Relief had weakened my legs and I had to lean against the car as we unpacked the boot. I kept checking the highway, wondering if the wrong-road guys were following, until Gretchen snapped her fingers my way.

'Come on, Tess. It's over.'

Our motel was a low-slung box with a tin-roofed veranda. Once shaded by four lollipop palms, the trees were now too tall for their shaggy tops to cast anything. Seeking a feeling of comfort and safety, an escape from the exposure of these flatlands and the simmering threat of the afternoon's events, I looked further up the highway into town, hoping I might pick out signs of activity. A mini-mart squatted at the next crossroads, its empty car park home to a sign urging drivers to Slow Down, Save a Life. Beyond that, next to a corrugated barn slowly rusting in the sun, a tow-truck dozed on flat tyres.

An insistent desire to leave pulsed like a drum.

Later that evening, in our twin room, Gretchen worked on other projects while I watched the highway from the window. Just one night, I kept telling myself.

We'd rise early and shoot at dawn before security were out of their beds and, within twenty-four hours, we'd be on a plane back to Gatwick.

Turned out it was never going to be that simple.

21

I must have dozed. The next thing I recall I was breaking the surface of sleep. I rolled stiffly onto my side, still mostly dressed, bladder full, teeth fuzzy and skin slick with sweat.

I sat up, light-headed, and unzipped my tent slowly and quietly, not wanting to disturb anybody. Cool salt air, wind in the nearby canopy and the woodsmoke scent of the dead fire. Sleeping bodies in the circle of tents. I wasn't in Kern County, I was on an island at the edge of the world. Still some oppressive sense of threat remained, as if my recollections had been vivid enough to summon a man with a machine gun more than a thousand kilometres across the ocean.

I pulled myself out on my knees. The balls of my bare feet hurt against the rocks so I made my way outside the circle of the camp gingerly, eyes adjusting. The mountain was an oil-dark backdrop but the sky above the ridge was incredible; stars like spilt milk. I briefly wondered what sort of exposure I'd need to film, but despite the blue-white blaze of the moon, there was no way I was hobbling back to the tent to set up my camera.

The tops of the trees were just visible, dipping in the wind, but the wood itself was the impenetrable black of roofing tar. For a few moments I did nothing but watch, adjusting to reality, shivering slightly. The sibilant hiss of sea and woodland, the kind of sounds unheard here by the human ear for half a century. Further out from the camp, I located a soggy depression and squatted against a stand of spiky seagrass to empty my bladder.

Relieved – and promising myself I'd stay off the wine in future – I tiptoed my way back to camp, feet hurting at the scattered rocks. Nearer the tents it took me a moment to reorientate myself and identify which was mine. I crept forwards.

Then I heard movement somewhere nearby.

The gentle placing of a foot. Scrub springing back as something passed. A sharp note of alarm sang between my ears, emptying me of thought. It took a burst of monumental effort to flay myself into movement. I cowered against the back of my tent and made myself small. My t-shirt, sour-smelling, clung to my shoulders. The soles of my feet stung.

All was silent. Just the ocean breathing stickily beyond the ridge. I waited. Had it just been my imagination? It had been the kind of day that shook convictions and eroded confidence. That blaze of obsession I'd felt in the presence of Clay's body, the team's calculated evasion, the key I'd found in the dead man's stomach; swirling together, they threatened sanity. No wonder I was on edge.

Just jumpy, that's all. I straightened, my thighs burning. Again, I got a sudden sense of presence. This time it was enough to lift the hairs at the nape of my neck.

A figure blundered out of the dark towards me.

I tried to scream. Nothing came out but a hoarse, airless yelp.

'*Merda!*' a voice croaked.

It was Vinny. My pulse was a storm against a seawall. 'Jesus,' I whispered, rising to standing, a hand on my breastbone. 'What the fuck?'

If daytime Vinny was a shaggy, grey-haired sloucher, his nocturnal alter ego was wilder still; a mane of tousled hair, stubby jowls, football shirt over boxer shorts, eyes wide. 'Tess,' he said; he raised his gaze to the stars, briefly crossed himself. '*Graças a Deus.* You scared me.'

I indicated his sandals. 'Where've you been?'

He swallowed, regained his breath, pointed. 'I was up at the woods. Call of nature.'

'Same. Enjoyed your wine a little too much, I think.'

We stood together in silence. I fancied he too was waiting for his pulse to steady.

A minute or so later, he folded his arms across his chest and shivered. 'Incredible night sky.'

We turned and stood, side by side now, examining the ridge against the flurry of stars, and listened to the tangling woodland canopy chatter. Some way off, the sound of the rollers soothed. Soon the heat inside dimmed and the sweat on my skin made me shiver.

Vinny yawned, hugging himself. 'OK, I'm going back to bed,' he said, his voice low.

I murmured an affirmative, eyes probing the landscape. I'd brought along a thermal imaging module on the off-chance; a smartphone attachment. I'd used one before – it could film passable night-time shots with a decent resolution. I wondered what it might capture out there in the darkness.

Vinny tipped his head towards the tents. 'Night.'

We parted. I washed hastily at the bucket and scrubbed my teeth. Back in my tent I straightened my sleeping bag, lay back down and stared at the roof, thinking about Steven Clay alone on the beach, sightless eyes pointed at the water; about the key in his belly; about the lighthousemen who lost it out here.

There were nicer ways to fall asleep.

THIRD DAY

22

I woke, pillow damp and bag knotted around my legs. I'd been imagining Steven Clay, overboard and thrashing slowly along a chain of islands, link by link, until he reached the last of them. Light rolled lazily across the roof of my tent as I untangled myself and sat up, my back and shoulders sore. Would a boat tip over in calm weather?

I shook myself free of the thought and dressed.

Outside, my colleagues made a sad tableau: solemn and wordless, Vinny and Mike ate breakfast while Alex, lost in thought, her planner and itinerary on her knees, sat by the ashes of last night's fire studying the toes of her hiking boots. In spite of everything, the morning around us was beautiful; clean and cool, the sea breeze as fresh as mineral water. Seabirds, their underbellies impossibly white, chased updraughts, calling to each other. My hair smelled of woodsmoke and mosquito repellent so I repeated last night's ritual, dousing my flannel and washing myself in sections. I ate bread rolls, wolfed a palmful of Brazil nuts for energy, and packed my camera bag, pushing two bottles of water into the outside pockets.

I watched Alex master herself. Her eyes wore dark circles. 'OK, everybody,' she said, indicating her notes, 'Tess is filming from the lighthouse today. It's going to be dangerous up there, so we travel in pairs. Mike, you're going with her.'

Mike gave a subdued cheer.

Alex gave the two of us a look of cool insistence. 'Don't split up, watch each other carefully.' She was unspooling a length of rope from the supply tent. 'Deck rope,' she told us. 'About fifteen metres of it. I want to see you safely tied before you go, OK? Don't want to lose you in a landslide.'

Mike worked a loop around his waist. He'd clearly done this before. 'Deserta Grande was the same,' he said in response to my doubtful expression.

'That looks clever,' I said, watching him tie a complicated knot.

'Let me teach you.' He smiled, undoing it again. 'It's a lifesaver. I did my fair share of sailing as a kid. This is a buntline hitch, not a climber's knot but good enough. Stand here.'

I positioned myself next door to him, our shoulders touching, and watched as he demonstrated slowly. 'Round your waist like this. Good. Now make sure you've a decent amount of slack in your right hand. This much.' He waggled it. 'Ready? Over to the left, under to the right. Over both and pinch, like this. Then through the small gap.' I practised a couple of times. 'That's it,' he said. 'Superstar.'

Alex raised a thumb in approval and tried for a smile. 'Good stuff,' she said. 'Mike, you've got the map so you lead. Got your GPSs?' Mike waved a waterproof pouch that he wore on a lanyard around his neck.

'Flare gun?' she checked.

I volunteered to dig one out, padded across to the supply tent, unzipped and pushed my head inside. Spare butane canisters, tinned food, powerbox and phone cables, first aid kits, seal sedatives – I scanned them all. Vinny's speargun was stowed carefully towards the back, I noticed, wreathed in the plastic wrapping left over when we assembled the transceiver. And beside it, a flare gun of chunky orange plastic, safety catch deactivated by a thumb, flare already inserted, trigger waiting to be pulled.

'Got it,' I called.

'Right.' Alex examined the peak against the vivid blue of the sky. 'An hour up, an hour back. An hour for filming, Tess?'

'That should do it.'

'So, we'll all be back here by early afternoon.' Alex cleared her throat. 'Be safe, everyone. Stay focused. I know it will be hard with everything but . . . ' she gave a shrug. 'We do our jobs, we look out for each other.'

Remembering Mike's words from last night, I felt for Alex, trying to imagine the grit necessary to push through. Especially since I couldn't rule out disappointing her even further than I already had. We waved each other off, and Mike and I headed towards the mountain path, our rope hanging slack between us.

Further up, we examined Mike's map. It wasn't exactly OS-standard, but in conjunction with our GPS devices it would do. He traced his finger as he spoke.

'We're here,' he said, indicating a spot inland on the northern tip. 'We follow this trail here and we take it up to here, Pico da Chaminé – the lowest of three, then climb the back of Pico Íngreme, then across the top to Pico da Olho Queimado. This is the lighthouse.' He looked up, checking the terrain ahead, then back to the map as if to confirm a calculation. 'Like Alex said, I reckon an hour, but it'll be slower in parts.'

I examined the section he was indicating; a whorl of contours tighter than a fingerprint. 'Looks steep.'

We climbed for twenty minutes, following the memory of a path I'd found yesterday, and reached the place where we'd conferred last night. We studied the copse at the edge of the cliff. I pictured the pathway beyond, the route down to the little cove.

Mike caught my eye. 'I can't get my head around all this.'

'I know. Maybe we should just keep moving.'

We turned and headed upwards, leaving the shade of the trees behind and breaking new ground. It was slow-going on that ridge; dusty and hot, a scramble through bulbous cacti and broken rock. Another twenty minutes climbing and we took a break. Mike restudied his map, I checked the GPS and we both drank. The air up there was herby, fennel-like. Under our feet, last year's leaf-fall covered the beginnings of fine-grained soil. I felt the weight of yesterday's terrible trauma begin to lift. As long as we were here, it felt strangely as if Mike and I were inured against the horrors of present-day Navigaceo and, instead, existed in its past, retracing the steps of its last occupants. The brutal beauty of the place was a balm I hoped he felt too.

'Pico da Chaminé is just up here,' my companion said, mopping his brow with a handkerchief. We were both breathing pretty hard but the blood-rush of exercise in clean salt air was exhilarating. We'd gained enough height now to see both coasts of the finger of land we were climbing. To a marine biologist like Mike, a vista of endless ocean was commonplace; as inconsequential as an urban patchwork of commerce and traffic was to me. In my eyes, though, the water was stunning; a plain of supple glitter stretching all the way to sub-Saharan Africa on one side, and on the other, six thousand kilometres of mirrored sky shifting beneath the trade wind. My camera couldn't possibly do it justice.

We set off again. Climbing further, the path became more treacherous. Where once we'd woven idly across broad flanks of rock, now the mountain dropped away steeper at each side. I was glad of the rope as we negotiated these sections; soon, we were threading ourselves across a knife-edge outcrop on a trail no wider than my boots and I was clinging to it with damp palms. I'd long ago stopped filming, directing all my attention at where I planted my feet, when we came to a section of path that skirted the edge of a curved cliff face.

'Pico da Chaminé,' Mike said, shuffling towards a dizzying drop over a series of sheer outcrops. Chaminé, I thought as I studied its curved shape, almost a vertical half-pipe. Chimney. We continued our climb, and the pathway was thankfully leaving the cliff edge as the spine of the mountain widened when, out of nowhere, Mike said, 'I couldn't sleep last night.'

For a while I didn't answer; I just wanted a little longer with the sunlight and emptiness. But reality was going to intrude sooner or later. I wiped my eyes. 'Me neither.'

'So weird to think he's dead.'

I paused, hands on hips, blew my fringe from my eyes and dug out my water bottle. 'One thing I wondered,' I tried experimentally, 'was whether he took his own life.'

Mike didn't respond immediately. I watched him struggle with the suggestion, run a hand across his cropped hair, and I used the time to casually ensure I was recording.

'I'm not sure it makes much sense,' he said.

I drank and wiped my mouth. 'Yeah. Taking a boat feels more considered, as if there was a plan of action.'

We began climbing again. Mike worked his way around a boulder, arms out for balance, and having pondered this, turned to me. 'Plus the things we found around him.'

'I was thinking that too,' I said, joining him. 'Hat, torch, wallet – you're not going to need any of that if your plan is to . . . '

Mike nodded and examined the sea, the wind whipping at his zipped jacket. 'He was a pretty robust guy.

Tough, opinionated, determined. I couldn't imagine him becoming – I don't know, depressed? Hopeless? That wasn't him.'

'So tell me what you remember of the night he went missing.'

He held a breath for a moment, eyebrows raised as he travelled back to those brief days two years ago. 'Well,' he sighed, 'it wasn't the easiest trip. There were tensions.'

I began to burn again. 'What about?'

'I suppose . . . ' He stopped, examined the backs of his hands. 'Look. I'm going to say something here. But I don't want you leaping to any conclusions or thinking any worse of him.'

'Of course.'

Mike cupped his chin and rubbed. 'Well,' he said. 'It was Vinny.'

23

My companion was in confessional mood. I checked the mic and kept my voice light. 'OK. Go on.'

'Well, back then,' Mike said, 'Vinny hadn't met Sofia. He was a bit of a wreck, if I'm honest. I mean, he enjoys a drink now, right? Let's just say Sofia's changed him a lot. Before her, Vinny could *really* put it away. When I saw he'd only brought two bottles of wine this time – wow, a miracle. I was so relieved, you know? He's a great guy and a good friend. But there were times back then when I thought some sort of intervention might be necessary.'

So Vinny was definitely the drunk. Alex was the one on the verge of a nervous breakdown. Did that make Clay the fake? Or was that the man I was talking to right now? 'Sounds like it made work difficult,' I said.

'Oh yeah. Vinny was up half the night. Long after we'd finished playing cards and gone to bed he'd sit at the fire, or you'd hear him clattering around the kitchen when you were trying to sleep. And he was good for nothing until lunch each day. Alex was constantly having to work around it. They've been friends for so long she's got used to accommodating him but it just made things worse.' Mike's expression darkened. 'And that wasn't the half of it. Everything that could go wrong on that trip did. It turned out our camera guy had Covid, so he spent a couple of days isolating in his room. We had to leave food outside his door. He ended up having to abandon the project early, so Alex was even more frustrated and angry with everything.'

So Lukas had got ill. Maybe that went some way to explaining his ranting at Seawild; if his film went unfinished he probably hadn't been paid. 'And what about the night Steven went missing?'

Mike rolled his lower lip between his teeth. 'Steven was insular, even more than usual – not that he was depressed, you know, just quiet. He went for a walk along the water's edge in the dark after we'd eaten. And Vinny had finished a bottle of wine to himself by dinner. I went to bed to get away from it all.'

'Vinny was out of it that night?'

'Yeah, I mean not fall-down drunk. He functioned well with a skinful, he was used to it. Although . . . '

I waited. We continued climbing, the rope slack between us, the wind swirling and thudding. Eventually I had to nudge him. 'What, Mike?'

'Well,' he said, hands in his pockets, 'I couldn't sleep that night. Vinny had come in from the fire and done his usual performance in the kitchcn, banging around the drawers looking for food. I remember a couple of hours

155

later I got up to get water.' Mike cleared his throat, weighing something up. 'And I went past Vinny's room and the door was open. And he wasn't in his bed.'

'Out by the fire?'

Mike shrugged, raised his hands. 'Don't think so, but look, it's nothing. Just one of those things, he was probably taking a pee.'

That made me think of meeting Vinny outside the tents last night. He'd had sandals on and had walked all the way out to the woods.

The steep section to the next pico left our legs burning and we drank deeply from our water bottles once we'd battled our way to the top, enjoying the chill wind that came at higher altitude. The mountain had levelled off now, and the last leg of our journey was simpler; a gradual ascent to the final peak.

Mike fought the map as the wind attempted to unfold it. Our shared moment of honesty seemed over. 'This is Olho Queimado,' he said as we approached. As quickly as we got there, the path descended slightly, heading towards the final outcrop, lower than this high point but flat and broad; the only place big enough for any sort of building I'd seen on the entire route.

And there it was.

The old lighthouse was directly ahead, a mottled, off-white stripe against glorious blue. 'Olho Queimado,' Mike was saying, raising his voice over the roar of the wind, 'means "burned eye". Maybe a reference to looking too long at the sun.'

'Or the lighthouse.'

We picked our way across the rocks. The building was an astonishing sight; constructed of stone and brick, a low-slung section on the landward side dominated by a tower rising ten metres from a flared base on huge stone footings. The place was haunting in its isolation. I reminded myself as we approached that this had once been occupied, and marvelled at the sheer bloody-minded determination of people.

We descended, catching ourselves in a pocket of rock protected from the relentless wind. 'Amazing ... ' I grinned at Mike ' ... look at this place.'

He was sweating and panting, smiling like a kid as he surveyed the natural clifftop platform ahead of us. 'Can you imagine?' he asked, and I knew exactly what he meant.

He was thinking about what it might have been like to live out here.

I'd forgotten the name of the three Portuguese lighthouse keepers in Vinny's tale. On the first night, still ignorant of the horror we were to discover later, and by the light of a crackling fire, the telling had been charged with a child-like thrill. Now, in these new circumstances, I felt instead a strong sense of sadness pull. I could imagine how a three-month stint out here might drive a man mad. The relentless wind alone would test all but the hardiest of characters; down at the shore it had been pretty assertive, up here it brawled and bullied, stripping the senses and making the ears throb. The desolation prompted a stab of homesickness. What I wouldn't give, I thought briefly, for a café table and some decent food. But the thought brought others with it: Brixton Police Station, DCI Rafiq. Shivering currents of anxiety returned. Two more days before my appointment, I told myself, returning my gaze to the lighthouse, hauling my mind back to the here and now. She couldn't touch me for another two days.

'Come on,' I said.

We approached, losing the privilege of shelter and re-entering the white noise of the wind. The weather had taken its toll on the building. The gallery beneath the cupola was wrapped in badly degraded metalwork. Most of the panes were gone, and if the flotsam and guano were anything to go by, colonies of gulls had spent decades calling this place home. There was an exterior ladder descending from the high balcony, its iron rungs bleeding red rivers into the stone, but it ended nowhere, its lower half missing. A carved date picked out, 1857, just beside the rusting ladder, had accrued a frosting of bird shit. Both building and tower had once been rendered white, but the paint had long since been shorn from the stonework, so the place was lichen-grey. The only flash of colour now was the raw red of the entrance door, recessed for shelter and sealed shut with a padlock that surely belonged in a museum.

Mike's fingers worked at the rope and we freed ourselves from each other. He was alert, eyes sweeping the exposed rock as we approached. He was looking, I realised, for a good place to sit and draw. He dumped his bag and dug amongst its contents, pulling clear his sketchbook and pens. Like him, I began considering how best to capture the view. The position of the sun would be important. I shrugged off my bag and set to work on my camcorder with cold, clumsy fingers as Mike took in the topography of the area and made his first tentative strokes against the paper. We had maybe thirty square metres of relative flat up here before the sides of the peak dropped in steep shelves. Leaving Mike to his drawing, I headed across the rock towards the lighthouse, filming as I went. I lost my footing. Lurching sideways, my body jagging with adrenaline, I steadied myself. This was not the kind of place to accidentally take a tumble. I imagined pitching over the side and bouncing downwards, rock to rock until I struck the sea. There were equal parts beauty and brutality here. I'd need to stay focused.

I made my way down a series of natural steps, fancying I could detect again the curve of an ancient path beneath my boots, and reached the stripe of shadow cast by the lighthouse. I put my camera down, pulled my earbuds out, flexed my fingers and checked on Mike. The pages of his sketchbook danced madly and he was leaning hard against them as he drew, his face a mask of concentration.

Up close, the lighthouse's dilapidation was even more evident. Given long enough, the wind would flay this place flat. Anything iron was scabbed in rust; tiny plants sprung from joints of the stonework. The single-storey building looked sturdy enough closer to the tower, but had fallen inwards at its landward end, bricks scattered. I approached this outhouse first. Towards the collapsed section, its windows had become eyeless sockets, the wood around the holes gnawed to spongy rot. Hoping to film the interior, I drew closer. It was clear there was a complete room, probably still watertight closest to the lighthouse, but the second outer one had fallen in. I could see the door to the first – sheet metal, locked with a padlock – exposed in the interior wall of the second. Inside the roofless room, a scramble of plants flourished among the bricks.

I turned my attention to the tower itself and its red door. All around the base of the lighthouse were bones, scattered like matchsticks. Some of the skeletons were partially decomposed and furred with feathers – the remains of unfortunate birds who'd smashed against the stone. Approaching the main door, set back in the circular body of the tower itself, I found myself unable to resist the mischievous temptation to push at its cold metal.

The strangest thing happened. The door shifted slightly in its frame, pushing the padlock against the corroded hasp. I'd somehow expected it to be sturdily immovable. I checked the padlock. For a second I couldn't quite credit what I was seeing.

The curved shackle wasn't in the locking bar. All it would take was a twist and I'd be able to work the bar free of the hasp and get inside. I leaned in, checked again.

I was right. No shearing, no bolt cutters, just an open door that appeared, from a distance, to be securely locked.

24

I turned, feeling the dry snap of bird remains under my boots as I did so.

'Mike!' He couldn't hear me out there in the wind. I had to climb back up to him, waving my arms until he looked up from his work. He tucked his picture away and followed.

Once we were back in the shelter of the building, I explained. He frowned at me. 'That can't be right.'

'Come and look.'

My companion stared. 'Well, would you believe that,' he whispered. 'I guess fifty years ago, they were in such a hurry to leave that they forgot to lock it.'

I twisted the hasp. 'So, are we going in?' I'd need to make sure there was enough light to film. I rooted through my bag, found my LED and cupped a hand over it to check my battery would give me sufficient brightness.

Mike seemed to hesitate. 'I don't know.' He shrugged. 'I'm thinking of Alex . . .'

'Come on. We're not missing this opportunity.'

'Listen.' Mike licked his lips, seemed to change his mind. 'If you're sure.'

It took some effort to work the old lock free but I snaked it from the hasp and set it aside. Then I steadied the camera and gave Mike a nod of encouragement. He pushed the door inward and we moved into the darkness of the interior.

The door lifted a veil of dust from the concrete floor. Mike moved forwards, grit spitting beneath his boots. Two more doors. To our left, a locked one which I guessed gave access to the single-storey structure; to our right, one standing open, leading through to the living space. Ahead of us, against the far wall, three cast-iron sea-green barrels with brass fittings; storage for the lamplighters' oil. A peeling label gave faded instructions under the heading *whale oil vapour burner.* Below it, a pressure gauge slept beneath a blanket of dust.

But none of that drew our attention right now. Instead, we found ourselves staring at the collection of objects in the corner.

There were two jerry cans in red plastic, plus a pair of sealed crates sitting one atop the other. I struggled to make sense of what I was seeing. It contradicted everything we'd been told about this expedition. Whatever illusions we might have had that we were the first to set foot on the island since the seventies were abruptly and finally shattered. It may have been scuffed and sun-bleached, but this was modern equipment.

'My God,' Mike breathed, making his way forwards

across the broken tiles. He nudged a can with the toe of his boot. It wouldn't shift. 'Full,' he said. I filmed as he unscrewed the cap, sniffed and wrinkled his nose. 'This is MDO,' he said.

'What?'

'Boat fuel.'

'What about the boxes?'

Mike unclipped the lid of the uppermost and slid it aside. 'Water. Litre bottles.' I approached, framed the crate's interior as his hands counted off the contents. 'Thirty litres?' He plucked one out. The label pictured a snow-capped mountain in hazy blue, beneath which were the words *Sidi ali. Eau mineral naturelle.* 'Moroccan,' he said.

'This is bottled water from Africa?'

Mike shrugged, spun the bottle, checked the reverse. A further label; Arabic writing. 'Or Gran Canaria,' he said, lowering the top crate and beginning to explore the one beneath. This was stuffed with food and bedding. Packets of biltong in sealed bags, their tearaway tabs untouched. Two bedding rolls, a sleeping bag.

'Food and water,' I said. 'And somewhere to sleep. Doesn't look like it's been touched recently. There's a coating of dust.' A two-year coating, I added mentally. Did that mean the cache was here at the same time as Clay? Surely they were linked. I caught Mike's eye. 'Has someone been hiding out here, you think?'

'I doubt it,' my companion said, continuing his rifle through the supplies. 'This is just a storage space for fuel and water. If I had to guess, I'd say illegal seal-pelt trading, something like that.' He replaced the crate lid. 'This stuff hasn't been used in a good while.'

I stopped shooting, testing this theory. It didn't hold up. Seal-pelt traders would keep their stash closer to the shore; there didn't seem a good reason to haul it miles uphill. Whoever was using this space had chosen it because it was sheltered, dry and invisible. I tried another angle. What if, for some reason, Clay was intent on disappearing? Alex had said last night he had no immediate family, no one to question his absence. If he was planning on reinventing himself, starting a new life, he might have arranged to be collected on the island. There was plenty of supplies here for someone lying low. Except something had clearly gone wrong. Clay had never made it up to this building.

Mike was eyeing the door to the next room now.

We crossed together. He loitered, stayed out of shot and motioned for me to lead if I wanted to film. I pushed the door further open.

Floor tiles scattered like crazy paving; a spray of broken glass, the carcass of a seabird. Iron buckets punctuating the space, placed to catch leaks; the remains of a burgundy rug with its corner upturned and the skeleton of a big, weather-beaten dresser, its drawers missing. Glass crunched underfoot as we made our way inside. The notion that people once lived here struck me again, as cold and hard as a clifftop gale. This was an outpost so distant and defiant, any normal rules of behaviour wouldn't apply. Day by day and week by week, life would surely become indistinguishable from survival.

'Lookee here.' Mike nodded towards the far corner of the room. A winding staircase hugged the circular wall, wooden slats supported by an iron skeleton, rising into the space above us. He paused at the foot of the slatted stairs, checked I was still close by for backup, then tested the first step.

I was charged with explorer's excitement, ready to film whatever I found. 'Come on,' I said. 'Let's go.'

I ascended, Mike followed. The wooden slats took us up into a bedroom. Two more buckets – for carrying the whale oil up to the burners, I guessed – an upturned desk, shards of fallen plaster scattered, and the sagging metalwork of a single bed.

'You fancy risking going up to the top?' I asked, thinking of the shots I'd get from the cupola.

My companion craned his neck, peering up the next staircase to the space above us. 'Doesn't exactly smell great up there,' he breathed, then set his jaw.

I patted his shoulder reassuringly and, despite his reluctance, we climbed again. Ravaged by rust as it was, the metalwork still felt solid but the wooden stairs were soft beneath our feet this time. I held my camcorder against my chest to steady my shots and kept to the outside edges of the stairs, hoping they might be better able to support our weight.

We emerged at the top of the tower. Glassless windows were choked with layers of guano; hardy plants, bent double by the barrelling wind, thrived in the fertilised pockets of the sills. The smell of dead fish was surely the whale oil chambers that lined the cupola, metal storage tanks designed to feed the great lens that dominated the space. Rising from the floor in the centre of the circular room was an elongated sphere of convex glass plates, each pane tough and thick.

The huge swollen lens rose taller than us right to the metal ceiling; the area within its walls, where the stored oil would have burned brightly, was easily big enough to fit an engineer who'd have doubtless slithered inside from the access points below to light the device.

Mike ran his hand along the bulging glass panels of the great lens. It still turned, grinding against the rust in its mechanism. I filmed, moving around the ovoid. *Olho Queimado.* This was surely the burnt eye that gave the peak its name; an all-seeing lens suspended high over the tiny boats below. Watching and guiding. I wondered what a lens like this might reveal if it could record what it saw.

'Incredible,' Mike said, peering through the magnifying panels to study its interior. 'Looks complicated. Do you think it would still work after all this time?'

I grunted, distracted. The views through the windows were so stunning I could almost convince myself I was seeing the curve of the planet. I made a slow 360, careful to position myself close to Mike and keep him out of shot. To the west, a rolling plain of water, spun through with pulsing darkness, and somewhere over the horizon beyond a distant anvil of cloud – the Carolinas, Georgia, and the Florida Keys. Northwards, a borderless expanse of water all the way to Iceland, and behind us to the east, the dusty coastal settlements of the Western Sahara. To the south, across the glittering water somewhere beyond the scope of my lens, Gran Canaria.

'Are you up for a stroll on the balcony?' Mike quipped, indicating a small door that gave access onto the mesh-metal parapet that ringed the building. Through the broken windows I could see sections out there; the railings, stripped of their paintwork long ago, were a series of uprights topped with rusting finials.

'You're kidding.'

'Well, now that we're here ... ' He approached the door and I followed, feet crunching through drifts of paint-peelings; off-white curls that had flaked from iron rivets and forged grab-handles. We were looking at a hatch with a draw-bolt. Mike ground it back and pulled the door open. It swung inward, revealing the parapet beyond. Noisy air brawled through.

My stomach gave a jolt as I saw, through the gaps in the mesh-metal of the walkway, the distance to the clifftop rocks below. 'I don't fancy that.'

'If it's anything like as bad as the stairs,' Mike said, 'that thing will collapse as soon as we set foot on it. Look at the rust.' He stooped and crawled half-out, hands on the metal. 'Incredible view though,' he called back, the wind lifting his t-shirt. Palms flat against the parapet, he gave it a push. 'Feels pretty solid. Shall I risk it?'

'Just be careful.'

Mike wormed through and, arms aloft tightrope-walker style, rose to full standing, his back to the exterior stones, only his legs visible through the doorway. He stayed there, no doubt scanning the horizon as the wind bullied him, then, like he'd completed a school-yard dare, he dropped to a crouch and executed an ungainly reverse back inside. Brushing his clothes down, he laughed. 'Amazing views down to the water. Scary. Not sure it'd hold two people.' He clapped rust from his hands, palms still carrying the impression of the metal grille. 'Well,' he said, assessing the eye of the great lens once more, 'it's been fun. But I think we should get out of here.'

Footage captured, I took one last look at the curved glass, then we circled our way back down the spiral stairs, testing each slat as we went.

25

Downstairs, relieved to be back at the entrance again, I paused at the locked door that led through to the single-storey building. Earlier, we'd been so surprised by the stash of boat fuel and supplies, we hadn't had time to consider this door. I hadn't even noticed the padlock. Now I did.

It was a brash, modern thing in polished steel. I gave it a tug, hoping the same thing would happen as before, and I'd find it unlocked. It wasn't.

'Look at this,' I said as Mike passed.

He stared at it, eyes narrowing as he calculated possible explanations, then, following some train of thought, turned back to the fuel storage. 'Whoever hid this,' he said, nodding towards the plastic crates, 'probably attached this.'

Outside he turned, hands on hips, and studied the exterior. When I joined him, he said, 'So if it's become some sort of trafficking outpost, I think we should lock this place up.'

'Absolutely,' I agreed, happy to be back in the sun-shine, despite the circle of bird-bones that surrounded us; little ribcages and still-feathered wing-joints scat-tered like broken flags.

Mike's attention was caught by our bags in the wind. His was unzipped and his sketchbook was flickering, threatening an escape. 'Shit.'

As I packed away, I remembered we'd agreed to lock the lighthouse. Neither of us had dealt with it.

Mike was absorbed, so I crossed to the door and twisted the bar into the hasp, cursing the rust. As I did so, a possibility struck me. The thought came suddenly and hard – banged the underside of my breastbone as it surfaced.

Dumping my bag between my boots, I unzipped the lid and pushed a searching hand inside. It was a crazy idea but something about the age of the padlock made it possible; it hadn't been cast as a single piece of metal, but was instead riveted together, with a sliding tongue to protect the keyhole, a design which looked ... I tried figuring it out. Well, it stood to reason it was fifty years old at least, attached when the island was re-designated a reserve, but it actually looked even older.

I dug out Clay's key and tried it with trembling hands. This was old too, with its circular shaft of corroded metal.

I pushed it into the lock. Clay's key was precisely the correct shape and size. I twisted.

My heartbeat broke from a trot, upped its rhythm to a canter. Then a gallop. It required a strong twist, but once the rust had shifted, it locked and unlocked the hasp with ease. I did it again to double check. 'Oh my God,' I breathed, a thrill in my fingers.

Steven Clay had swallowed a key to the door of the lighthouse.

I turned. Mike was still drawing; hadn't seen my discovery. I pocketed Clay's key then made a performance of repacking my bag in case he looked. All the while I was burning. This confirmed Steven Clay had come to Navigaceo on purpose. He'd been planning on staying at the lighthouse, where a cache of food, water and bedding was waiting for him. Did that suggest he had an accomplice? The story seemed unlikely, but the evidence was right here in my pocket. Clay had . . . what, swallowed the key to avoid it being found? But, by whom? And how had he ended up dead on the beach?

'Tess!' Mike had been calling but the noise of the wind and a fever of speculation had prevented my noticing. I blinked myself back to reality, forced a smile and waved.

We made our way back across the summit. The conditions required concentration, the rooting of feet with each step. A raw wind lifted the rope between us and spun it like a playground skipping game, flaying us until our ears ached. Our descent felt treacherous, the mountainside seeming to fall away more vertiginously as the path wove downwards. The hardest section was the Pico da Chaminé. We went slowly and wordlessly, skirting the cliff face with lungfuls of held breath. Sweat beaded in my eyebrows. It was a relief when the path wove inland, affording us an escape from the edge. Feeling the sun's warmth out of the wind, we paused for breath, untying our rope now the dangerous sections were done. The relative safety of the spot encouraged the return of a crowd of thoughts. Perhaps Mike's speculation about seal-pelt trading did have a role to play – maybe Steven Clay had been involved. It didn't fit with those descriptions of a principled ecologist, but hadn't Mike hinted Clay might have deserved what happened to him?

'Ready?' he said, capping his water bottle.

'You go ahead,' I told him. 'I'm going to do a little more filming.' I had a plan that necessitated shaking my companion off. Free of Mike, I figured I could go back down to the cove and capture Clay one more time. Now I knew where the key belonged, I could grab more footage while I still had time. I was never coming back here again. Always better to over-shoot and dump a ton of stuff in the cutting room during the edit.

He thinned his lips. 'Come on, Tess. We shouldn't really split up.'

'Don't worry,' I said, aiming for reassuring. 'We're past the difficult bit. I'm just exploring along the forest edge here. I'll be careful.'

'How about I wait? How long do you need?'

'Another thirty minutes at least.'

He assessed this. 'Half an hour? OK, well, I guess I'll go and check on the others and we'll meet at camp.'

I waved Mike off, then, while he was still in view, put on a show of shooting the cliff path. Once he'd disappeared, I packed away and set off. In fifteen minutes, I was back down at the turn by the copse of trees. There were the fallen slats of the fence and there the route beyond. The prospect of revisiting Clay sent a shiver of dark excitement through me, the movement of it weakening my legs as I crossed the threshold of the tumble-down fence. In a matter of moments I could search the beach and nail the footage once and for all. I felt the fever of story-obsession strengthen. Strange to think that only yesterday I'd been here in the spirit of carefree exploration, light of heart, mind untroubled.

Now I knew exactly what was waiting for me at the bottom of that descent.

26

At the water's edge, the lonely ugliness of the place struck me again. Rotting bottles, the cheap Hallowe'en ghosts of plastic bags, clots of frayed rope like wet hair; the tatty trash of our everyday lives. I crossed the sand, weaving between the washed-up flotsam, and the body manifested itself again; Steven Clay on the rocks by the sand, pushed up against the thin trunk of a shrub, entwined in a net of branches.

Piece it together, Tess. Clay could be part of some gang of wildlife criminals or, more likely, the stock of supplies at the lighthouse might be fuel for some onward journey, the room up there a place to sleep away from the water and out of the wind. He could have been leaving one life behind and beginning another. But if he'd made it to the lighthouse, why did he return here? I tried picturing him collecting food or supplies maybe, then descending back to the beach. Was he meeting someone? Was another vessel picking him up? It wasn't a completely convincing explanation.

I was disturbed by a noise somewhere behind me. The unmistakable rustle of movement on the path above. *Shit.* Mike had come back.

I didn't want him seeing me here. Jesus, the trouble Alex would make.

A giddy wave of adrenaline propelled me. I scrambled up onto the rock alongside the body, then worked my way beyond him, pushing into the tangled border of shrubs. I had to wriggle between tough twigs and branches, eventually finding protection between the painful, scraping growth and an outcrop of volcanic rock. Mike was down on the beach now, I could hear his movement. I waited, my back pushed painfully against an irregular boulder, until the sounds stopped. Then I risked a quick look.

It wasn't Mike.

Vinny Perriera was standing before the body on the beach below. I didn't like what that suggested. Vinny was supposed to be down at the haul-out with Alex. Which meant he wasn't passing by, he'd come on purpose, and against the wishes of his boss. Alex's warning hadn't deterred me, but I was the outsider, not the crew member. I adjusted position, slowly and carefully, until I had a better view of Clay's newest visitor.

He approached the body with caution, and waited. He was deliberating. My stomach tightened. He moved forwards with the kind of reluctance that was born of revulsion, his head angled slightly away from Clay's face, then began probing the dead man's midriff; checking the Seawild hoodie, tugging at it. I watched him steel himself, brush aside the fallen leaves and accreted dirt, then peer closely at Clay's belly. Did he know about the key? Was he looking for it? He stayed, studying the body for a minute, then withdrew, rose to standing.

Vinny's posture told me everything I needed to know.

Now he was stiff with alarm as he checked the beach with a quick, wide-eyed glance. He left hurriedly, hauling himself up the rocks towards the cliff path again.

I waited until I was certain he wasn't returning then fought my way back down onto the sand – I was scratched and scraped painfully – and crossed to where Vinny had been. Something had frightened him. I forced myself to look at the body. It was immediately clear Vinny hadn't been looking at the place I'd found the key. Clay's hoodie was pulled out of shape. He'd seen something wrong with the clothing. So had I, I remembered, in the footage I'd shot yesterday. I moved in close, began a slow examination, hoping my eyes might snag on something.

He hadn't been near the boots or legs, he'd been more firmly focused on the upper torso, so I scanned upwards, passing the belt and finding myself studying the zip-up Seawild hoodie. Worn grey cotton, the logo still visible beneath layers of grime. Two winters' worth of Atlantic squalls had turned the dust of the island's rock into a red-brown glue that caked his boots and coated his clothes, but there was nothing remarkable in that; my own gear was beginning to stain and I'd only been here three days.

Leaning in, I noticed the odd feature my footage had

picked out before. Clay's right shoulder was larger. It was bulked out by something beneath the fabric of his top. Had Vinny seen this? I peeled the hoodie back until I could see the bony joint where shoulder connected with torso.

A cross-body bum bag was looped over his arm there, hidden beneath the fabric.

Sun-drained to pale yellow, it was the size of a student traveller's cash-belt, the kind I used to wear around my waist under my clothes, keeping my passport and replacement batteries safe. I stared at it, my pulse jacking. I was pretty sure Vinny hadn't noticed it, or he'd have explored it, maybe even taken it with him. The wind and rain had scattered most of Clay's stuff along the rocks; animals had dragged the contents of the poor guy's pockets about. But he'd kept this bag carefully hidden under his clothing. I thought about the things I'd said to Alex as she'd tried dignifying Clay's passing by corralling the dead man's belongings. This hidden sling bag could be an inflexion point; one I could ignore, cutting off the project's oxygen, or one I could use to pick a route forwards.

I knew which it had to be but that didn't make the doing any easier. I reached in, unclipped the bag and pulled it carefully from under Clay's skeletal arm, then placed it on the rocks. I unloaded my camera and thumbed the on-switch.

'Hidden beneath Clay's hoodie,' I whispered, panning across the beach and back to the body, 'I've come across this. Never noticed it first time round but it looks like he was cradling it carefully. Its contents could reveal something of how Clay ended up here on the island.'

I kept the camera rolling as I leaned forwards – all in now, no going back – and unzipped the lid of the thing, releasing a mist of trapped dust. I peered inside.

My heart leapt. A transparent plastic bag protected car keys, a neatly folded wad of low-denomination euros, a map of Deserta Grande, and a phone.

'This surely takes suicide out of the picture once and for all,' I narrated. 'Who would plan on ending their life but take their phone and a set of hire-car keys with them?'

I unpacked the contents, arranged them on the rocks beside me and began a careful, fingertip exploration. First the phone. It was an older model, its screen cracked and casing scuffed. It was, of course, dead, and I didn't have a charger to fit it. Next the car keys. These belonged to a rental; a Peugeot with a Sixt keyring. That matched the paperwork I'd found in the wallet yesterday. I pictured Clay with the waterproof sling bag secured across his arm, beating out across the ocean, and began re-packing its contents, thinking. Should I bring the bag back with me? I didn't like what might happen if I returned to camp and was caught with Steven's belongings. The phone, though – I could hide that. Maybe recharge it somehow. I slipped it free, pocketed it. Then I reattached the bag to Clay's bony shoulder and lowered the hoodie back over.

And that's when I saw the thing I'd been missing.

The thing Vinny had seen. I ran the tips of my fingers across the hoodie, flattening the creases, brushing away the dirt. And found the fabric was torn. Just in one place, and not the rough-edged snag of undergrowth. It was a neatly ripped line. I pushed a finger into it; a two-centimetre-wide tear as precise as a zip. The ground dropped away beneath me.

The stains across his clothing weren't volcanic rock dust. They were blood.

I was looking at a hole made by a blade.

Vinny hadn't been searching for the sling bag I'd just found. He'd been looking for *this*. Everything I'd been speculating about was wrong. Clay hadn't thrashed across the water to Navigaceo to wait for a boat. He hadn't come here to collect a cache of supplies from the lighthouse, to make a new life for himself.

He'd been stabbed and dumped.

And as I backed away I realised something even worse.

Two years ago, Clay had been one of four members of a closely monitored research expedition. Red tape prevented anyone else coming close to the shoreline. So his killer had to be someone present on Deserta Grande back then.

The other three members of that expedition were with me now. And this time, we were even further away from help.

27

I leaned forwards, hands on knees, and waited to throw up while the cove whirled above me. Eventually I regained sufficient control over the battering ram of my pulse and tried putting it together. Maybe Clay had taken someone else's key – just like he'd taken Vinny's card – and that someone had killed him. Did the fact that Vinny had returned to examine Clay make him more likely to be the perpetrator? Or was it Alex who, with her stern warnings about returning to the body, clearly didn't want anyone down here? Or Mike, whose cheerful demeanour might be nothing but a mask? All three of them knew about the tides, which meant either one of them could have known this day would come.

And now they were back to clear up the mess they'd made. The *Auk* wasn't due for another day. My hands were jittering.

I hadn't felt cornered like this since Kern County.

★

Back then, the first signs of trouble had come at four thirty in the morning, the day after we'd found Redfern in his car and had the encounter with the wrong-road guys.

Gretchen and I left our key at the McKittrick motel reception and were re-packing the car in the lot out front, the dawn air already promising heat, when we heard a vehicle on the road. Oil tankers had toiled past in the night, but this sounded different. We slammed the boot shut, opened the car doors and hovered. A black SUV passed at speed, heading south out of town, a widening wake of dust rolling outward behind it.

'That was the security guys,' I said, my mouth suddenly dry.

Gretchen pursed her lips. 'Looks like it.' She frowned, tied her hair back and climbed into the car.

'Hang on,' I said. We shut our doors against the dust. 'You said they'd be in bed.'

'Guess I was wrong.' She smiled, clicking her seatbelt on and putting the car in gear. 'Tess, don't worry. They were heading south in a hurry, we're driving north. You ready?'

We had our cameras on the back seat: spare batteries, radio mics, wide-angle lenses. Once more I quelled a wriggling anxiety. This was Gretchen Harris, for God's sake. Who was I? 'Ready,' I said.

Outside town, the highway split. We stayed on the 33 north towards Blackwells Corner and soon we were deep into the Midway-Sunset fields. In the dawn light around us, pumpjacks nodded like dashboard dogs, and beyond the fences overground piping systems shuttled oil through miles of tubing. Gretchen drove and I worked from the paper plans, trying to pinpoint our exact location – hard when the only landmark was a highway as straight as a plumb-line passing through a featureless rockscape. Eventually a building emerged in the distance beyond a shallow cutting. It was tall and silver in the rising sun and a tangle of chimneys pumped blurred clots of burn-off. At least I had something to work with.

'That's some sort of treatment plant,' I said. 'Which means we're here. Another kilometre or two and we should pass a crossroads – a track running diagonally – then we're in the right spot.'

'Shouldn't we be seeing them now?' Gretchen leaned forwards over the wheel to examine the desert ahead. The sky was a vivid pink. 'How tall are these things?'

All my research confirmed carbon-capture required substantial heating chambers. 'Can be up to ten, fifteen metres, so with luck we'll be able to—'

'Shit.'

I looked up from the map at this. A pair of headlights some distance away were approaching. My stomach became a slick knot. 'Another oil tanker?'

'That, or our friends are up early and about their business.'

There was no point in *but you said*. I remember a thought flickering just briefly: did Gretchen Harris make things up as she went along, confident that events would fall in her favour? If so, I had no idea where that kind of conviction came from. Back then, I interpreted its absence in me as conclusive proof of my significant personal shortcomings. I know better now. 'What do we do?'

'Hold our nerve,' Gretchen said. 'It's just another car heading in the opposite direction, right?'

'What if they recognise us?'

Gretchen yanked the driver's sun-visor down. 'They won't.' I followed suit, shading my face. The vehicle passed us; one of yesterday's black SUVs, its tinted windows grime-caked. Just as Gretchen had said, it didn't stop, but I watched her studying it in the rear-view, chewing her lip. 'See?' she said when it had disappeared into the heat haze. 'Nothing to worry about. Whoa, crossroads, Tess. Is this the place?'

And there it was – the track I'd identified, passing across the road ahead and winding through low scree towards the treatment plant to our left. 'No CCS towers,' I said. The enormity of the discovery hit me. 'No CCS towers.' Back in the UK I'd requested the Chase plans, trawled their websites, dug through the company's paperwork, and predicted there'd be zero sign of construction on this precise site. And I'd been correct. 'Oh my God!' I managed, amazed. 'I *said* it would be like this. I *bloody said*, Gretch.'

My companion pulled up at the road's edge, our tyres spitting gravel as we slowed. 'Let me see.' I handed her the plans and the road map. She studied it. 'OK. So according to this, construction began almost a year ago . . . ' she matched the two documents '. . . here.

This section of land, beyond that bluff.' She looked up, checked the map, looked again. 'Holy shit,' she said, and began laughing. 'You're right, Tess. It's all a con. Come on.'

She pulled out again and we cruised another kilometre, eyes on the fenced-off land, the treatment plant belching smoke in the distance. I was still blushing with pride at *you're right Tess* when we found a way off the road and rolled down an uneven verge. Gretchen parked where a storm drain tunnelled beneath the highway. We switched our phones off and tucked them into the glove compartment. Our car wasn't easy to spot from here, I reassured myself, as we unloaded the cameras – I'd bought a brand-new Red MX – and approached the fencing.

'You should do the honours,' she said, passing me the wire-cutters. Even in the afterglow of my partner's praise I must have hesitated because she grinned, 'Come on, Tess. It's going to be your name on this film; you get to break the law in the pursuit of truth.'

And so I clipped the fencing wires carefully, working my way up from the ground until I had a flap I could squeeze through. Gretchen held back the wire. I pocketed the cutters, cradled my camera, and crawled into the compound, then, attention focused on my monitor, began filming.

I'd got into the habit of narrating dummy audio back at university, so that's what I did, my courage and confidence building as I moved forwards across the desert. 'This is the spot where Chase Industries claim to be running their carbon-capture storage project. They're backed by tens of millions of pounds' worth of UK government funding. Ordinary tax payers' money has been diverted away from schools and hospitals. And what do we have for our investment?' I moved further inward as I talked. 'It seems we have nothing. But that's not the story the Chase website is telling us.'

I made my way up and over a low ridge, ensuring I was capturing the full extent of the unworked land, and was descending the far side when I heard something on the road. I turned; saw two things happening at once. The black SUV, sun shimmering against its windows, was arrowing north out of McKittrick towards us. And Gretchen, who'd followed me through the fencing, was caught in two minds. She hovered briefly, her gaze flicking between me and the approaching car.

Heart banging high in my chest, I threw myself to the ground and, thinking of reflecting sunlight, capped my camera lens. I lay in the dirt and risked a glimpse over the ridge. Gretchen was back through the fence and heading for our car.

A terror, real and sharp, passed its blade across my belly. I felt cut in two.

She was leaving me. I heard the driver's door slam, and watched as our Chevrolet laboured up the verge and back onto the road, its rear wheels summoning clouds of grit as Gretchen hit the accelerator. For a second or two – no more – I nurtured a fragile hope that the wrong-road guys might follow my partner as she fled and leave me be.

They didn't. They pulled up.

I was going to die out in the desert.

The fear was so intense it drove me to sobbing. I slithered down the bank away from the road and tried to run, but my legs, nothing but a blaze of pins and needles, wouldn't respond. Eventually I got them working and looked back, just once. There were two figures at the fence. One was examining the damage I'd done, talking into a radio. The other had swept his gun around his body so he could better slip through the gap. He was following me in.

I remember staying low and just running, face wet with tears, into the wilderness.

28

Up until that point, our circle of tents had been a comfort, but as I approached our camp, following the beaten-back ferns along the edge of the wood, an entirely different feeling worked its way through me. This time, our little pocket of civilisation appeared corrupted.

I was approaching a place that felt less a source of support, more a trap. One of these people had killed Clay.

The camp was empty. Alex was out at the colony and Mike, who was almost an hour ahead of me by now, must have gone to join her. Vinny would need to account for his movements, so he'd be heading back there too, I guessed. At least I could take a moment to calm myself before facing them all. I unzipped my tent, unloaded my equipment, repositioned the transceiver's solar panel for maximum charge, and plugged my phone into the powerbox.

Then I paced, wrestling with thorny possibilities. Surely the last thing Clay's murderer wanted was a nosey filmmaker asking awkward questions. And though I couldn't have witnessed their objections when I was commissioned, I could surely detect their animosity now. Alex's suspicion was bordering on disdain. Did that make her a more likely candidate for Clay's murder?

The rip of a tent zip made me jump.

From behind me, beyond the firepit, Vinny emerged from beneath his flap. 'Hey. How was the lighthouse?'

It was the second time he'd surprised me like that. I removed my hand from its startled position against my chest. I tried to laugh but it came out strangled. Could Vinny have killed Clay?

'Sorry,' he said, rising to his feet with a groan, dusting grit from his knees. 'I've just been checking on the transceiver, charging the laptops. Going back to the colony in a minute.' I knew this to be a lie, but didn't know what to do about it. He must have seen something of the conflict in my face, because he asked, 'Are you OK?'

'I'm fine,' I began, then faltered. If Vinny was innocent, he'd be feeling just as I was. Frightened by the possibility that Clay was murdered by a colleague. Replaying the events of the night two years ago, hiding in his tent and worrying about what to do next. He might have come here to switch the transceiver on and make contact with his superiors at Seawild. I could be disturbing his attempts to request immediate evac. None of this appeared evident in his face, but that didn't mean it wasn't boiling away somewhere beneath. I could confide I also knew about Clay's murder, but I had no idea whether it was the right thing to do. I stared at him dumbly.

He ran a hand through hair knotted by salt. 'You don't seem fine,' he said. 'Did something happen at the lighthouse?'

I wasn't going to be sharing my discovery about the key. But since Mike had witnessed the rest with me, I proceeded cautiously, checking his responses. 'Actually, yes. We found something.'

A brief shadow clouded Vinny's features. Maybe I was watching a man preparing himself for a blow; a man who knew exactly what I was about to say. I watched the bob of his throat as he tried to swallow.

'There's a stash of fuel there,' I said. 'Food, a sleeping bag.'

His face slackened. 'What?' Either it was real, or he was an adept deceiver. He inflated cheeks grey with stubble. 'And it's recent?'

I nodded. 'Something strange has been happening here.'

Vinny swayed, placed an uncertain hand on the upright of his tent, threw a glance around the camp, wiping one hot palm on the thigh of his shorts. It looked like shock to me. 'Seawild will need to send a team out,' I said. I thought about Mike's words up on the pico. Vinny's drinking, his room being empty the night Clay went missing. 'Can I ask you a question?'

Vinny slumped into a fireside chair, his gaze pulled beyond the tents to the woodland boundary. I took his silence as an invitation.

'The night Steven went missing,' I said. 'Do you remember what happened?'

He blinked, recovering himself. 'It's a long time ago . . .' He thought a little, then wiped his face. 'Steven was different on the trip, not his usual self. When he'd first come to us, he was full of energy, a really positive guy. But that changed.'

I let the silence between us extend, constructing a narrative. Clay had got involved in something on this island and was killed for it. 'Changed how?'

'He had a lot on his mind. Each night he'd walk along the waterline on his own.' Vinny returned his gaze to the woods, a troubled frown creasing his forehead. 'I used to stay up for him, wait at the fire. He'd come back and I'd try and talk to him, but he didn't speak.'

'Was it a work problem?'

I watched him gnaw at his lower lip. 'OK. Listen. In the cove, when you found my card, I said I didn't know why it was there. But I do know. Steven had asked for it before. And . . . I had given it to him.' He shook his head. 'Twice he'd borrowed and returned it. Stupid thing to do, I could lose my job. But he was my friend and he kept telling me he needed it.'

Interesting. 'Did he tell you what for?'

'No. But he asked for the card all the time.'

'Is there something yours can access?'

Vinny watched the woods. Something was distracting him. 'Mine gets most places,' he said vaguely. 'Labs, offices.'

I changed tack, thinking of Mike's story. 'So I guess you were up waiting for him the night he left.'

'Yeah. The whole trip made me unhappy. Steven was

strange, Alex was stressed. Even the camera guy caught Covid and was coughing every night. It was a relief when he quit.'

'When exactly was that?'

'Well, he didn't make it to the end ... ' Vinny levered his cap upwards and ran a hand across his brow. 'Three nights in? Something like that. He went back to the mainland a couple of days before Steven went missing.'

'And the night itself. Were you up waiting? Did you see anything?'

'No ... ' He ran a knuckle across his teeth, his focus broken again.

'Vin. What's wrong?'

I remember, as I asked the question, thinking things couldn't get any worse. That seems laughable now. Vinny rubbed his eyes, checked the woods again and cleared his throat. 'I think there's someone on the island with us.'

The shift of topic threw me. I didn't know how to respond. 'What do you mean?'

'This is going to sound strange,' Vinny continued, his eyes darting along the treeline as he cupped the back of his neck. 'Did you see someone else on your way down from the pico?'

Apart from you? I nearly asked. Instead, 'Mike came down before me. I stayed to do some filming.' Something about Vinny's expression tugged anxiously at me. 'What is it?'

'About an hour ago, were you filming in the woods along here?'

'No, Mike and I were still at the lighthouse.'

'Both of you? And you didn't come down here to film at all?'

'Vinny, what is this?'

He pushed his hair back, two big palms against his temples. 'Alex was down at the haul-out. I came back to charge the laptops, turn the solar panel, check whether we'd had our first tracker-data delivered. And—' he shrugged unhappily '—there was someone out here with me.'

My first thought was: he's lying. He's been down in the cove checking on Steven Clay's body and he's needed a cover story; one he can stick to and confidently re-tell. Even so, my skin itched. A tale about an impossible visitor was a bizarre method of misdirection. What could I do but play along? 'No,' I said. 'We were still up at the pico. You must have imagined it.'

Vinny's posture loosened as he unburdened himself. 'I was looking at my screen, reading the data. Sitting just here. Then I heard a noise from the path and I looked, but my eyes . . . ' he fanned a hand vaguely. Despite just having lied to me about his whereabouts, I got the strong impression he might be telling the truth about this particular experience.

'I understand. It's hard to refocus quickly.'

'Right. There was a noise. Something moved in the trees but I didn't see what.' He sighed. 'I saw him, it . . . ' Pausing, he placed a finger alongside his eye. '*Olhar de lado.*'

'I get it,' I said. 'But Vinny, you can't have. Alex hasn't

192

followed you back, she's surely down by the shore. And if you're right about the time, Mike and I were both up on the mountain.'

'Well, I saw someone.' He removed his cap, passed the brim between his fingers. The sweat band was dark with moisture. Airborne seeds clung to his tanned skin.

I was reluctant to endorse Vinny's story with further questioning but something about his manner made me probe a little more. 'Can you describe the person?'

'No. A shape, a movement. I turned and I couldn't see what it was.'

'That could have been anything,' I said. 'Maybe the wind blowing the canopy ...'

He gave me a look. 'It wasn't.'

'I guess we should ask the others,' I offered. My palms were clammy, my clothes sticking to my back.

'I've been thinking that. Maybe I'm just seeing things.' Vinny replaced his cap, pulled it low to shade his eyes. 'One more day,' he said grimly and I was struck by the desolation in his voice. Here was a man desperate to get home. Did that make him more guilty, I wondered, or less?

'I guess we need to tell Alex about the lighthouse.'

Vinny nodded, hauled himself up from his chair. He glanced once more at the woods, I noticed. 'Let me tell her, OK? She's under enough pressure. It's better coming from me.'

'If you think so,' I said, before a thought struck me. 'Vin, can you tell Mike to collect my GoPro?'

'Of course.'

Watching him cross the *faja* towards the haul-out, I

realised what a big man he was; broad-shouldered and imposing. He could overpower someone with little effort.

I felt anxiety close a fist around my stomach. I was trapped in a horror I didn't understand.

29

Vinny's behaviour had me on edge. This time I confirmed I was entirely alone by opening every tent and checking each interior.

Mike's held a neatly arranged sleeping bag and half-packed rucksack topped with a sealed plastic bag; the shells he'd gathered for his daughter. Alex's came as something of a surprise, an explosion of personal effects with a dramatic blast radius. I almost didn't check Vinny's since I'd seen him emerge from it, but, I reminded myself, that didn't mean it was empty. Inside I glimpsed cigarettes and lighter, a paperback in Portuguese. Nothing else.

There was definitely no one here but me.

Suppressing all other concerns for a moment, I pulled Clay's phone from my back pocket and squatted at the powerbox in the supply tent, checking the charging cables. Two types didn't fit it but a third did. I plugged in the phone and studied the screen. Nothing. I checked the cable was secure – it was – and plugged Clay's device back in, studying the polished black emptiness of its display. The euros in Clay's waterproof body bag had seemed completely dry, but there was a chance the bag had leaked and the phone had got wet. Phones and cameras shared a complete aversion to saltwater; drop a camcorder in the sea and you're never filming a frame again.

Just as I was thinking this – almost as if it were proving me wrong – the screen changed.

It didn't light up entirely, instead went from black to slate grey. I got an old-style empty-battery icon. I'd need to leave it for two or three hours. I wondered if I'd be able to do so without the others recognising our new impostor-phone. Certainly, whoever owned the cable would quickly realise there were four people but five devices. I'd have to do the charging in shifts. It'd be crucial I didn't forget it was there; as soon as the others were back, I'd need to hide it in my tent. I could finish charging it overnight.

A noise outside alerted me. Boots on the rocks; the sound of my colleagues returning. Guilt flared and I tucked the phone away with clumsy hands. 'Hey!' I called, doubtless overcompensating with mock cheer. 'Glad you're back. I'm starving.' I scrambled to my knees, unzipped and crawled out. 'I'll warm some soup,' I said, rising to stand.

There was no one there. In their tents already? I hadn't heard the familiar scratch of drawn-back zips. 'Hey!' I called, still genuinely expecting a response. I circled the firepit, fake-knocking the tent roofs. 'How did it go?'

Two tents through my circuit, I felt a flush of embarrassment. Our camp really was empty. But I hadn't misheard – there'd been the noise of an approach. Away to my left, the tide was a heartbeat at the edge of hearing. I scanned the tops of the tents, then the open ground beyond. The same breeze that plucked at our guy ropes stirred the woodland canopy.

I wasn't frightened. Not then at least. Even so, I broke the magic circle of the camp carefully, rounding the outside of the tents as if I expected to find someone crouching there. I didn't. Of course not, I reminded myself. Vinny hadn't seen anyone, he'd concocted a lie in order to—

I turned.

A bone-like snap had echoed from the woodland. My skin tightened. That was the noise of something moving between the trunks, I knew it as plainly as I knew anything.

I watched the wood, wondering about the age of the trees, the likelihood of ancient branches just falling. For a few moments I did nothing but watch.

Another crack.

By some aberration of human biology, my heart had risen between my collarbones and was announcing its new position with a tattoo. I held my breath, willing a little rationalisation to come. No further sound. That was good, right? I knew from my information pack that the largest land animals were feral rabbits, rodents and a rare wolf spider the size of an open hand. I was probably listening to the canopy shedding. Who knew how salt weakened the structure of the wood, what fungi might be rotting the branches from the inside out?

This was a reassuring line of thought. I realised what a persuasive combination some sounds were out here; how the hiss of the sea or the whisper of the wind created an aural hallucination, so that even the most experienced scientist might find themselves spooked.

I went back to the supply tent and checked on Clay's phone. The screen was still obsidian, empty but for the charge icon. It'd had thirty minutes, it's battery slowly filling after two years empty. I spent the next quarter of an hour watching to the north. The woods stayed silent.

When I eventually saw my colleagues, I returned to the supply tent, unplugged Clay's phone and hid it in my rucksack, then watched their three distinct and familiar shapes making their way back towards me as the afternoon faded into early evening. One of them was a murderer. But I was safe for now, I told myself. The killer didn't know I'd figured it out.

Mike returned my GoPro and began assembling the night's fire. Vinny started work on dinner. Alex had been able to distract herself with work, but now the lighthouse was a topic she could no longer avoid, and I was beckoned away from the others.

'Mike says there's supplies up there,' she said. 'Water, food.' She began furiously cleaning the lenses of her glasses on her sweatshirt as I confirmed the story. When she spoke next, it was with unexpected venom. 'I don't know what's going on here, Tess. But I think I know what you might be doing.'

'I'm sorry?'

'Oh, come on.' She thinned her lips. 'Asking Mike about Steven's last day. Then interviewing Vinny. Don't you think you're beginning to appear a little too interested?'

'I was just . . . '

'Don't pretend, Tess. You've been hired to make a documentary about the island. I think you might be up to something else.'

Behind me, I got a strong sense of movement temporarily suspended; of Vinny and Mike watching silently. Was Clay's killer warning me off? 'Come on, Alex.'

'To me, you seem intent on raking up trouble.'

'All I want to know is—'

She interrupted with a firm shake of the head. 'Tess, no. I'm not interested. No one wants you asking questions. I believe Leo made that completely clear last night. Did you sign the documents he sent through?'

'Not yet,' I admitted. She gave me a look that was part weary expectation, part disgust. 'I've not had a chance. Once we get the transceiver powered up tonight, I'll download them and get it finalised.'

She appraised me. 'Good idea,' she said. 'No more questions, Tess.'

And that was it. I was left on the edge of camp, smarting from a conversation that had been as firm and unyielding as a slap. Mike and Vinny had answered my questions. Alex had chosen to warn me off.

That surely meant she had something to hide.

30

Dinner that final night was cheerless. Soup and potato cakes, dried apricots and the last of the wine, two centimetres each. Our candles were nothing more than pools of wax, our fire a low glow, when Vinny sat forwards in his chair. 'I've been thinking about something I saw this afternoon,' he said.

I saw a flash of dismay in Alex's eyes before she composed her expression. 'What's wrong, Vin?'

'I saw a man.'

There was a moment of tense silence. Despite my prickling skin, I think I managed to appear calm. Vinny's story had been aimed at me when he told it earlier; a justification for his presence at the camp and a cover for his visit to Clay's body. I hadn't expected it to be repeated. Surely sharing it further served no purpose.

Alex said, 'I guess it must have been one of us.'

Vinny shook his head, swirled wine in his glass and examined it. 'No. You were at the water with the seals.

Tess was filming, Mike was with her at the lighthouse. I was alone. Apart from the man.'

Alex smiled – an attempt at a dismissive gesture – but there was something else in her expression now. When she addressed me, she avoided eye contact. 'Tess, could it have been you?' I shook my head in response. 'Well then, that's not possible,' she said, and ran her fingers across her lips before adding, 'There's no one out here except us.'

'I don't think that's true,' Vinny said.

He stared at the twilight slopes, the chalk-mark of the lighthouse beneath the shapes of birds dreaming on the day's late updraughts.

'Listen, Vinny,' Alex said, 'out here, perception is different, particularly at the close of day. The light's so clear, the colours are bold, noises are exaggerated and our imaginations do the rest. I completely understand why you might think it was something moving around.'

'Did you see him clearly?' Mike asked.

'No. A . . . *olhar de reflexo*, I don't know the word. Just for a moment.'

'So can you describe him at all?'

'A shape at the edge of the woods,' Vinny said.

Alex's gaze was intense. Her jaw was working. 'The trees in the wind?'

'I once thought there was someone on the boat with me.' Mike grinned, rolled his eyes and indicated the day's-end glitter of the ocean. 'The team were diving. I was the only one aboard but I swore there was someone on the stern beyond the sails. Like Alex said, the light can play tricks on the water, clouds move quickly, re-flections on the surface. Turned out it was just shadows. It'll be the same with you, mate. Shadows.'

Vinny rubbed at his face, a stiff offshore tugging at his t-shirt. 'I've thought of all that. But this was a person.'

Alex raised herself, straightening her cargo pants with quickly moving fingers. 'Well,' she said, 'if you're certain, it must be Arnaldo, back with the *Auk*. Or a fishing boat has got into trouble and put ashore. They're the two most logical explanations.' Even though there'd been plenty of fishing boats ploughing the water in the distance, Alex didn't sound certain. When she shielded her face against the lowering sun, the visor of her palm darkened her eyes.

'I don't know about you guys,' Mike offered, 'but it's not easy to get a good night's sleep with everything that's happened. We're all tired, right? And when you're tired, you're prone to misreading movement. Particularly if you get a quick glance.' He threw his arms out in demonstration. 'A big seabird takes off and, for a second, it looks like a person.'

Vinny listened patiently, then cleared his throat. 'So no one else has seen anything?'

My pulse stuttered like a firecracker. This all meant he was telling the truth. I glanced into the gloaming, trying to talk myself towards calm. *The noises this afternoon.* I'd heard boots, and called out. If someone had been there, they would've had a chance to retreat as I'd blundered out and checked tents. Was it possible?

'Nothing,' Mike said. 'Sorry, bud.'

Alex lifted a shoulder. 'I've been so focused on the seals, I haven't looked up all day,' she said, before rehashing her previous position. 'Listen. Like Mike says, you're just tired. One day left, Vin. Arnaldo's here tomorrow afternoon. Why don't you get the transceiver up and running? I need to get in touch with Leo.'

Alex's call was a long one, so I took to my tent and began my hour of connectivity with a check of my email. Excitement blazed as I spotted an unopened message.

Lukas Larsen had finally made contact.

My fever soon cooled, though. It was a website-generated auto-reply. *Hey*, it said, *thanks for getting in touch. I'm afraid I'm away from my desk at the moment finishing a project, and don't expect to be back for a period. If you have any pressing issues or emergencies, you might be able to reach me on my mobile, but I'm working with only intermittent signal out here. Hopefully we'll be able to connect soon. LL.*

The number he left was the same as the one I'd texted back in Funchal. He was probably in a jungle somewhere. Much as I wished I could speak to him, it was off the cards. Next was Leo Bodin's NDA. I wiped my eyes, fatigue tagging at me, and accessed the documents. If I was to be summoned to discuss my behaviour with Leo, I should at least have the damn papers signed. I scrolled through, attached my electronically generated signature to the bottom of each page, and updated the file.

I read Lukas Larsen's auto-reply a second time, feeling my obsession harden.

I had a few minutes to check his social media. It

didn't take me long to track down his Instagram feed. Back at the start of the craze, everyone in my line of work thought social media would establish itself as the new way to find commissions, and we'd all spent hours filling our pages with video. It had worked for a while. We'd all fastidiously commented-on and favourited each other's stuff, until we'd found ourselves sharing clips and pictures in the same echo chamber. When the work dried up, we all went back to tending our websites. I'd stopped updating my feed years ago, and so had Lukas. Back when he'd been more active, though, there was a whole slew of desert shots. Roads cutting across dunes. Big trucks barrelling through dust storms. According to the descriptions, the pictures were all taken along the N1, a motorway in Morocco running from Agadir all the way down the Atlantic coast into Western Sahara.

I felt my shoulders stiffen. Could that be a coincidence? Scrolling further, there was nothing to connect Lukas's investigation to our lighthouse. Instead, he'd been inland from the coast, recording the movement of big vehicle convoys. I squinted at the branding. It was hard to see through all the dust, but I reckoned the trucks had 'NRM' on their sides. I opened a search engine, typed 'NRM Morrocco', and scrolled through the results until I found what I was looking for.

An organisation called National Recherche Minieres. The website was in French. A translation described them as an *'Atlantic margins mineral extraction company with 100 years of mining experience in the Moroccan subsoil.'* Their maps and infographics had them operating within the disputed Western Sahara territories. Inland from Dakhla, a goldmine in the middle of the desert was marked. Pins indicated extraction points, lines showed transport routes.

Did this mean Lukas Larsen had left the Seawild expedition – ill with Covid if the stories were true – and made the short crossing to Africa? If so, why? What had he been up to?

'Tess!'

Alex was summoning me for my meeting with Leo. I rifled through my stuff, located Clay's phone, and brought it with me for some extra charge.

Leo was dressed in a black running top in technical fabric and was calling from somewhere outside the office. The whitewashed wall behind his desk was so rustic it had a large, elaborate crack running down it, a vein of darkness illuminated by an Anglepoise lamp that threw sideways shadows.

There was a second of silence. I wondered whether the connection had hung, and opted to fill the space. 'If that's your new office,' I said, pointing at the crack in the wall, 'you better have a word with your builders.'

He turned to assess his surroundings. The joke became clear. 'It does look a little worrying.' He laughed, blurring his background. I heard the scrape of boots against concrete as he adjusted position. 'One of the interesting things about this job,' he continued, 'is never being in one place for too long. Every day different.' He cleared his throat. 'I see you've signed the documents I sent through. *Merci.*'

'Sorry I didn't get to them earlier.'

'They're done now, that's the important thing. You'll be aware they prevent the use of any audio-visual material related to the investigation into the unfortunate death of Dr Clay.' He ran a hand through his fringe and continued. 'Alex was telling me you'd been ... ah, a little inquisitive? Tess, you're a documentary film-maker, curiosity's in your DNA, so I understand your fascination with Steven's story. But gruesome as the circumstances are, I have to ask you to refrain from further investigation. The police will do their job when they arrive, and you'll no doubt be of great assistance to them. In the meantime—' he touched his desk with an extended index finger, smiling emphatically '—we're doing such important work here. The preliminary data the team have sent back suggests a significantly healthier seal colony than just a few years ago. We've seen an increase of almost twenty-five per cent; the impact on marine biodiversity can't be overstated.'

'That's great news.'

'It is! And we're so lucky to have a filmmaker of your calibre on the ground to document the impact. With your help, we can ensure there's no move to open up access to the islands. Your contribution is crucial, Tess.' His voice had a flat echo, as if he were calling from a cellar.

'Thanks, Leo.'

'And in the edit, you'll be sure to emphasise the fragility of the colony and the necessary extension and enforcement of the permit system?'

'Of course.'

Leo shifted position. 'Keep up the good work, Tess. And – I'm sorry to repeat myself – let's leave the unfortunate events to one side now and focus on the project in hand, OK?'

I took a steadying breath and returned his smile. 'I will,' I said.

31

I attached a charging cable to Clay's phone, tucked it away so it wouldn't be noticed, returned to my tent and zipped myself in.

I still hadn't checked the GoPro footage from the cave so I settled cross-legged and ran it through once before rewinding. Night one looked OK, but night two was significantly better; thronged with activity – the seals huffed and hauled themselves through the darkness in an almost human fashion. Reminiscent of those docs that followed insomniac sleepers' night-time movements in bed, they rolled together, slumbering in pairs and groups, before shifting and flapping, lazy movements becoming theatrically exaggerated at speed. It was over too quickly so, greedy for more, I scanned backwards and picked up from the halfway point again, looking for the best point to clip it.

I slowed the film, pulling up frames one at a time. Empty cave, a blur of movement triggering the motion sensor, then nothing for seven or eight frames. That seemed odd. One shot every thirty seconds meant four minutes of empty cave. Why was the camera filming without seals there? Either the movement sensor was glitching or I was missing something in shot. Frustrated, I re-wound and played again. At first, nothing.

Then, like a ghost, a shape appeared.

A soft-edged blur manifested from the black before being re-swallowed. It came from the cave wall, breaking away, limbless and globular. Whatever it was, it moved upright. Which meant it wasn't a seal. One frame later it was gone, the lighting too poor to provide any definition.

It must be that I was seeing things, or mistaking the movement of something else. Water? A colony of bats moving together? Any explanation I could summon seemed ridiculous apart from the obvious. There had been someone in the caves last night.

OK, I tried reassuring myself, I must be looking at one of the Seawild team. But hadn't we all been together? My thoughts spiralled back to Vinny's story. It was obvious he'd thought he was telling the truth earlier. Maybe he actually had been.

'Switching off in a few minutes, folks,' I heard him call.

I set the GoPro aside, pulse fluttering through my fingers. If I took the strange events of the last three days separately, though they each might appear odd, they could all be explained. Together though, they grew much darker. Clay, the key, the lighthouse stash,

Vinny's paranoia, and now the shape on the time-lapse footage: the fear summoned in me seemed to compound until, considering them all at once, my throat tightened and my heart throbbed like an injury. If I thought about it all for too long, I was going to lose my mind.

I tried to concentrate by addressing a second mystery, one that at least had some internal logic. I went back to the Lukas Larsen Instagram photos and the National Recherche Minieres website. Examining the mines indicated by pins and the mapped routes, checking them against the truck convoys in the feed, this was the kind of sifting and probing I was used to from my days on *Spill*. What exactly had Lukas been up to? Surely there was no point in snapping pictures of the vehicles unless they were evidence of something. I opened a search engine, typed 'NRM mining company scandal', and began scrolling through the meagre results. A Reuters article looked promising.

'Just one minute, Vinny!' I called, skim-reading.

It was a piece about sanctions. Western administrations imposed trade bans – for human rights violations, mostly – leaving African governments struggling to raise money. One way around these restrictions was to trade natural resources on a growing black market. Some countries had set up illegal deals with mining companies. These outfits were based in Europe and had legitimate export licences, and shipped African gold in large but unrecorded quantities out to Paris and London. A proportion of the profits found their way back to the governments in question. 'The goods go to gold trading companies on the continent,' one contributor explained, 'and clean money flows back.'

My tent vibrated as Vinny tapped the roof. 'Powering down now.'

I switched off my laptop and stared for a few moments at its empty screen. This, at least, was starting to make sense. I needed to disregard Mike's theory about seal-pelt trading and consider something else instead; that these islands were being used as a stopping-off point for gold smugglers asset-stripping the Western Sahara – a back door into Europe – and that Lukas Larsen knew about it. The boat diesel and supplies in the lighthouse made more sense now. What I still didn't know was how Clay had become involved.

Tired, I wiped my eyes and switched my attention to backing up the day's footage. I had some lovely shots of the lighthouse interior, crucial to my secret film.

I dug through my camera bag for my SSD hard drive. It wasn't there.

No alarm at that; it'd be on the tent floor, mixed up amongst my lens-cleaning equipment. I located what I thought was the drive, but the object under my towel was an extra battery. Must have missed the drive in the side pockets of the camera bag. I unzipped all pockets and pouches.

The SSD wasn't there.

I checked my groundsheet again, foolishly running open palms over sections I'd already searched, lifting my bed roll, unzipping my sleeping bag, going through the camera bag's storage pockets – places I already knew were empty.

'Shit,' I hissed, a prickle of panic rising. My hard drive was missing. 'Idiot,' I spat at myself, fists clenched. I took a breath and reconsidered. No. Backing up your footage was filmmaking 101. I hadn't lost it, I'd put it in here last night. If it wasn't here now, it was because . . .

For the first time I tuned into the talk from the fire-pit outside. Low voices in discussion. I thought about the sequence of events the day before yesterday. I'd discovered the body, filmed secretly, and then returned to the cove and found the key. Mike had met me as I climbed back to the path. Though he couldn't know for sure, he'd expect me to have been filming. Alex and Vinny knew nothing of my visit, unless Mike had told them. He surely had. Alex seemed to know about everything. Her distaste for my recent questions wore its disguise pretty lightly. There was another possibility: had I left my camera out anywhere? I didn't think so. And since I'd backed up last night, my hard drive had stayed in here.

What should I do? Pretend nothing had happened?

I gnawed at a knuckle. No, that wasn't an option. I needed the storage. Always over-shoot, that was the rule, get a ton of footage in-country or you end up tearing your hair out during the edit because there's no going back. If Alex had taken my kit as punishment for my behaviour, I'd have to assert myself. And be careful as well. I was dealing with someone dangerous. But after everything I'd been through with Gretchen,

I sure as hell wasn't going to end up dead due to an investigation.

I hovered. Fighting down a grey fear, I unzipped my tent door and wriggled out.

Someone, Vinny I guessed, had opened a bottle of spirits, and poured a small amount into the plastic tumblers lined up along the firepit's boundary. There wasn't one for me, I noticed. Solemn and quiet, Mike was examining the label on the bottle, a book splayed face down by his chair. Alex and Vinny were talking in low voices. They ignored my appearance, though Mike at least had the good grace to look up.

'Hey.' He smiled, raising the bottle. 'We're trying this brandy. Fancy some?'

Vinny's conversation with Alex faltered. 'Macieira,' he said. Some of his old enthusiasm returned. He raised his glass, pursing his lips with pleasure. 'This stuff's even better than Cognac.' Staving off the silence, he continued, 'Back in Porto I knew a guy who owned this bar. It's named Capella – it's in an old chapel, so inside, there's still the altar. I used to go there with my friends on Thursdays. Fado on Thursdays, you know fado, yes? Very beautiful music, very sad. We drank brandy there. Try it.' This was his cue to realise there was no cup set out for me. He scanned the kitchen gear, suddenly embarrassed.

Mike pulled my chair out for me to sit but I stayed standing. 'I'm missing an SSD.'

There was a beat of silence. Alex sipped her drink. Mike's smile cooled and he asked, 'A what?'

'External hard drive,' I said, suppressing my irritation. 'I've been using it to download my footage.'

'Oh no,' Alex said. I'd grown accustomed to ice in every word, but her voice was sympathetic. She made to rise. 'Can we help look for it? It can't have gone far.'

If any one of them had been involved in its disappearance, they weren't likely to admit it. Nevertheless the offer of help was unexpected; I'd banked on surly denial. I stared at my colleagues. 'It was in my bag,' I said. 'I put it there earlier and now it's gone.'

Vinny considered the others, scratched his beard and offered, 'You're sure?'

'Yes, I'm sure,' I snapped.

'It's only a small camp,' Mike said, standing up and addressing the group. 'Can't have gone far. We can find it, I'm sure.'

'It's not a case of looking. It was in my tent and now it's gone.'

Alex removed her glasses, breathed on the lenses and began cleaning. 'Have you checked the floor? Mine's a mess,' she said. 'I often think I've put something somewhere, only to find—'

'There's no need for me to do that. It was in my bag.'

A heavy silence now. All eyes on me. Mike sat down again, smiling nervously. Vinny was leaning on his elbows, one hand against his jaw.

'I don't mind doing the filming with the seal tagging again,' Mike said, all sympathy.

Taking her cue, Alex brightened. 'How much

material have you lost? Could we try and get it all again tomorrow morning? I can adjust the schedule.'

I boiled internally. Without my footage from the cove, my secret documentary was stripped of its stand-out footage and someone knew it. There was no way I could re-film exactly what I'd lost. 'Where do I back up my stuff from now on?' I asked. 'There's not enough memory on the camera itself.'

Alex cleared her throat. 'Laptop? You could put a bit on each of ours. There must be a way around this.'

Convenient. That way, all my film could be checked. 'Can everyone just listen a second? The issue is that my SSD is missing. It was in my tent and now it's gone.'

'But you can't be . . . are you suggesting that it's been stolen?' Alex asked, her forehead creased. It had been said now. The air tightened, though night birds away along the water's edge still called over the pulse of the tide.

'Someone's taken it,' I said, as firmly as I dared. 'That's the only explanation.'

32

Two sounds: the spitting of the fire as the wood resettled, and the ocean breathing.

'That hasn't happened, Tess,' Alex said, her voice cooling. She rose. 'Let's all have a good look for it now. I'm sure we'll find it somewhere.'

I was suddenly conscious of their pity. I was being treated like the kind of undergrad intern Seawild doubtless had in crowds. The smiles around the firepit seemed sympathetic but the three pairs of eyes told a different story. A clot of worry in my chest glowed, pushing heat to my skin.

Vinny was rubbing his hands together, business-like. 'I'm great at finding stuff,' he said. 'Especially cigarettes.'

I squirmed, patronised. 'Someone took it!'

All movement stopped. Mike gave me an agonised look. Alex brushed her lips with her knuckles, then spoke, her voice harder and colder. 'We've talked about the importance of togetherness. That's an inappropriate accusation, Tess.' She placed a palm on Vinny's knee.

'We're working in close quarters here and it's important that the team trust each other, treat each other with professional courtesy and work effectively.'

An idea, suddenly illuminated, announced itself. Reality was being reinvented right here in front of me. I was getting gaslit. The act of dragging air inwards and forcing it out again took the fullness of my focus. I couldn't look at Alex.

'It's been a horrible couple of days,' she continued. 'We're on edge. Tess, no one has taken your hard drive. We're all pretty mixed-up and we're all going to make mistakes. Yours won't be the last. Isn't that right, everyone?'

There was murmured agreement. If her speech had been designed to cripple my convictions, it had worked. She was good. I genuinely began to think I'd mislaid the drive. Had I checked the tent's side pocket? Was it tucked inside my waterproof jacket?

'So let's get searching,' Alex concluded. 'Start with you own tents, folks, in case we've dumped something accidentally when we've tidied up. Then grab torches and we'll meet back and have a look around the camp.'

I found myself frozen in confusion. Without my engagement, the others hovered.

'Tess?' Alex said. 'Describe what we're looking for.'

The possibility of some distasteful charade of an organised search felt too humiliating. We weren't going to find the drive.

Mike came to my rescue. 'I'll help,' he said to me, before turning to the others. 'Tess and I will sort this. You guys enjoy the brandy.'

Alex shrugged, victorious. 'You're sure? Fine. Just shout if you need us.'

Mike approached, took me by the arm. 'Let's begin around the outside,' he said loudly, 'and work inwards. It's an old trick, but it's a goodie.' I allowed myself to be led. Out of earshot of the others, Mike leaned in and whispered insistently. 'What's going on, bud?'

Had I just stood helplessly by, while Alex orchestrated a search for an item she'd taken herself? And had Vinny just pitched in precisely the right amount of self-deprecating humour to render the conversation harmless? I flapped cool air against my stomach and lower back, my face glowing furiously. Those few moments might have been the most humiliating of my career.

That, or I really was going mad.

'What are we even doing?' I managed. 'My drive isn't out here. It's been stolen, Mike.'

He held out his hands, palms down, a neatly executed calming gesture. 'You don't know that. There's no reason for anyone to do that.'

The problem was, he didn't have the full picture. No one did but me.

There was an obvious solution, of course. I could tell him everything.

Except that, despite the fact he seemed like a genuine man, warm, helpful and reassuring, he'd been on the same expedition as Clay two years ago. I'd only been more convinced of Alex or Vinny's guilt because of circumstantial evidence; Vinny missing from his room,

Alex closing down my questions. The fact that Mike had a sketchbook and a warm smile, and was hunting for seashells to add to his daughter's collection, didn't make him any less likely to be Clay's killer.

I could test him, I decided. Tell him about the stab wound and gauge his reaction. Vinny had seen the injury on Clay's body but he certainly wasn't going to acknowledge it, Alex was out of the question and I'd lose my mind trying to pick my way forwards without testing potential allies. But once the words were out there was no packing them away again.

'Tess.' Mike was an arm's length away now, head tipped as he tried to catch my eye. He touched me lightly on the shoulder. 'This isn't just about your hard drive, is it? What's troubling you? Let me help.'

I looked back through the gauzy tangerine of woodsmoke. Vinny was pouring Alex a second shot of brandy. The firelight through the bottle turned his hands blood-red.

'OK,' I said to Mike, my voice low. 'There's something I need to tell you.'

Afterwards, I went back to scour my tent again.

The more I looked, the more stupid I felt. A second search wasn't going to suddenly conjure the missing item from nowhere. I tried resting, but each time I closed my eyes, I inevitably ended up at Brixton Police Station two days from now, so I had to stop. In the end I sat up and flung back my sleeping bag, blinking away fear until I'd firmly returned to the present.

I'd told Mike about Clay's wound.

I could still see his expression; that open face a picture of wide-eyed dazed shock as he'd listened. Once I'd finished my story and urged him to keep it to himself, Mike hadn't got past the whispered disbelief phase before Vinny was skirting the camp to ask how the search was going, and we'd returned to our places at the fire.

I couldn't bear to stay and talk and so here I was, stewing under canvas while the others enjoyed a drink. I watched the firelight play a diorama of shadow along the tent walls while I thought about why I'd told Mike. Maybe I should have continued to try and shoulder the burden alone. I wasn't sure, but tonight felt like a turning point. It was likely all of us now knew about the true manner of Clay's death.

I set out my equipment as I brooded, not in another hopeless search for the drive – that was long gone – but in preparation for later in the night. If there was any repeat of this afternoon's noises from the woods, I wasn't going to hover on the *faja* while my imagination conjured images of feral beasts. I was going to film. I laid it all out and practised locating the thermal imaging module quickly in the dark.

I was just about done when I heard Mike call my name. Much though I wanted time away from them all, I couldn't hide forever.

'Tess, come and look at this,' he called. 'Come on.'

I could smell Vinny's evening cigarette, hear the spit of the fire. I unzipped and peered out. The three of them were sitting around the brick circle, the brandy bottle a quarter empty, mosquito candles long burnt out. They were all looking in the same direction – up over the foothills towards the lighthouse – with the fire's dying embers shining in their eyes. Vinny was blowing badly behaved smoke rings, fragile loops that shivered and broke. I crawled, straightened, and looked in the direction of their collective gaze.

The stars were gone.

Sometime in the last hour, our island had been de-capitated by a slab of heavy cloud, as if a black anvil had crashed into the pico. Only the charcoal-grey foothills were visible below the line of thick fog. Clinging to the cliffs, it insulated us from the moonlight above and beyond. What stars were left glittered in scattered patches.

The air was different too, brewing rain. Further west, over the ocean, another bank was suspended; a great grey wall had risen from water which now shivered with spume-topped wavelets.

Vinny seemed unsurprised by the change in condi-tions. 'Happens a lot,' he said, smoking. 'On Madeira, you get sun on the beach and snow in the mountains on the same day. You know Fanal? A forest on the north coast? Always foggy there. Visitors go to take photographs.'

'Does it last?'

'Depends on where you are, the strength of the wind.' Our fire had become ragged now, and, as if on cue, our circle of tents pulsed and flapped.

'What does it mean for tomorrow?' As soon as I had

my footage back, I wanted off this bloody island. It was getting so that Brixton felt like a welcome distraction.

'Not sure,' Alex said. 'We're back online again. Mike's been in touch with Leo. I'm trying to get hold of Arnaldo, double-check he's confident he can come and get us.' She smiled. 'Oh, did you find your hard drive?'

Later on, crawling into bed, I thought about that question, dropped in lightly as it was: a thoughtful caring touch.

Either that, or some sort of psycho-emotional torture.

33

My final night on Navigaceo served only to emphasise how far we'd fallen since that first day.

I lay in my tent, desperate for the comfort and sanity of Funchal.

Eventually, I drifted off, thinking of Lukas Larsen's Instagram pictures. The ergonomic curves of desert dunes; sand-clouds summoned by truck tyres; the liquid blur of a horizon heat haze. The brutality of those Saharan spaces reminded me of the day I'd spent ten years ago, frightened and alone, on the Kern County oilfields outside McKittrick.

★

Gretchen had taken the car and left me.

And I'd spent hours without water, hiding in a baking landscape of gravel and bluff, navigating only by pipe-ways. Chase Industries had a network of these tubes – arteries for crude oil – raised a metre or so from the ground on huge steel brackets. Once the initial terror of pursuit lessened, I realised their value. They cast thick lines of shade; they hid me from the wrong-road guys and, best of all, as long as I was careful for rattlesnakes basking in the cool, I could navigate by them. So I started filming again and found the act of speaking into my shotgun mic comforting. I narrated my way along the pipes, tongue thick with thirst, grit in everything from my hair to my boots, working my way through the wilderness. Whenever my thoughts galloped forwards to that future moment I might die of exposure, I tried corralling them back; started talking again as I filmed.

That endless day passed through increasingly desperate stages. During the morning I was intent on returning to the hole in the fence where I'd entered, and a couple of hours were spent navigating by the sun as I tried to find the cut section, whilst avoiding imaginary assailants. Hopelessly lost, and with the sun at its highest, I ditched that plan and opted to head for the treatment plant until, after toiling towards it for an hour, I spotted a CCTV camera mounted on a weather station and retreated again. I panned my camera endlessly along the highway, hoping for Gretchen's return, cursing the fact she'd made us switch off our phones and leave them in the car. Delirium must have closed in by the afternoon, because at one point I recorded a desperate message for my dad, telling him I missed him, apologising for borrowing so much money without paying it back.

After that, something changed in me. Fear and despair became a grim determination to do the right thing. I'd become convinced, by that point, that I couldn't have my evidence confiscated or destroyed; that I was going to preserve the film I'd got by any means. So the plan became finding a storm drain like the one we'd initially parked by. It had been choked with tumbleweed, I remembered, which would make it a good hiding place. Once I'd convinced myself I wasn't being pursued, I was going to ditch the Red MX in a drain, make a note of its location, and escape along the road. Then, when I had a car again, I'd drive back and rescue my footage.

By mid-afternoon, I'd worked my way back to an unfamiliar section of the compound fence. Despite a dizzying hunger and thirst, I crouched alongside a pipe and waited for half an hour until I was convinced there wasn't an ambush waiting for me at the highway's edge. An oil tanker hissed by, followed sometime later by an articulated truck, and once, a Winnebago heading for the hills. Eventually I took a chance and ran for the perimeter. Hands slippery, I cut an exit hole and raked my arms and legs pushing myself through.

I headed south – at least I thought so at the time – and, briefly energised by the relief of escape, made good progress scrambling along the verges of the road, desert dust sealing my torn skin. Now I was free, terror and despair were replaced by florid bursts of anger. One moment I'd be consumed with burning injustice; *what the fuck had Gretchen been thinking, leaving me like that?* The next, unlikely as it sounds, I'd be telling myself she had ten years' experience in the business and this was how it worked. She was simply strategising; she was a pragmatist making decisions for the good of the project. Investigative work like this wasn't about anything as naive as friendship or loyalty; it was about getting the job done, and if that meant risking your life, that's what you bloody well did – you trusted your partner to fight through and emerge with the footage. And you certainly didn't moan about it. But then, sweat stinging at my cut skin, I'd return to my former position: *She made me cut the fence, she made me go first, then she fled. She was a coward and a fraud.*

So absorbed was I by this internal debate, it took me some moments to hear the sound of a vehicle.

A Pavlovian rush of horror forced me to the ground. Pressing myself into the verge, I prayed the angle might conceal me. It didn't feel like it would. I scanned wildly about for tree cover, a sandbank or drain. Nothing.

I had moments to hide the camera. Those men in combat gear could come for me but they weren't going to destroy my footage. I still remember that old Red MX well; tough as rocks it was, compact and chunky as a hand grenade. I was still using it years afterwards, and on that day I could have thrown it down a well and fished it out later, scuffed but ready to shoot. Having no well to hand, I opted, in my sunburnt madness, to try and bury it. I scooped at the ground with bleeding fingers as the engine approached, and had it pretty much covered by the time I heard the wheels crunch to a stop somewhere above me. I lay over it and prepared to meet my maker.

A door opened and a voice said, 'Tess! Oh my God!'
Gretchen Harris was at the top of the verge.

Later, in the car with the air-con blowing, she told me everything while I tried not to bleed on the upholstery.

'I wanted to draw them away,' Gretchen said as I drank from her water bottle, cracked lips singing pain. 'You know, circle back and get you once I'd shaken them. But they pulled up.' She shook her head. 'Tricksy bastards, eh? So, plan B: I pulled over and watched from the next gate. Used a zoom lens. I could see one guy calling for backup while the other tried tracking you. Jesus, Tess, you were amazing, he couldn't keep up. Figured you'd use the pipes to work your way across the compound.'

I listened, shell-shocked, starving and totally conflicted.

'So I drove further along 33, and found a side road. It looked like you might emerge there. I set myself up as your getaway. But you didn't come.'

'Tried to work my way back again,' I croaked.

'Huh. Yeah so I waited, realised I'd got it wrong, went back to the spot where we'd started. The SUV was gone, but I saw them in the distance, circling the compound. I began searching myself, making sure I could track you down without being spotted.' She whistled. 'Hell of a day.'

'Hell of a day,' I managed.

'But it's what we do, right? You were brilliant, Tess. Couldn't have done it better myself.'

A year earlier, if someone had said Gretchen Harris

would be levelling this kind of praise at me, *in person* while we worked on a project together, I'd have been starry-eyed and frothing with delight. Moments like the one in the car, heading to the airport with our footage intact, had been the kind of thing I'd only dreamed of up to that point in my career. But I vividly remember the journey not feeling that way; that instead, I rode back beyond betrayed, brooding on the events of the day as we followed the signs south to LA. Was this really how things worked in the industry? Were filmmakers working in partnership expected to fend for themselves like this? I didn't know. And I didn't know any better.

A precedent was established out there in the oilfields – one that held for the last six months of that doomed project. Gretchen's job became scoping out the day's filming, suggesting shooting schedules, and projecting an air of bullish confidence while she worked on her laptop.

And I got to be the one who crawled through gaps in security fences.

34

Darkness and the slow hiss of the sea.

I was awake, my scalp tight and my head aching. I wasn't in London, I was trapped on an island three hours from Madeira. I felt my heart break. Something outside had woken me. I lay on my back, senses tingling. A minute of stiff silence later, the tidal pull of sleep returned, until I jerked awake again. This time I knew for sure.

Movement in the wood again, just like the afternoon.

I unzipped my bag and swung my legs from my camping mat, feeling for my laid-out camera equipment with open palms and thinking *the boat will be back to pick me up in a matter of hours.* It couldn't come soon enough. It took me a few moments to locate the thermal imaging module. I switched my phone on and attached the extension.

Outside, the woodland emitted another echoing crack.

There was a yellow-orange blast of heat when I turned

my phone-camera towards my legs. Thermal-imaging working, I pulled on socks and trainers, yanked a t-shirt over my bra, and unzipped my tent as quietly as I could. The night was immediately different; spongy and damp with salt, the soft air opalescent. A wind was coming in off the breakers, gusting clots of mist, and the moon looked trapped under ice. Fog squatted on the peak. In the wood, twisted trunks were a net for night-time shadows. I checked my phone once more – my splayed hand was rendered the comic orange of a rubber glove – and made my way towards the trees.

At the edge of the wood I faltered. Some instinct stirred itself awake, and when the noise came again, I found myself responding with an instinctive duck-and-cover, huddling low with my arms over my head. I rose and pointed my camera with shaky hands. At first nothing, but then the attachment worked and the screen gave me a blue and burnt orange treescape, branches holding on to the day's heat despite the mist; the undergrowth warm. A mammal flitted between rocks, a soft white blur, then vanished.

I hit record and climbed the slope, legs hot with flight-energy. I could hear birds moving in their sleep and the wind-stirred treetops. The louder noise that had woken me had gone now. I almost let myself believe I hadn't heard it at all. Then it made a reappearance, a clatter and a snap; something blundering.

'Hey!' I shouted, swinging my phone in its direction.

I was picking up tiny movements among the roots and rocks. Then I caught a jellyfish of warmth, and took a

230

few steps towards it. It vanished, so I pushed into the trees, calling out. 'Hey!'

Aware of the sound of a tent zip opening back at the camp, I blundered on. Another snap. I banged my shin against a fallen branch and tumbled into slippery ferns. Dropped my phone like an idiot, and had to spend a minute sieving the undergrowth with clawed hands. Another volley of cracks somewhere in the blackness. Then the night-noise changed.

The grey glow of my phone must have been enough to render me visible, because whatever it was, sounded like it had circled. Clattering stones, the crackle of understorey, and it was coming back in my direction. I reversed, robbed of sight. There it was again: the sound of movement. Undisguised, blatant, alarming movement – undergrowth yielding as something pushed towards me.

My blood iced. The thing sounded the size of a fucking bear.

I turned and stumbled. My night vision had improved enough for me to pick a route and I floundered forwards, my heart in my throat. My world became a terrifying montage of shadow, but I crashed onwards. The thing was closing. *Weren't animals to scare easily?* Jesus, the ground was impossible. Salty pools conjured into life during storms, trenches of leaf litter – I fell spectacularly but found my feet. Fought my way up a bank before risking pausing in a pocket of phone-light to listen. There it was again, close now. Someone called my name, and I swung towards the sound, moving as fast as I dared. Struck a tree hard with my shoulder, kept going. I vaulted a fallen trunk and lost my footing.

Before I knew it, I was slithering down a muddy trench and rolling, clinging to my phone, into a soggy, leaf-filled depression. Ragged instinct told me to freeze. Holding my breath was almost impossible, such was the banging in my chest.

The silence was sudden and profound.

I waited. Nothing. Once I'd mustered enough courage, I held my phone close and turned on the thermal imaging.

There was a wall of heat directly above me. I yelled. 'Tess?'

'Shit,' I croaked, lowering the phone. 'Alex.'

'What's going on? We thought you were in trouble.' She turned and called, 'Got her! She's OK.'

I fought my way out of my trench and leaned a hand against the damp bark of a tree, breathing hard. Alex was in unlaced trainers and a strap-top. She had scratches on her arms from fighting through the undergrowth, and tangled hair. Such were my levels of adrenaline, I checked to see if she was armed, thinking of Clay's body, wondering whether she was coming to finish me off. She was empty-handed. I chided myself. 'I heard something out here and came to investigate.'

'Tess, there's nothing larger than rodents on the whole island.'

'I haven't been running away from rats, Alex.'

'Noises can seem louder at night. What's that?'

'Thermal imaging,' I said, holding my phone up. 'I managed to get something – just a glimpse – but it's bigger than a rodent.'

Behind her in the darkness, I heard Vinny swear as he picked his way towards us. Alex shook her head, her lips thin. 'Tess, this has got to stop. We have half a day left. I don't want you wasting time chasing shadows.'

'I'm not,' I said. 'There's something in here. And *it* was coming after *me*.'

'You've had the rest of us up looking for you when we should be focused on the work we're here to do.'

'Alex . . . '

'I have to ask this, Tess. Are you in a fit state to do the job you're here for?'

'Fuck's sake, what sort of a question is that? There's something in here.' I felt reason return. If Alex had stabbed Clay two years ago, this is exactly how she'd behave now. My questions and snooping were a threat and she needed to do something about it. Discrediting my ability, and my sanity, would be a good first step.

Vinny emerged from the darkness, loping towards us in his Motörhead t-shirt. He tucked his hair behind his ears. 'You're OK?'

'I'm fine,' I said. 'Sorry.'

'Did you see anything?'

'Rats,' Alex said. 'She was chasing rats.'

We worked our way back, following a channel of floating ferns, Vinny guiding Alex, me bringing up the rear. Maybe I'd got it wrong. As the expedition leader, Alex had to impose herself on proceedings. I was mistaking her leadership for guilty defensiveness – she was just doing her job, keeping her crew in line.

Something shifted beneath my trainers as we walked.

I toe-poked it. 'Alex, you dropped this.' I stooped to collect her chunky GPS tracker. She held out a palm and I handed it over.

At the edge of the wood, Mike was waiting for us, hands in the pockets of his checked pyjamas. 'You found her,' he said. 'Hey, Tess. Everyone OK?'

We worked our way back to the edge of the *faja*. 'Listen, everyone,' I said, 'I'm really sorry. I heard a noise in the woods, I went to look. I thought I could do it without waking anyone, I didn't mean to cause alarm.'

'I thought something really serious had happened,' Mike said. 'What a relief!'

'You guys heard it too, right? Something big.'

The silence that followed was awkward. Alex pushed her hair back. 'I just heard you,' she said. 'You were pretty noisy.'

'It broke branches.' I'd expected some sort of support. Were they doing this on purpose – Vinny working in league with Alex in a replay of the hard-drive mystery? 'You must have heard it,' I said. 'Something big. I've got footage. Just a blur, I admit.' I swiped my phone awake, rewound my recording and held it up. It wasn't much, I realised as I showed them. A wet screen and a palette of blues disturbed by a cloud of orange with a white-hot centre; an amoeba that quickly bloomed and retreated. 'That's at head height,' I said, 'so we're not talking about a rat. Look at the size of it.'

'OK, that's big,' Vinny said. I knew what he was thinking: the figure he'd seen in the afternoon. Anxiety creased his forehead. 'What *is* that?'

'Tess, rocks hold heat,' Mike said kindly. 'It's most likely an exposed boulder, a gap in the canopy. It's been sitting in the sun all day before the fog closed in.'

That wounded me. 'It moves,' I pointed out.

'Or maybe it's you who moves,' Alex said. 'It's hard to keep your footing out there. Listen. Old forests aren't managed, right? These are ancient trees. We're just hearing them drop dead branches. Come on, let's go.'

The four of us headed back to the tents. Once, we all turned in response to an echoing crack from the woods and waited, watching. 'See?' Alex said, a hand held out in demonstration. 'Dead branches.'

Back at the tents, before we returned to our bedrolls and sleeping bags, Alex handed the GPS tracker to Vinny. 'You dropped this,' she said.

Vinny looked it at. 'Not mine.'

'Mike?' Alex said, holding it out. 'Your tracker.'

I stiffened, knowing the answer before he gave it. 'I wasn't in the wood,' he said. 'It'll be yours.'

Alex stared at the object in her hand. 'Tess?' she asked, her expression caught between hope and desperation. I shook my head and watched while Alex pulled a second tracker from her pocket. 'Well, it's not mine,' she said, raising them, examining the two handsets beside each other. They looked identical. 'Check your tents,' she breathed. 'It has to be one of ours.'

Vinny and Mike stooped and unzipped. The canvas

shells were beaded with moisture, which ran in streaks as the torches went on and the two men searched. Alex and I watched their silhouettes scrabble through personal possessions before both emerged. Each man was holding a GPS tracker. A coldness curled in the pit of my stomach.

'I must have packed two,' Alex said. 'Or left one in my bag last time. They both look like they're from work. Yes, that'll be it.' She gave a bright laugh. 'My turn to apologise. It's been a tough few days.'

Our grins, forced at best, quickly evaporated.

Something had caught Vinny's eye. He'd wandered away from the camp following the wires from the supply tent towards the transceiver. Now he was on his knees, leaning in close to the equipment.

Alex turned his way, the GPS trackers still in each hand. 'What's up, Vin?'

'*Merda*,' Vinny hissed before turning. 'Folks. I think we have another problem.'

35

'Everything OK?' Back in Funchal three days ago, Alex's voice had been all carefree energy and enthusiasm. Now it was cracked through with hopelessness.

I could sense Mike felt the same air of inevitability as we regarded Vinny's back. The older man was on his knees. His t-shirt had ridden up, revealing a swag of middle-aged paunch. His hiking boots were turned inwards, touching at the toes, his treads thick with red mud. Something about his posture made him appear suddenly vulnerable; a lost child working on a broken bike.

Mike padded over. 'What's up, bud?'

The two of them, heads almost touching, adopted the hands-on-knees pose of the troubled tecchie while Vinny toyed with the control panel. Attempting to still a rising nausea, I folded my arms across my breast. It wouldn't go away. Alex and I joined the others.

I knew a dead machine when I saw one. Illuminated by Vinny's pencil torch, the satellite transmitter's panels were lifeless. 'Maybe it's moisture,' I offered, 'with the fog coming in.'

Vinny was prying at a panel cover with his army-knife screwdriver. 'We had plenty enough brightness for the extra use earlier,' he muttered. 'We pushed it a bit, but we didn't run it down.' He illuminated the cables back to the supply tent, then followed them. 'Are we running everything off it?'

'You reckon we've got battery issues?' Mike asked, studying the solar array.

'Maybe.' Vinny grunted and returned his attention to the transceiver, twisting open one of the side panels to examine the interior.

'Don't tell me it's broken,' Alex said.

'It's broken,' Mike said, mock-cheerful. 'We've lost power somehow.'

Vinny clicked the panel back into place and sucked his teeth, evidently unhappy not to have discovered something he'd hoped for. 'I don't like this.'

A chilly trickle, a winter raindrop on a window, slithered in me. If this was Vinny's work, he was the ideal person to discover it. Was this an elaborate act in which he was innocently investigating damage he'd actually caused himself? And had Alex done exactly the same with my hard drive earlier?

I put as much of the evidence together as I could. Clay had Vinny's ID in his wallet. Yesterday, Vinny had secretly visited Clay's body, probably because he'd been searching for something – evidence of his part in the crime. Now, he'd wrecked our communications so we couldn't contact Leo. Vinny probably botched Clay's killing; knew the body would surface one day; knew the local currents well and had incriminating evidence he absolutely had to take care of.

Alex touched him lightly on the shoulder. 'Let's see if we can fix it,' she said. Her voice was calmer and softer than before. 'Take your time, Vinny. No problem, OK?'

'The *Auk* can't come fast enough,' Vinny said. Then he knuckled his eyes and added, 'there's something really wrong here. I don't want to spend another minute on this damn island.'

'Listen,' Alex said, palms raised. 'We're just trying to get through. It's been such a terrible time. Let's just stay focused.'

'Screw that,' Vinny barked. We all recoiled, wordless. The waves beat beyond the ridge. This didn't look like an act, this was a man in distress. 'Why aren't we talking about this?' he asked. 'There was someone here at camp earlier, I saw them. Now noises in the woods. And then this.'

'You think they're connected?' Mike asked. 'Mate, this is just bad luck, OK? It's not like there's someone sabotaging our stuff.'

Vinny ran a forearm across his brow. Sweat gleamed at his temples. 'Whoever it was, dropped their GPS tracker.'

'That was me,' Alex said calmly. 'I packed two without realising.'

Vinny jabbed a finger. 'I don't want to hear explanations. I saw something, OK? And Tess filmed them in the woods.' He gave a growl of frustration. 'Now they're messing with our communications. We have to get off this island.'

'One more shift,' Alex said. 'We just have to do our jobs tomorrow morning. By the afternoon, Arnaldo will be here . . . '

'One shift?' Vinny said, pointing out into the darkness. 'Look at the fog. He isn't coming in this.'

The gruesome possibility we were trapped here seemed to whisper through the mist. Alex blinked, wrung her hands. 'If we have to wait another day or two it's not a problem. We have enough supplies to last.'

'Maybe we can fix this,' Mike said, returning his attention to the transceiver. 'Come on, Vinny,' he said, all pseudo-brightness, 'let's think. It's like Tess said – sometimes they get glitchy in damp conditions. If we power-down, give it a clean and reassemble, who knows, we could get a call-out and ask them to come now.'

'No chance,' Vinny said. 'Not in this weather.'

'Well, let's all get some rest then,' Alex said. 'We're not exactly doing our best work out here in the dark. Why don't we look at this fresh in the morning, OK?'

Despite the suggestion, no one moved. Alex included. I looked out over the ocean, assessing the chances of the *Auk* pushing through thickening banks of fog to collect us. The feeling of suffocation was suddenly so strong I felt my chest constrict and bile rise.

'Come on,' Alex said with a gesture of impatience. 'Let's deal with this tomorrow.'

*

Sleep wasn't going to come anytime soon, I knew as I pulled my clothes off, so I packed away the thermal imaging module, made another entirely pointless search for my hard drive, then lay on my back listening to night sounds, half expecting the woods to stir again.

I got nothing but the wet breath of the ocean; water unspooling against rock, just as it had, unheard, for the last half-century.

Needing reassurance, I tried mentally repeating Alex's mantra – *one more shift* – as I stared at the roof of my tent. It didn't work. Instead, another feeling announced itself with the uncanny certainty of a premonition.

The *Auk* wasn't coming to get us.

36

A voice beyond the canvas hissed my name.

I shuddered upwards onto my elbows, blood coursing cold. I hadn't been asleep long; my muscles were still nursing a post-adrenaline exhaustion and my thoughts were slow and confused. 'Hello?'

'Tess, thank God you're here,' I heard Alex say.

The phrase struck fear into me – where else would I be? I asked hoarsely, 'Is it morning?' knowing it couldn't be; I was still aching with lack of rest, and besides, outside the bright blade of a torch danced.

'Come out here,' Alex hissed. 'There's something wrong.'

Not again. I wiped my face, tired eyes burning. Tried for reassurance. Pulling on my hoodie and dragging a pair of cargo shorts over tired legs, I told myself: just a few more hours and we'll be gone. Please let the fog have lifted. Please let the skies be clear and the sun – or stars – be bright. Please let the *Auk* come and get us. Futile hopes, I knew, ringing as hollow as they had before I slept. I unzipped.

Alex leaned in close, her breath still strong with brandy. 'He's gone.'

Two things struck me, both bad.

It was still dark. And the fog had descended further as the night-time temperatures had dropped. We were hemmed inside a shifting sea which turned everything the hue of riverbed pebbles.

I knelt, pulling on the socks I kept balled up in my walking boots. They were damp. My feet hurt and I was hungry. 'What are you talking about?'

'Vinny's gone.'

Tying my laces and rising to stand, it didn't take me long to realise Alex was different. The mask of calm professionalism had slipped a few times over the last three days – now it was entirely absent. She was wide-eyed and jumpy. The change in her was unusual enough to trigger a mirror anxiety. I'd had two main suspects involved in the death of Clay, and both now seemed entirely undone by our situation. Alex swept a torch across the tent roofs. Our world had shrunk to this tiny encampment. All around, great ghostly walls shifting in the darkness.

'Come and look,' she urged.

'He's just gone for a pee,' I said, remembering he'd done the same on the first night and, if Mike was right, on the night Clay had vanished.

We crossed to Vinny's tent. In seconds, mist was clinging to my eyelashes and gathering in the damp folds of my clothes. The night felt like a flotation tank. The beam of Alex's torch sketched a million tiny droplets and, by its light, I could see Vinny's door-flap drifting loosely on the wet breeze, moisture streaking in rills and pooling on his groundsheet. I stooped and pushed the doorway inwards.

Alex's torchlight probed. 'I think his boots are gone.'

The foot of Vinny's bedroll was visible beneath a tangle of sleeping bag. Further in I saw his packet of Chesterfields and a lighter, two inside-out t-shirts, and a paperback. 'Hey Vinny,' I whispered. I checked his rucksack, lying unzipped along its outer edges.

'So where's he gone?' Alex asked. 'What do we do?'

I squatted, my calves stiff, my head aching under the burden of two dozen competing thoughts. What if, two years ago on Deserta Grande, Clay didn't leave by boat alone – he left with Vinny. It would explain why Mike found his room empty; Vinny left with Clay, then stabbed him, tipped his body overboard and returned to the research station. Only then did he discover his ID card was missing. So Vinny finds himself trapped in an agony of indecision – there's an object lying around at some future crime scene that will directly implicate him. If that was the case, he'd surely jump at the chance to revisit the islands and recover the evidence. That's why he lingered after us on the day I discovered Clay: to clear the scene. Except I'd found his ID card before he could. He'd been forced to return later to check the body over again. Everything fitted.

'Tess. We should search for him, yes?'

And I was here asking awkward questions. Filming. That surely made me his biggest threat. I felt panic begin to pulse. If I challenged him, who knew what he might be capable of? My tent was hopelessly flimsy protection, a barrier of social convention only. The fact I was breaking that convention right now, peeking into Vinny's private sleeping space, only served to underline its fragility.

'Tess?'

I let Vinny's tent flap drop and stood again, rubbing my face, my skin sheened in mist. Should I tell Alex what I suspected? Not if she was involved. Vinny might have killed Clay at her instruction. Except that now, she seemed undone by the events of the last three days. Last night's sabotage had undermined what little confidence she'd had left. Vinny had been the same last night too; frightened and desperate to leave. Could both be innocent? If so, that left Mike. Maybe it had been a bad mistake to tell him about Clay's stab wound.

'We need to wake Mike,' I said. 'It'll be quicker and safer searching with all of us.'

We circled the firepit to the other man's tent. Alex hissed his name and got nothing. She played the torch across the carapace, illuminating a diamond-field of moisture. Some of it had poured in streaks to the floor, which implied movement. I crouched by his closed door. 'Mike,' I said. 'Wake up.'

We waited long enough for him to surface, then Alex hissed his name again. Another pause. I tapped on the tent, sending further streams running. 'Hey, Mike. We need your help.'

'Open it,' Alex said.

'Give him a second.'

We did. I tried listening, but the dominant sound was the roll and pull of the ocean. Eventually I said, 'Mike, I'm opening the door, OK?'

I unzipped, pushed back the flap and Alex dipped her torch into the space.

Mike's tent was empty as well.

37

Four people alone on a remote island had suddenly become two.

I drew back, gathering with Alex at the firepit. She was moving from foot to foot, illuminating the grey walls of our prison as they drifted. 'What's going on?'

'Vinny's tent flap was open,' I said, 'Mike's was closed. Does that mean anything? Does Vinny look as if he might have gone in a hurry?'

'How does that help?' Alex's glasses were beaded with gems of airborne water. She handed me the torch and tried cleaning them on her sweatshirt, her hands shaky.

'I'm just trying to picture it,' I said. 'Did one leave with the other, or did one follow the other?'

Alex nodded, understanding now. 'Right. OK. Vinny wouldn't leave his door open unless he was coming back. He wouldn't want his cigarettes getting wet. He can't have gone far.'

'I didn't hear either of them,' I pointed out. 'You?' Alex shook her head. 'I need to get my stuff,' I told her.

It's strange how momentous events arrive – and often pass by – entirely unannounced. This would be the last time I returned to my tent; the items I collected the only kit I'd ever recover from those islands. Thank God I grabbed all my equipment. Camera and bag, lenses, GPS device.

'Vinny told us earlier that he didn't want to spend another day on the island,' I said. 'So, what's his plan? What's he taken with him and what's he left behind?'

'His coat isn't here,' Alex noted.

'Check Mike's tent, see what's missing. I'll have a look through the supplies.'

Our storage tent told its own story. Someone had been through it. The torch lit a groundsheet of scattered items: a laptop, a jumble of tinned food, the powerpack lying on its side. I didn't know what that might indicate, and there were things here we'd need, so I shrugged off my bag and added dried fruit, nuts, two bottles of water and the rope Mike and I had used on our trip up the mountain.

Then a thought struck me, hard as a flat palm between the shoulder blades.

Clay's phone. I went back to the powerpack, sifting the cables. Mike's was missing, I noticed, but Vinny's was still here. Clay's was gone. I checked Vinny's a second then third time, as if repetition might transform it into the one I was looking for. It didn't. I moved everything aside and searched. I knew I'd re-plugged it, tucked it carefully out of sight and left it, but I managed to concoct a dozen ridiculous reasons for why it might still be here; it had been accidentally kicked towards the back, Vinny had mistaken it for his and moved it, I'd forgotten exactly where I'd plugged it in. I hunted through the tangled equipment bags, the torchlight summoning slices of shadow.

Moments later I had to concede: someone had found Clay's phone, realised its importance, and taken it. Which meant Vinny or Mike. I hissed a stream of curses, a furious *no, no, no*. I'd lost my best potential source of information. *Tess, you idiot.*

The hot torrent of self-loathing quickly cooled, leaving a raw and ragged fear pulsing in its place. Someone had taken the phone because they knew what was on it. Whoever it was might assume I'd already examined its contents. That put me in danger.

But without the phone I couldn't complete my film. The phone *was* the project. I had to get it back. If that meant forcing someone to hand it over, I was ready to try.

A thought surfaced — too slowly, it was the fatigue — that we could take the speargun we'd found on the shipwreck.

I hunted, but that wasn't there either.

'Alex?' I called, and when she emerged from Mike's tent, 'Vinny's speargun?'

'In there,' she said.

I pulled out. 'It isn't.'

Alex looked at me, her expression breaking like a wave. 'Oh God,' she said.

The absence of the speargun pushed a line of sweat down my back as I completed my search. One of the missing men had it. So did one of them perceive a threat so significant they needed protection? Or had they taken it with the intent to kill? A further hasty, palms-down search got me nothing. *Shit.* The two men might be hunting one another. Or one could be coming for me. If I was to get Clay's phone back, I'd need some sort of weapon of my own. Flares. I rooted for the two snub-nosed orange guns Mike and I had taken last time we visited the lighthouse. They were gone as well. My search took on the frantic desperation I'd been trying to suppress since we found Clay on the beach. I had to force myself to stop, to breathe. This development suggested Alex wasn't the threat. I'd rifled our supplies: no speargun, no flares. *Concentrate, Tess.* Was there anything else we could use?

I found myself rifling the box of seal equipment, pushing aside the few tagging devices left, fingers clawing through blister packs and swabs until I reached the vials and injector pens.

Alex was with me now, stooping at the door. 'Mike's stuff has gone.'

'What, all of it?'

'Clothes, boots, food and water.'

'His phone too,' I said, reversing from the tent. I held up the vials and injector pen. 'I think we should take these.'

'The sedatives? Why?'

'Protection.' In response to her expression, I added, 'Alex. This whole trip is seriously screwed.' Her throat worked, words rising but drying. 'Someone killed Clay when he was out here last time.'

'What? Tess, he drowned.'

'You're really going to persist with that? Come on. He was stabbed, I've seen the wound.' She was silent. Fog glistened on her pale skin.

'Steven was stabbed . . . ' she said numbly, shuddering.

'You know he was.'

She gave me a glazed look. I recognised shock when I saw it. 'I suspected something,' she said and straightened; a dignified summoning of courage and energy. 'Pass me the injectors.'

I'd been tucking them into my bag with everything else. 'What?'

'I'm keeping the sedatives and injector pen. That's Seawild property and it's dangerous stuff.' I paused for a moment, staring. Her expectant palm was upturned. A tentative faith in Alex might have been shoring itself up, but it was still fragile. I didn't want to hand the drugs over. 'Come on, Tess,' she continued. 'You have to work with someone, you can't do this alone. And I'm not a killer.' Hand still outstretched, a steely look in her eye, I watched her fingers curl. 'If we don't trust each other, we might be dead out here by morning.'

It was Mike or Vinny who'd removed the speargun and flares. One or the other who'd taken Clay's phone and abandoned us. This mess wasn't Alex's work. And I was going to have to ally myself to someone. I handed the sedatives over. She gave a tight nod, then weighed her GPS in her palm. 'OK. Let's go and find them.'

If one of the men were coming after me, moving would be better; even so, leaving our camp felt like turning our backs on safety and heading into the wild. We picked our way inland a little, then looked back. Already, our little home was gone, concealed behind a thick curtain. I looked beyond the trees, attempting to check the mountain above us. The nocturnal world was wet cotton wool. Somewhere, the moon glowed like a thrown coin.

'You suspected something?' I asked, repeating her earlier words. 'What do you think's going on, Alex?'

'I don't know for sure. I've just been trying to stay out of trouble, you know? But it's all falling apart.'

The fog, opaque and unstable, made anticipating danger difficult. Cutting it with my torch, I felt my stomach shrink to a wet knot. 'What's falling apart?'

She slowed, cleared her throat and turned. Everything about her posture told me, before a single word was spoken, that she was revealing something shameful. 'We both had a written warning after the last visit,' she said, and her eyes immediately shone with tears. 'Vinny and me. Not a great experience. I had to go before a panel. The CEO was there. They blamed us – me, mostly – for Steven's death. They said I hadn't planned properly, that my risk assessments were poor, I'd been negligent.' She wiped moisture from her glasses, her jaw tight. 'It wasn't true. I'd done the work. If Leo hadn't intervened for us, we'd have been dismissed.'

I remembered Mike telling me a little of this on our search for shells, and felt a sharp and sudden sympathy for my current companion. Her obsessive focus on safety, her micromanaged itineraries, her insistence I stayed away from Clay; everything she'd done was an attempt to avoid a repeat of a professional disaster that had tailspun her career.

She was trying, against all the odds, to right some wrongs, to recover her self-respect, her reputation.

It was a feeling I knew well. I'd spent ten years attempting the same thing.

38

The September after our trip to McKittrick, Gretchen and I submitted a rough cut of *Spill*. Then we convened to plan our final expedition, a visit to an onshore gas terminal in Saltfleet on the rural coast of northeast England. It was to be the last nail in the Chase coffin; we'd blow the lid on a scandal happening on our own soil, and the footage we'd collect would provide *Spill* with its climactic closing scenes.

But then an email changed everything. Forwarded from Channel 4, it came from the parliamentary aide to a cabinet member.

Even all these years later, I'd rather not name the MP who sent their representative to meet us that day. This person was prominent in public life at the time, a cabinet minister with enough cachet to be a regular guest on radio and TV. We were to meet their aide late morning in a restaurant tucked away amongst the Georgian terraces of Pimlico. We were the day's first customers. I remember sitting with Gretchen in a window seat with my camera in my lap, my phone ready to record, watching the traffic outside. If it had been the MP themselves approaching, spotting them wouldn't have been a problem – everyone on the street would have known them instantly – but we didn't know who we were looking for that day. The tension was slick between Gretchen and me as we drank expensive sparkling water and waited.

'We've trodden on someone's toes,' she told me. 'We're going to get a dressing down from some special advisor. This could be gold.'

Gretchen was fizzing with mischievous energy, but the possibility of a public bollocking had me jumpy, and the fact that my partner had abandoned her no-phones policy only served to further underline the severity of our situation.

I didn't expect what happened next. It was like something from a movie.

A glossy black car pulled up in a bay opposite and a man and a woman emerged. The woman – trouser suit, steel-grey hair, sharp chin – led, and the man followed. He was on his phone and wore dark glasses and a knee-length coat against the chilly sunshine. They checked traffic, crossed towards us, and entered the restaurant.

The man removed his shades, tucked them into a breast pocket. 'Leave your things,' he said. 'My colleague here will look after them.'

The woman, communicating with discreet monosyllables and gestures, had us switch our phones off, leave them on the table with the camera and turn out our pockets. We had to raise our arms while she ran cupped hands along them. Once we were checked, she nodded at her partner, settled into the seat I'd just vacated, and scrolled her phone.

The man inclined his head towards the car. We were going for a drive. Weak with anticipation, I got in. We went nowhere in particular and heavy traffic meant we never surpassed cycling pace. I recognised Victoria Station, a pub I'd been to in Belgravia, but mostly I was too frightened to focus on the world outside.

The man turned to address us. 'I have to say, I admire your tenacity,' he said. 'You've given us quite the headache to deal with. Steps will be taken to ensure there is no further misappropriation of government money, and we're happy for your film to be broadcast largely intact.' He gave a smile so cold the ambient temperature dropped a degree. 'However, it would be a shame to see three years' work go entirely to waste. Stop now, and the project can see the light of day as it is.'

Rigid with anxiety, I couldn't find words. My mind remained unfettered, though. What we'd committed to film so far – and that meant the entire sequence we'd shot in Kern County – was acceptable under the terms of this agreement. Which suggested the problem was with what we were about to shoot; our visit to the Saltfleet gas terminal. This meant two things: the man knew what our next steps were, and he'd been instructed to prevent them happening.

'We're not finished yet,' Gretchen said. I'd had my

issues with her in the shoot up to now, but this was the Gretchen I'd fallen in love with as a teen, and I glowed with fear and pride to see it again. 'There's still a section we still need to film.'

The man bore his teeth. 'It would be better if you consider your project complete as it stands. Its revelations are sufficiently dramatic. And the coverage will do your cause no harm at all.'

'As it stands,' Gretchen mimicked, 'there's no ending. We need to shoot a final sequence.'

I found my voice at last. 'The trail leads to one more location,' I said, under the impression he might need our position explaining. 'Everything we've discovered points there. It's a matter of public interest. To stop now would betray that.'

'Stopping now,' the man said patiently, 'would mean your film gets broadcast. Carrying on might result in us having to extend the process of vetting.' He tipped his head, looking upwards in mock calculation. 'I'm only speculating, but I'd say our legal team might require access to all your key documents, footage and court filings. We'd need to be sure all information had been obtained lawfully; wouldn't want any issues with your public-records requests, or problems with republication liability. And we don't want you ending up with an expensive defamation claim, do we?'

My legs felt soft and boneless, my body a blur. Years of work for nothing.

He smiled. 'All of that could take time. A very long time.'

'We're willing to take that risk,' Gretchen spat.

'I have the authority to make an appropriate settlement,' the man said with blithe disregard, removing a pair of documents from an envelope. 'Take a moment.'

He turned, settled in his seat.

Carefully studying four pages of small print whilst moving through Sloane Street traffic was nigh on impossible, but I flicked, arriving at the page with the figure he'd mentioned. Gretchen had got there ahead of me and I barely had time to register the amount – it went off like a flare beneath my ribs – before she laughed. 'I'm sorry, but this is ridiculous. You heard Tess. We're following an important story.'

'Take a moment,' he repeated.

'Thanks,' Gretchen said, 'but no thanks. We'd like to get out now.'

'I'm going to ask you to— '

'I said we'd *like to get out.*'

The man sighed, touched his forehead lightly. 'If you wish.'

At that moment we'd been queuing at a set of lights by a Patek Philippe outlet, so I still have this vivid memory of stepping out of the car and standing on the pavement, unsteady on my feet and prickling with sweat, in the glitz of a Boodles storefront, having just turned down enough money to clear my debts twice over.

Gretchen touched my arm. 'Bet his boss has capital invested in Chase. Paid a retainer for consultancy, has a seat on the board, something like that.' She grinned.

'One thing's for certain,' she told me, putting on her sunglasses, 'this means we're really on to something.'

It was a long walk back to collect our phones. We passed it in silence.

FOURTH DAY

39

There was one big difference, among many, between Alex's situation and mine.

While I'd fled my mistakes, reinvented myself and tried to bury my past, Alex had demonstrated the courage and decency to face up to hers. 'So ever since your dressing down,' I said to her, 'you've been staying out of trouble.'

'And you've been making that extremely hard.' She sighed. I passed her the torch and switched my camera on, checking the quality of the image. 'Case in point,' she noted, nodding at it.

'I've not been the only one making it hard though, have I?' We walked, tracking the treeline, our bootsteps deadened. I watched the grey world braiding at the touch of the wind.

'Steven had found something out.' Alex sighed. 'I don't know what, before you ask. Something he didn't like. He wouldn't tell me what it was.'

Clay had found something out. Of course. Through the

right lens, the soft edges of unrelated shapes were suddenly sharpened, turning an impressionist cloud into a clearer picture. A picture that told a very different story. Clay wasn't the perpetrator of some crime. He was the investigator. He'd been using his African contacts and his on-the-ground expertise to expose something linked to gold mines and smuggling. Clay had got Lukas Larsen fired-up about it – not hard to do; if ever there was a warrior looking for a cause it was Lukas – and together they'd tried enlisting Vinny; persuaded him to relinquish his access card. Whatever Seawild's secret was, it was connected to the stash in the lighthouse, and it was valuable enough to be worth killing for. But was it really possible Alex had no idea what Clay had been investigating? 'I guess you ended up helping him,' I tried.

'A little. But when we were out here last, he'd become frightened. I kept pushing him to share but he wouldn't. Whatever his fear was, it had him properly spooked. He really wanted Vinny's ID card. We ended up arguing.'

The Lukas Larsen blog made further sense. Tension, anger, alcohol and dispute. I tried piecing these new revelations together. Clay had found out someone was running a smuggling operation. Someone on the team. If I was right, that put Mike squarely in the frame. Mike or Vinny.

And both of them had disappeared.

'Damn,' Alex spat. 'We'll never find anything in this.'

She tucked the torch between cheek and shoulder, and we conferred around our GPS devices. The island was a featureless blue-green wedge glistening under condensed moisture. Without a paper map, all the handset was good for was orientation and proximity to the water. The lighthouse wasn't even marked.

I dried the screen of mine. 'So why did Steven want Vinny's card?'

'Access to Seawild labs,' Alex said. 'Vinny's clearance was higher. But Vinny knew whatever Steven was up to, if leadership ever pulled the access reports, it would show him in those labs, not Steven. He didn't want to get into trouble and he refused. At least . . .' she rolled her lower lip, eyes loose and unfocused. 'He started by refusing. But Steven had the card when we found him, so I guess Vinny must have given up objecting in the end.'

'Or he stole it.'

Alex considered this. 'Vinny'll be able to tell us when we find him. Look, how shall we do this? We could split up. You head north to the colony, I head south beneath the cliffs here?'

I had a decision to make. So far, Alex had seemed believable. But that didn't mean I trusted her. Of the three of them, she'd been the one most eager to shut down my investigation. She could be trying to restore her reputation and keep her job, but equally, she might be Steven's killer. I didn't like the idea of being alone. 'I say we stick together.'

'I'm relieved you've said that, to be honest.' She gave a nervous smile. 'I don't fancy getting lost in the fog.'

Interesting response. 'So, where do you think they're heading?'

'Given what Vinny said last night,' Alex said, turning to face south and checking her screen, 'I'd guess he's heading for the boat.'

'You think they're planning on leaving.'

She didn't answer that one. The fog wouldn't stop shifting, making orientation difficult, so we kept having to stop, assess our blue dots in a pool of torchlight and go again. Pretty soon mine froze entirely, refusing to track further movement. Signal issues. Looming to our left, the slips of scree at the base of the cliff face emerged from the grey, making it clear we'd veered too far inland. I piloted myself partly via my monitor so I could check the eerie quality of the film I was getting; the land ahead revealing itself in ghostly three-metre increments.

A few minutes' walk along the base of the cliffs, the boat still somewhere beyond the scope of our vision, there was a dead seal.

It was a long way from the water.

'Oh my God,' Alex said.

The tight horror in her voice told me she was seeing something different to me. I looked up from the monitor. The shape had changed.

It wasn't a seal.

It was Vinny.

40

He'd landed on his back. The base of his skull was crushed flat against the rocks. Blood pooled in oily rills. His limbs were thrown out and his torso twisted, the spine inside displaced, and his eyes were lifeless as sea-glass.

'God,' I croaked, stumbling backwards, stunned into stillness. I stared at Vinny's open mouth and felt my blood charge in hot pulses, thudding across my palms as I willed myself to move. My stomach rushed upwards. I summoned enough control to turn and stagger on puppet-legs, then lowered myself to my knees and hung over a gap in the rocks, a fever-sweat pouring from me as I heaved.

'Vinny!' Alex sobbed.

My head began as a spongy nothingness, but at some point I became conscious of a single thought slicing the fog like the sweep of a lighthouse beam. Get this on film. I crawled across the rock to where my camera was – it was like willing someone else's arms to work – and somehow managed to hold it up and point it. I shot a montage of shaky fragments. The process helped clear my head. My temperature came down as the wind chilled the moisture on my skin and I started shivering, my sweatshirt sticking to the small of my back.

Alex, white-faced and stunned, was looking into the fog above us. 'He must have lost his footing,' she whispered.

I was sitting on my arse, my legs thrown out before me, the camera in my lap. As much as I tried, I couldn't drag my eyes away from Vinny. The rocks had smashed him into a new shape, a rag-doll thing that defied nature. 'He had the flare guns,' I said. 'He was heading for the lighthouse.'

Alex swallowed back a sob, following my gaze. One had been blown apart by the impact – coils and casing blasted into jigsaw pieces. The other was still pushed into his belt beneath his broken ribs. 'He was calling for help. A distress signal.'

I felt my stomach broil afresh and turned away, heart-beat drum-rolling. Vinny had the flares. That surely meant Mike had the speargun. 'Could it be that some-one pushed him?'

We could've been anywhere along the foot of the cliff, but I remembered the Pico da Chaminé somewhere up there, the path that skirted the edge. I'd traversed it tied to Mike. The thought of Vinny's fall sent fingers of horror crawling. There was a chance he'd lost his footing and plunged, but more likely it was something far worse.

Alex, reading my face, gave a determined nod of agreement. 'Vinny said there was a visitor on the island.'

Only last night, she'd dismissed that story, argued for a trick of the light or a fishing vessel putting ashore. If her position was changing now, it was because she knew something I didn't. 'The extra GPS device,' I managed. 'The one I found in the wood. You told us all it was yours. That you'd packed two.'

'I was trying to keep Vinny calm,' Alex breathed, wiping her eyes. 'It wasn't mine. Someone's here, Tess. Earlier tonight, they were in the woods. And Vin saw them yesterday afternoon. They must have been watching him down at camp.' She shuddered, dragged an inward breath.

Could there still be two people out there in the fog – Mike and the stranger? One could be hunting the other. Mike could have been woken by noises in the wood again, taken the speargun and given chase. Vinny might have followed.

'Whoever it is,' Alex whispered, 'they sabotaged our transceiver. And I didn't believe Vinny,' she gasped, tears rushing again.

I placed an arm across her shoulder, soothing her as best I could as she cried. We were a union of two, trapped in creeping cloud. Beyond the fog bank, the nearest people were fifty kilometres away. If we screamed out loud, our voices wouldn't carry the ten kilometres required to reach the next island. Could we take the boat and cross to the research station on Deserta Grande? Even if it was empty, there could be supplies there; we might be able to hole-up and wait for the police. I could row, I reckoned, if the water was calm enough. But how would we navigate?

I made it to my knees and moved across to Vinny's body. 'We're going to need his stuff,' I said. 'Come on.'

She looked at me, hollow-eyed, cheeks streaked with tears, then stirred herself.

Searching him was mercifully quick. Shorts pockets, front and back. A grotesque patting-down of his smashed chest in case he'd tucked something into a money-belt. Pouch pocket of his Seawild hoodie. Socks.

He didn't have the speargun, and he didn't have Clay's phone.

I pulled the surviving flare gun clear and held it up. Alex, crouching next to me, reached for it. As she did so, something slipped from the pocket of her cargo pants and skittered onto the rocks at our feet.

The sight of it made my heart ignite.

I was looking at a squat slice of moulded plastic I knew so well it didn't need a second glance. Only shock stopped me from reaching for it. The blood beat behind my eyes, insistent enough to summon stars. Alex had my hard drive.

She looked down at it, then back at me. 'Tess,' she said.

I ran.

I might have been staggering on locked legs, but it only took a second to lose her. The fog was so thick, the world shifting and seething with such strange energy, I was alone before she'd risen from kneeling. I fled, sense of direction entirely disabled, focused only on staying upright and keeping moving. The wind had risen, and the fog-walls were drifting now. Even when I risked stopping, standing for a brief moment to steady my breathing, it felt as if either I, or the island beneath me, was still in flight. The only landmarks I had were Vinny's broken body, the cliff wall behind him, and the sound of the sea. Instinct drove me towards the water.

Sometime later, I realised two things. First, Alex had been shouting for me. I couldn't hear her now – nothing other than the sound of the ocean rolling – but seconds ago, had I caught her call my name? I thought I had. Unless I was hallucinating. The second thing was this: I still had the flare gun.

There it was in my hand, gripped tight in white knuckles. Reason returned. I had to put some distance between me and this island. Find the boat, I told myself, and as soon as I was safely on the water, fire the gun. Lightheaded and nauseous, my legs made of modelling clay, I kept moving, imagining watching as the hot red parabola of my flare split the cloudbank. Rescue boats coming to get me. I wiped terror-sweat from my forehead with a sleeve. 'Come on, Tess,' I whispered, summoning whatever courage I had left.

The sound of the ocean grew steadily louder for five minutes' run-walking until, looming from the mist ahead, a shape appeared. The sign at the water's edge, the one that had warned us away as we'd first made land.

The sign meant I'd come too far, managed to miss the pulled-up boat somehow. I recalled us walking it slowly inland three days ago, the four of us puffing and blowing with exertion, a pair at each side of its hull. Those moments of triumph and cheer felt as distant as Funchal's festival streets. A penned-in closeness fermented in me.

I turned around and tracked back. As I did so, I found the noise in my head had dropped to a low murmur. I could think again. *Alex had stolen my hard drive.* What a performance she'd put on when I'd announced its loss – the sympathy as she'd witnessed my distress, the brisk purposefulness of the planned search, the admonishment when I'd challenged her authority. And all along she'd had it with her. What the hell was I to make of that? I tried constructing a version of events where she'd stabbed Clay and tipped him into the black water. Perhaps Steven Clay, with Lukas Larsen's help, had discovered Alex's role in a gold-smuggling operation. Knowing she was exposed, Alex conspired to kill him. Deed done, she'd rowed back to Deserta Grande in the middle of the night and returned to bed, calling the police the following morning. Distressed team leader was a role she was clearly capable of playing; after all, she'd been so persuasively believable all week.

So why was Vinny lying broken at the bottom of the Pico da Chaminé? He must have known something too. Alex and Mike, working together, had silenced him. She had the footage, he had the phone. Now all they had to do was get rid of me.

I had to find the boat. It couldn't be far, unless someone had taken it. The possibility ran a jumpy current through my stomach as I back-tracked to the sign again, using it as the central point of a compass, circling through the fog and returning, expanding my search each time. And each time, the queasy feeling rose.

There it was. At least I didn't have to untangle what the hell was going on here any more, I could just push off into the water, fire the flare, and pretty soon . . .

The boat wasn't how we'd left it.

I remembered tipping it upside down three days ago, aligning it with the wind direction, and tucking storage bags neatly beneath its carapace. Now its position seemed somehow wrong. Nevertheless, I failed to suppress a surge of hope as I drew closer. I set the flare gun aside and stooped to flip the boat, hooking slippery fingers beneath its edge. Trying to right it was like rescuing a huge beetle trapped on its back. My hands slithered against its wet wood as I fought it up at knee height. Then I noticed what should have been obvious from the start.

My fear was so palpable it felt like an extra layer of soaked clothing.

There was a hole in the hull.

41

I lowered it back against the rocks. Stared out into the grey, elbows out, fingers interlaced behind my neck, listening to oily rollers heave themselves against the border of this horrible place.

Without a torch I hadn't observed the damage immediately, but once it was seen it couldn't be ignored. Something big and heavy – my guess was one of the rocks on the waterline here – had been smashed hard against the hull, a repeated blunt force applied until the wood had collapsed inwards. The puncture wound, the size of two fists, made me think of Vinny's skull. I'd been with Alex since she woke me, so this must be Mike's doing.

For a few minutes I surrendered to a bleak and hopeless nothing. He'd visited the boat while I slept – hell, either of them could have done this at some point yesterday – knowing that I'd come down here . . . I rode a sudden, cold wave. Mike and Alex knew where I was. They could be closing in. I passed through a phase of paranoid fog-scanning, certain I was being watched until the obsession returned, beating out its rhythm.

I was going to locate my hard drive, retrieve Clay's phone and find another way off this island.

Which meant I needed a plan. I pinched the bridge of my nose, blinking away exhaustion. *Come on, Tess.* What resources did I have? I swung my bag down between my feet, unzipped the lid and searched. A coil of deck rope. Water and dried fruit. The seal-tracker Mike had given me three days ago. A broken GPS device, my camera, and the flare gun. It had one signal in the chamber. If I wanted anyone to spot something fired from an island two hours' sail from Funchal, and I couldn't leave by boat, the alternative was height. Which meant climbing the picos in the fog without a torch. Following the path up to the lighthouse presented a multitude of risks, but possibilities too – there was a chance I might get the big lens burning again, draw rescue that way. And since I didn't even know who I was running from, I could lock myself away up there, protect myself from both Alex and Mike. And hide.

I tried conjuring other possibilities, but struggle as I might, I got nothing. The lighthouse was the best idea I had.

I ate nuts and apricots, reserving some for later, then drank a little water. The sustenance steadied my nerves. Unpacked my equipment, wiped mist from the lens. There was an on-camera light – I'd have to watch it didn't drain the battery too quickly – its illumination limited but useful. Filming, like food, brought comfort, somehow normalised my situation. I was shooting a walk up to the peak, that was all. Challenging weather, but I'd worked in worse. I could do this.

And so I travelled inland again, cutting a route through the fog. The mountain was an invisible presence somewhere off to my right as I headed for the path I'd taken with Mike yesterday morning. Adrenaline made my muscles ache like flu, and the possibility Alex might be waiting for me somewhere strung my body taut. Another worry: I was beginning to feel a curious vacancy as if I were floating somewhere above myself. This, I recognised, was the prelude to a shock reaction. I wondered if I was going to be able to hold it together. It was a long walk up, and I'd need to find a way to keep breakdown at bay.

As I passed the wood, a sound silenced my thoughts.

That current of despair again. If Alex was coming to finish me, I had no resistance left.

The noise was nearby, and it was coming from the darkness, somewhere off to my left. I knew that sound. Movement; a ripple in the understorey, bracken yielding.

I stared into the trees. The interior was a gothic nightmare of twisted verticals, black stripes against boiling cloud. Instinct had me in a half-stoop, as if I might be harder to see that way. I tracked the noise, pointing the camera, moving vaguely back the way I'd come, every urge pushing me away from that place.

There was another noise, a gentle crackle of leaf litter. Then a click. Light sheened the shifting mist.

Mike emerged from the trees, torch-beam bouncing. 'My God, Tess,' he said, spotlighting me. 'What are you doing out here?'

Besides the torch his hands were empty, but he had a backpack on, straps tight against his damp sweatshirt, his appearance uncharacteristically ruffled. I noticed his boots were wet but his jeans weren't soaked dark to the knee, which suggested he hadn't been fighting through vegetation deeper in the woods, he'd been here at the edge. He knew I'd check the boat, and this was the only path back. 'I could ask the same of you,' I said, fear hardening.

He stepped carefully through the wet grass at the woodland's edge, drawing closer. Reading my change in posture, he slowed his approach. 'This must look crazy.'

'Somewhat.'

His eyes roved. 'You're alone?'

'I lost Alex,' I said before adding, in a whirl of desperate calculation, 'some time ago now. We were coming to look for you.'

'There's no easy way to do this,' Mike said, taking another step my way. 'I'm just going to level with you. First, switch your camera off.'

I was disturbed enough in that moment to comply with almost any other request. Not that one, though. Somehow I managed to say, 'I can't do that.'

I'd been searching his person for the speargun since he'd appeared, but hadn't seen it. A small part of me – the desperate *please God* part – was wondering if he had it at all. Turned out it was lashed against the small of his back by his bag straps. He dropped the torch, pulled the speargun clear and closed the gap between us.

Then he struck me hard with the butt. Square in the bone of the right shoulder, with a force that turned his expression ugly.

I was felled by white pain. Dropped the camera, found myself writhing foetally, my arm a roar of heat. I was sufficiently conscious – only just – to see Mike attack my camera with disturbing ferocity. The butt of that speargun came down again and again as he leant over and hammered, many more blows than were necessary, enough to split the case and for the disassembled innards to dance like beads of broken glass. By the time he'd finished, his face was a contorted mask of sweat, and I was insensible, my shoulder broiling.

He straightened, panting, then grinned. 'Been wanting to do that,' he hissed raggedly, 'for a long time.'

He pressed the tip of the speargun on the ground between his feet and, in one swift movement, stretched back the thick band of rubber and hooked it. That rubber was old and cracked, but its girth meant it held, taut and quivering, ready to propel the dart. He raised the gun, pressed the butt against his shoulder and pointed it down at me, that horrible hook-headed spike aimed squarely at my chest. Only the ground beneath my ribs was going to arrest its momentum. I'd be pinned to the rock for my final minutes.

'Here's what I need you to do,' Mike began, still breathing hard. 'Hand over the hard drive.'

Whatever sense I'd been slowly assembling – whatever

meaning I'd managed to sieve from the situation so far – dissolved at this. I managed to stammer, 'Someone took it.'

Mike gave a twisted laugh. 'Conveniently vanished, eh? Let's accept I saw through that ruse the moment you attempted it. Take off your bag.' The dropped torch provided grotesque back-lighting, and what I could see was fish-eyed by tears. He beckoned with the tip of the speargun. 'Take off the *fucking bag*.'

Removing it meant negotiating my throbbing shoulder. I worked slowly, pain pulsing in breakers; a tidal thing that dragged broken glass through me as it pulled out, then dumped it down my arm again as it rolled in. It took me an age to work the straps free.

Once I had, Mike tore greedily at the zip, tipped the contents clear, then glared. He was a man utterly changed. Beneath the mask he'd been wearing, his animal expression was cruel, his eyes icy. 'Where is it?'

I was too broken to resist any more. 'Alex took it.'

He rose to standing, raised the gun again and said, 'No more lies, Tess.'

And then the fog behind him slithered open.

Movement, a flash of an arm in the darkness and Mike lowering the spear, a palm cupped to his neck. 'Shit,' he said. When he spoke again, he'd turned away. Tears almost blinded me, but I could hear well enough and his voice was different: slower and heavier. 'What have you done?'

He wasn't talking to me.

Then the noise of a struggle, a shove and a thud. And

a moment later, another face above me. Alex, leaning in, pale-skinned, the lenses of her glasses streaked with water droplets, asking if I was OK.

I told her, in as colourful a way as possible, that no, I wasn't.

42

Alex recovered Mike's torch – it was dimming, its battery beginning to fail – and pushed painkillers from a blister pack in the weakening beam. 'Looks like your shoulder's dislocated. I reckon we can risk four of these.'

'Where's Mike?'

'Just here.' She placated me, eyes darting against the fog. 'It's OK. He's deep under.'

The sedative injectors. 'Night Nurse for seals,' I said.

Smiling weakly, she helped me stay upright, a palm against my good shoulder, feeding me pills and water. I wanted to stand, but every time I tried moving, I got a shriek of resistance. 'He wanted the hard drive,' I grunted, labouring to my knees, my stuff scattered about me.

Alex removed the hand from my shoulder and raised it. 'I'm sorry, Tess. I know it looks bad.' She hid her face in the crook of her arm, wiping her eyes. I waited. This needed to be persuasive. A moment later, she cleared her throat. 'After Steven died,' she said, 'I lost all confidence.

I tried to get it back. Just do things right for a few years, make no mistakes. I wasn't even sure I should have come on this trip. When I realised you were filming, I just . . . ' she touched her lips, blinked rapidly. 'I was trying to protect what was left of my career.'

I listened, thinking – as much as was possible with my shoulder howling for attention – and saw my snooping from her perspective. It made sense. The disaster of the Deserta Grande expedition, the dressing-down, the reputational damage; once Alex worked out what I was up to, it would have been imperative to stop it.

'I just needed to check what you were doing,' she said. 'I haven't even looked at it yet. I don't care any more, take it back.'

She placed my hard drive on the rocks between us and pushed it towards my strewn belongings. I nodded my understanding. Something about the loneliness of that island, the yawning distance between us and the mainland, the constant ache of fear and vulnerability, made me trust her. 'Listen. This isn't your fault,' I said, making peace. 'You've done everything right. Brought the team together. Sorted us out and kept us in line. Mike's the saboteur.'

Alex hefted the torch. 'Doesn't matter now. Everything's ruined.' That was a feeling I knew well. I held my good hand out, inviting Alex to help me. 'I'm so scared,' she said, hauling me to my feet.

Mutual exhaustion and despair had softened the space between us. 'Me too.'

'You? Really?' She gave me a tearfully uncertain look,

sniffing. 'I've seen *Spill*. The bit in those Californian oilfields.'

'That was a long time ago.'

'It's easier to be brave when you're young,' Alex said. 'You don't sense danger in the same way.'

That was true enough. Despite the meeting with the minister's aide, Gretchen and I had continued to investigate. 'After *Spill*,' I confessed, 'I nearly gave up altogether.'

She gave me a look that lingered somewhere between sympathy and pity. 'I saw something about your partner.'

That wasn't a surprise. If you knew the right Reddit threads, you could still find plenty of speculation about Chase Industries. Most discussions hadn't been updated for a couple of years now – I still tortured myself by checking every now and then – but there are theories about Gretchen, gossip about particular board members and information on failed lawsuits.

My name was mud in those places.

'I'm sorry,' Alex said. 'I shouldn't have brought it up.'

'We need to get to the lighthouse,' I told her. 'We still have one flare. We can use the height. We might even get the light going, draw someone's attention.'

Alex took a deep breath. Her throat convulsed and she dabbed at her cheeks with the backs of her hands. 'If we're going up there,' she said, strobing the dark fog with the beam of the flashlight, 'we'll need rope.'

I wasn't about to argue with that. My previous walk along the clifftop had been bad enough in the pin-sharp brightness of a tropical day. We unravelled the rope between us and stood side by side, just as Mike and I had done yesterday morning. He could've pushed me over the edge back then, I thought, but he didn't. *Why?* I hadn't yet discovered Clay's stab wound. Or the phone ...

'Search Mike,' I managed. 'Has he got anything with him?'

Alex stooped, ran open palms along his legs while I closed my eyes against the pain in my shoulder. The tide was up again, and with it, waves of glass. Moments later, I blinked away tears as the pain receded.

'Nothing we need,' she said. 'Cards, keys. A few euros. A phone.'

That set a firecracker banging in me. 'His?'

'Looks like it.' Alex held it up. Sleek and recent; not Clay's. Then, by the light of the torch, I saw her stiffen. 'What's this?'

She was holding up the seal tracker. 'Mike gave it me,' I remembered. 'On the crossing over. I've been meaning to drop it back in the—'

'It's on.'

'What?'

'He's been tracking your movements, Tess. Oh my God, Mike, what are you up to?'

That explained his position at the edge of the wood. He knew I'd been out at the boat, and knew I was heading back. Where else? The lighthouse; the cove for a second time. And of course, last night I'd confirmed his suspicions by telling him everything I'd learned.

'We need to go,' Alex said. 'Midazolam doesn't last forever.'

'Speargun,' I said. 'Don't leave it with Mike. And unhook the restraint. Looks like it'll snap and fire at any moment.' Alex nodded, trembling as she gathered our resources. 'And can you help me collect the bits of my camera?'

She eyed me. 'Did you miss what he just did to it?'

I shook my head, holding my breath against another pulse, weaker this time. Hallelujah, the painkillers were kicking in. 'Might be able to recover the hard drive. Just put what parts you can into my bag.'

She set aside the things we no longer wanted or had room for – spare batteries, hiking socks, seal tracker, broken GPS. We finished a bottle of water and left the empty next to Mike. Alex began re-packing my bag for me, smashed camera first, and I watched, ensuring she returned my hard drive. 'You can't carry this,' she said, hefting the speargun. 'I'll take it. You've got flare gun, cereal bars. The last of the water. I'll take the GPS and map.'

Packing complete, we returned our attention to the rope. Slack in my right hand, I tried recalling the bunt-line hitch. How did it go? Over to the left, under to the right, then over both and pinch? I had to get Alex to remind me. Once we were secure, we assessed her GPS screen and turned ourselves around until we faced the mountain path to the north.

It was one dying torch versus an Atlantic fogbank in the witching hour. A grey current curled feline about our ankles. The moon kept closing its eye. We set off, the rope loose between us, splashing our ghost-light against the wet wasteland of rock.

It was a long climb, and pain began probing my arms, exploring my hands and fingers. It turned out the best distraction was to talk. So I took a deep, shuddering breath and told Alex my story.

It was the first time I'd done so since that first police investigation ten years ago. 'I guess you know my partner died,' I began.

Alex nodded. 'I'm sorry. Leo and I did some background checks. I thought you were too good for this job. A big, successful documentary-maker wants to film seals, it seemed odd. But I get it now.'

'Gretchen and I were just finishing up *Spill*,' I started.

And something in that beginning loosened the floodgates. I told her the story of the Saltfleet gas terminal and the shoreline marshes.

43

Gretchen and I stayed the night in a thatched pub opposite a primary school. It was as remotely rural a landscape as you could possibly imagine by day: flat fields of spinach and cabbage, long, single-track straight roads edged with drainage ditches, village greens and churches.

Once the sun went down, the place took on a more sinister character.

We were a handful of kilometres from the coast, and as twilight loomed, a rough salt wind came hammering at the windows of our room. The empty expanse of marsh and reclaimed farmland offered no barrier. Out in the darkness, distant refinery chimneys blazed.

There'd been evident security at our drive-by of the gas terminal earlier in the day; the usual combination of high fences, checkpoint cabins and ID-operated barrier-gates, so we'd been waiting for nightfall before going back. From a *Spill* point of view the situation looked good; the Chase website had dedicated page after page of lavish graphics to illustrate the carbon-capture process and celebrate the award of fifty million pounds from a government-managed research-and-innovation fund. Construction had begun renovating the terminal last year, so the website said, 'decarbonising the region and playing a key role in meeting the government's net-zero emissions target,' but it was pretty clear when we'd passed earlier that no work had been started. All we'd seen was a place long-since shut down – overgrown woodland spilling through the fencing; the cracked tarmac of its abandoned car park.

I'd been working on some version of *Spill* for over two years by then, and the meeting with the minister's special advisor had scrubbed my project of what little magic it had left. Gretchen had mentally moved on too; her investigation into the phone-tapping scandal was close to getting a deal and she was on her laptop late into each evening, managing every last decision. Our relationship – never quite the same after that day in the Kern County oil fields – had begun to unravel altogether. Conversations were terse transactions, long drives were conducted in chilly silence. I'm sure she couldn't wait to get the film finished and me off her back, so she could focus her full attention on her own upcoming release.

That night, as the rain began to fall, I was in no mood for nocturnal breaking-and-entering, and the tension I felt – rigid along my spine all day – was further souring my mood. The plan was we'd follow a dirt track raised above fields criss-crossed by wet pathways, and Gretchen would stay in the car checking for security while I captured footage. Climbing out of the car that night, leaving my phone on the dash and zipping my coat up to my chin, I had no idea how badly things would go.

I clipped my way into the rear of the site. There'd be things I'd see here that would finally confirm what I had always known about Chase. This was for me; for my gratification, more than anything else.

As expected, the site remained undeveloped. The old terminal buildings were badly graffitied, the metalwork blistered and the ground-floor windows vandalised. A substation spewed pipes that had rusted in years of rain. Everywhere, nature was reclaiming that which had been stolen – silver birch saplings had gathered in stands to form a mini-forest, mosses snaked in cracks, skeletal buddleia drooped from gutters and chimneys.

I started filming, kept the lighting low, capturing shadowy outlines, scoping the abandoned exterior. The process had me jittery, and when I heard a squeal of tyres somewhere out beyond the front gate, I hit pause and tucked my camera away, convinced I'd been caught by security, or worse; genuinely contemplating government officials descending on Saltfleet attracted by the tiny light of my camera. Once my pulse had thumped its way back down to steady, I crept around to the front of the building.

Another noise, this time closer, sudden and violent: an engine giving a guttural roar, tyres screaming against gravel.

Something banged hard against something else, then I saw lights. A Land Rover careered past, bouncing along the uneven surface of the access road, its lights spinning wild shadows from the trees. It shrieked around a corner and was gone. I had the unaccountable feeling it was travelling away from, rather than towards. Fleeing rather than seeking.

I ran now, tracking back around the rear of the terminal to the hole I'd cut in the fence, squeezing through and sprinting along the wet lane to the spot where we'd left the car. The interior lights were on and no one was inside. The driver's door was open and it was raining on the seats. I made it, gasping, and checked the interior front and back. The car was undamaged – good news since I thought I'd heard a collision – but no sign of Gretchen. And no response when I called. I circled the vehicle, wet darkness all around me. She'd gone. *She must have left in the other vehicle.* But why? I leaned into the driver's side and flicked the headlights on. The rain was coming down harder now, bright shafts shimmering in the twin beams.

'Gretchen?'

It felt stupid to call her name. Better to figure out why she'd left, try and contact her. As I reached across the dashboard for my phone, a possibility surfaced. It chilled my blood. *What if she'd struck a deal.* There was nothing stopping the MP's aide playing the two of us against each other. Gretchen had made some sort of agreement that involved abandoning me mid-shoot, springing a trap I couldn't yet see. I felt the hairs rise on my arms as I scanned the empty road. *Forget the rule about phones. Ring Gretchen.*

The raindrops on my screen slowed everything

down, but eventually I got the call going. And when it connected, matters became horribly clear. I heard Gretchen's phone ringing, then caught sight of it blinking up through the muck by the drainage ditch.

Near where the phone glowed, the grass had been torn up and the soil beneath wept streaks of glossy mud. Slippery loops suggested something had slithered down the bank into the ditch below. I approached.

At the bottom of the drainage channel, Gretchen Harris was face down in the water. She was still, except for her hair which bloomed upwards through the muddy current.

Both her legs were broken.

I could still see Gretchen on the gurney, the body bag zipped closed. Rain gathered in the places where the bag dipped. Her camera had exploded on impact. Wires and workings all over the place, gold under the ambulance lights.

The footage I got that night was never used.

44

Alex dipped her forehead against her hands, wiped a sheen of moisture from her face, and shook the torch until our light strengthened. 'I'm sorry,' she said. 'That must have been terrible.'

'Yeah. There was an investigation.'

My companion sketched an exhausted smile. 'Sounds familiar.'

When we reached the switchback in the path next to the fallen fence, we rested for a moment, watching skeletal trees strain fog with their fingers. Disarmingly lightheaded, I wondered if I'd faint. Alex and I both stared in the same direction as we got our breath back. Beyond those trunks, the path wound down to the cove where Steven lay. If I'd never gone down there on that second day, we wouldn't have known about any of this.

'Alex,' I said. 'I had Steven's phone.'

She looked at me aghast and drew back until the

rope was taut between us. Then she steepled her fingers either side of the bridge of her nose, lifting her glasses and wiping her eyes. 'Bloody hell, Tess,' she said eventually.

'I went down to the cove on the way back from the lighthouse,' I said. 'While I was down there, I found a bag around his shoulder, a waterproof one. There was a phone inside. I was charging it, but now it's gone.'

Alex's eyes, dull with exhaustion, narrowed. 'Is that why this is happening? Did you start all this?'

The obsession was aflame in me again. 'Something's happening here because of Clay. He found something out and someone killed him.'

'But what? What did he find?'

'Whatever's on his phone will tell us. But Mike doesn't have the phone.'

'Well, I don't have it,' she said flatly. Then she took a breath. 'Vinny?' She watched me shake my head. 'Which means there's someone else unaccounted for.'

'Exactly,' I said. Vinny didn't have Clay's phone. Mike didn't. It stood to reason we had a visitor. And I was going to have to recover that phone from whoever had it. 'All the more reason to stick together,' I said, 'and get to the lighthouse.'

We toiled upwards for a half hour, our pace slow. My wet clothes rubbed and my feet were sore. My arm was a blast furnace cooling beneath the lid of the drugs. I shuddered with adrenaline each time the fog shifted.

Soon we drew close to the Pico da Cheminé; I could

tell by the way our route swung between rocks out towards the cliff edge. We slowed, silently assessing the pathway, the lip of rock and the ghostly chamber of fog beyond. I guess we were both thinking of Vinny. Alex and I arranged ourselves so we could hold each other's arms as we skirted the edge. My companion's trembling limbs were a clear sign she suffered as I did. When our route moved away from the edge, I expected a loosening of tension but it didn't come. We stopped, the rope loose between us, and watched the grey world creep and glide. The tidal pain-pool rose again, my arm throbbing in time with my pulse.

A few minutes later our torch battery died. 'At least it'll be dawn soon,' Alex grunted.

We left it halfway up that damned mountain, and illuminated the rest of our journey with the fading light of our phones.

When the path flattened, I knew we were close but, sightless as we were, I couldn't pinpoint our location. Alex's GPS was no help; we were a blue dot on an island devoid of topography. In the absence of landmarks at least some contours would have helped, but we had nothing beyond our wits and the rope between us.

Soon it was clear we'd veered off course. Scrambling over a spine of rock I didn't recognise and picking our slow way across a ghostly field of ankle-breakers, I realised we were lost. We approached an edge, marvelling at the sudden absence of ground as it fell away. A featureless mist churned above the drop. The water below sounded hungry.

We turned, fought our way onwards, heading towards safety through smoked-glass moonlight.

I was so absorbed in pain management – deep breathing, happy thoughts – that the appearance of the lighthouse, looming like a church spire, came as a surprise. We'd approached it from a different angle.

The fog pulsed, stabilising for moments of dizzying stillness, then racing again. We avoided any further unexpected drops by heading straight for the tower, carefully checking each few metres of ground we could see ahead. Trying to find some sense of control, I decided to use the last few minutes of battery on my phone to film, and found that seeing the world at a remove helped quell my fear. The footage was irrelevant; it was the process that mattered now. *Do your job and stay calm, Tess.*

Wreathed in cloud, the place looked, if anything, stranger than last time. When the wind gusted it felt as if we were beneath a river, a grey eddy pouring through the broken cupola and kneading over our heads. Despite my wet and blistered feet, my burning shoulder and shock-response dizziness, I felt a faint flicker of hope. We'd nearly reached safety. We hauled ourselves onwards against exhaustion. I shot the iron ladder dropping vertically from the rusting balcony, the broken outbuildings, the filthy stones and carved date of construction. By the time we made it to the door I was shivering and numb, searching wet pockets for the key.

'Hang on,' Alex said. 'It's open.'

That little light of hope I'd felt was immediately snuffed out.

The door wasn't arranged in the same way as it had been last time. Padlock nowhere to be seen, building open to the elements. Maybe Mike had been up here while we slept, killed Vinny, then headed back down to the woods. That was a lot of ground to cover. The other possibility – the one that tightened the skin – was that the visitor might be up here. We crunched across bird bones and pushed the lighthouse door inward slowly, careful not to make any noise.

Even with Mike dealt with, I felt a bead of terror grow as I entered. The interior, dark for a moment, outlined itself in grey-blue as Alex's phone-torch sliced through rising clouds of dust. All was as I'd remembered: the cast-iron whale oil barrels with their pressure gauges and that jarringly modern collection of objects: the diesel cans, the sealed crates sitting atop each other. To our right, the door through to the room of smashed tiles and rotting rugs and the spiral stairs up the tower.

I heard Alex's sharp intake of breath and felt a jolt strong enough to fuse me to the flagstones.

The door to our left – the one that led through to the collapsing single-storey building – had been securely locked last time I'd been here.

Now it stood open.

Alex, reading my face, blanched and raised the spear-gun, its thick rubber catapult thankfully hanging loose. 'Is someone inside?'

I was wound so tight every muscle hurt. The interior of the new room was in darkness. No sound emerged from that half-metre gap between door and frame. I'd seen the room from the outside, so I knew it could only be small. Nevertheless, this could be the space that provided answers. Clay's phone might be here. 'Point your light,' I mouthed.

I followed Alex's meagre beam, took a step forwards, and pushed the door open. Fear clouded in me like blood through water as I stepped inside.

For a moment I wasn't sure what I was seeing. Phone-light ghosted across a desk and lamp, to find whitewashed walls beyond. The only thing on the desk was a heavy-duty torch, lens-down. This wasn't an office, though; it was something more like a lab. There was a curious gathering of equipment tucked into the far corner; a shallow tray with a rippled base had been propped against the wall, next to what I mistook for a small concrete mixer, hip-high, until I saw its rotating drum had holes in, like a big tubular sieve. It was some sort of wheeled machine for sifting, and next to it, glass jars and plastic bottles of hydrochloric acid. If I had to guess, I'd have said this might be the kind of equipment needed to analyse mineral samples: a shaker, some sort of drum for spinning mixtures out into their constituent parts, acid for cleaning. A mini-laboratory for assessing the quality of mined ore. Despite the equipment – as out-of-place as a dead man on an empty island – there was something familiar about the room itself.

I'd seen it before, though that was surely impossible.

The epiphany arrived at the second pass of the tiny beam, looking at the long crack in the plaster. It ran vertically, ceiling to floor behind the desk. I knew the shape of that crack; the way the lamplight had briefly illuminated it before Leo had blurred his background.

This was the office he'd called me from.

45

I leant against the door frame, my knees weak.

This was impossible. Leo was in France. Wasn't he? I scrabbled to catch up. The lighting, the bookshelves, the suit – he'd definitely been in Paris to begin with. After that, things had changed. Where had he spoken from each time we met? Different places. Firstly on the move somewhere; then at some railway station . . . no, I corrected, *an airport*. As soon as he'd heard about Clay, Leo Bodin must have made arrangements to fly out here. Which meant he'd been here for twenty-four hours at least. The shape on the GoPro footage. The woods earlier tonight; the Seawild-issued GPS. It was Leo's. And he was the one who'd sabotaged our transceiver.

Suddenly, his insistent brief made sense. The film was his boss's idea. He'd never wanted it made – of course he hadn't – but he'd been backed into a corner. Now I was here, he wanted a documentary designed to drive away visitors, emphasising the fragility of the seal population and discouraging ecotourism.

He wanted the island to remain remote. Just not to protect the wildlife.

Alex panned her phone again: chair, cracked plaster, desk. 'Tess. What's wrong?'

He must have a boat somewhere. He must have pushed Vinny from the pico. Was Steven's body even down at the cove any more? I guessed not. Bodin had surely done what he'd come here to do already. Except he was still here, which meant he hadn't cleared up everything. He was the one with Clay's phone. He had what he wanted, didn't he? Maybe he was waiting to be picked up. Unless he was still here because I had something . . .

'Tess?'

Leo had sent Mike to recover the hard drive. I had the last document of Steven Clay's body. Leo wanted my footage. And what he didn't want, was witnesses.

I moved into the office. 'Leo called us from here,' I whispered. 'He's on the island.'

'Oh my God,' Alex whispered. 'Leo?'

A noise disturbed us, the dull sound of movement somewhere above. Had to hurry. My tide of pain was out for a moment; the broken glass drawn down and away. I had just a few moments before it was back. I beckoned and, with Alex's illumination, checked the desk drawers. No sign of Clay's phone. It had been a long shot. I lowered my bag, placed it on the stones between my boots, extracted the flare gun, then straightened, all without crying out in agony.

Alex's gaze was pleading, so I turned my attention to her. Using the wicked tip of the speargun's dart, she indicated the ceiling in the dying light of her phone. Something was moving across the upper floors. 'We need to get out of here,' she whispered.

'I can't,' I said, and tucked the flare gun into my front pocket. 'I need Clay's phone.'

Alex took a step back, distancing herself from me. 'What? You've got to be kidding.'

'Listen. If I was Leo,' I hissed, trying to wrestle some control back, 'I'd have sent Mike to sort us out. And I'd have been up there looking out for his return. The fog's pretty thick but I bet from that vantage point you can see an approaching torch.'

'We have to go. Now.'

'But our torch died,' I continued. 'We lost our way, didn't even approach from the direction he was checking. Which means Leo doesn't know we're here. I need to stay. You can go.'

'Tess, what are you talking about?'

I took as calming a breath as I could, tried stilling the obsession that hammered in me. 'The phone's where all the evidence is – I know it sounds crazy but I have to do this. You can help. Listen, Alex—' I held a hand up, trying to release some of the pent-up fear in the air '—you can help. Do this one thing for me and then you can go.'

She managed a nod.

'Approach the lighthouse again,' I whispered, 'from right out at the front there. No, hear me out. You use this torch. You go a little way down the mountain, switch it on, emerge from the fog.'

She dragged in a breath, nodded. 'And he thinks I'm Mike?'

'False lights,' I said. 'He comes down to meet you.'

'Then what?'

My shoulder chose that moment to boil beneath my skin. I shut my eyes against the pain. 'You leave the torch on the rocks, then disappear,' I croaked when it calmed. 'Head down the mountain. The torch will confuse him; meanwhile, I get upstairs and have a go at lighting up the lens.'

'But when Leo sees it's a trick, he'll come back to get you. How do you escape then?' Alex pushed her hair up off her forehead and stared at the torch on the desk.

A thought occurred to me. 'I'll need the speargun.'

'Leaving me unarmed?'

'Set the torch down on the rocks and retreat. Stay well out of his way and you won't need it. Come on, we need to untie ourselves.'

The next quarter-hour was an excruciating balance of competing priorities; assessing the noise of movement from upstairs and watching for Alex's light. It would take her some time to position herself – we'd agreed she'd return the way we'd come, staying out of Leo's line of sight, which meant a treacherous looped route along the front of the building and away across some difficult terrain before returning. At least ten minutes for the journey out, we reasoned, then, protected from view by the fog and the curvature of the mountain, Alex would switch the torch on and mimic Mike's mazy return as he made his way up to the plateau.

I watched the fog folding itself, trying to rest my arm in a variety of hopeless positions while my shoulder thumped heat along my collarbones.

The outward journey seemed to take Alex forever. So long that at one point, watching from the door, I began to think she might have just left me. There was nothing stopping her taking the torch and heading back down to our camp. Why hadn't I thought of that? *Christ's sake, Tess.* She'd abandoned me up here.

Then, just as anxious speculation had calcified into certainty, her light appeared. The beam was strong and clear, weaving like a wrecker's waterline lantern. I padded carefully along the front of the building, then tucked myself against a tumbledown wall at a crouch and waited. Mist thickened and slithered. Eventually, I heard footsteps on the stairs, and saw a figure emerge at the lighthouse door.

It was Leo Bodin.

He paused on the threshold, eyes determinedly set on the light. After a moment's consideration, he set off, a windcheater billowing at his waist and wrists, his head inclined into the fog.

46

Once convinced of my safety, I worked my way back along the front of the building and re-entered, pausing inside at the foot of the stairs. The air felt different now, the place wrapped in silence.

The two curling flights of wooden slats – hard to navigate in the almost-dark – would take me up to the cupola again. Soon I was at the top, back within those two concentric circles; the outer space lined with ancient whale oil tanks, the inner a second chamber hemmed in by a huge lens in a circular track.

I placed the speargun on the top of a tank and located the access hatch to the interior of the lens. Stooping, one arm cradled against me, I managed to squeeze through the door. Inside, I rose to standing again.

I was in a chamber of toughened glass still capable of rotating around a single burning point. There was plenty enough room for the complex of chambers and oil-burning pipes as well as space for an engineer to circulate, accessing the interior of the great lens. Much of my new space was taken up by the vast central oil burner, a chamber encased in metal, thinning as it rose, until a solid-looking pipe emerged, feeding into a glass column.

The whole arrangement looked like a huge camping stove. Surely I could figure out how to light it. The metal housing below, its chipped paint peeling, had a hatch that stood open. By phone-light the interior looked alarmingly complex, a tangle of pipes with circular iron taps, some sort of storage chamber, a rubber cap attached to a chute. Those smooth, bottle-green chambers outside the lens must feed it somehow. So how did it burn? I checked where the tip of the tube emerged at the thick glass column. Twenty centimetres high, it sat on what looked like a valve with two twistable keys to regulate oil flow. I lifted the glass protector and peered inside. More incomprehensible workings, stinking of fish.

Cameras I knew, but this knot of piping was another language.

Crawling with doubt and sweating against the pain of my shoulder, I crouched before the lower workings, stuck a hand in and twisted both taps back and forth. Nothing. I tapped the chamber with a knuckle, heard it slosh and echo back at me. Not quite empty. OK, that was something to work with, but how did the oil travel upwards? Air pressure? Even assuming I managed to make sense of the system, I didn't know how I might light the oil as it reached the wick. I had no matches.

My synapses jangled, nothing connecting.

Then there came a noise at the stairs below me.

Leo was back already. He must have found the torch abandoned on the rocks. He'd know there was someone up here, that they'd arranged a distraction. How had he done all that so quickly? I didn't know what the speed meant, but it couldn't be good. A bitter desperation tightened like a fist beneath my ribs and I felt like I was falling. Leo's steps began two storeys below, slow and heavy. I was the only one left now. Mike would recover soon enough and then it would be two against one.

I tried swallowing a racking sob but everything was too much and it shuddered its way out. I couldn't get back down the stairs – he'd already closed off my exit. I didn't have time to figure out how this nightmare of pipes worked. Which meant no light and no rescue. His footsteps reached the first floor, then continued their upward rotation.

I only had twenty steps left before he'd be in the room with me. Sweat beaded in my hair. Fear clanging beneath my ribs, I tried to plan.

I'd have to fire the speargun at him as he reached the top of the stairs.

Abandoning any attempt to light up the great lens, I squeezed out through the service hatch back into the upper floor's outer space, and collected the speargun. The rusting metal was slippery in my hands. I'd have to pull the restraining rubber back and locate the thick catapult in the hook. I gave it a tug. The rubber, protected from the water in the old lockbox, was tough and hard to stretch. How had Mike done it? I'd been suffering too much to notice. I pulled again, one-handed, straining to get the band back far enough to trap it. He'd used two hands, that was it. Spear to the ground, both hands pulling the rubber upwards to hook it. But I didn't have two hands.

Leo was close now. I had ten upward steps to work with.

My fear was a vibrant, technicolour thing, surely glowing with enough intensity to attract passing ships.

I gave the restraining rubber the hardest pull I could. Somehow I managed to claw it up against the hook. But it was at the cost of my damaged arm, which roared and broiled. And the pain meant I accidentally depressed the trigger.

As soon as I'd got the catapult tight, the rubber pinged free and the bolt flew from the gun-tip.

I'd been aiming down.

Jesus, it was deadly – the spear struck one of the metal whale oil chambers that lined the cupola and, with a flat, wet bang, punctured it. The impact was centimetres above the floor and the resulting wound gulped greedily. Stinking oil pulsed out in a spreading pool, rolling for the stairs, pushing in a curved rivulet around the outside of the lens.

Blinded by tears, fuelled by a terror that cared nothing for logic, I found myself doing the only thing I could think of. I dropped the useless gun and ran for the balcony door. Raked my back along the jamb as I ducked out, and crawled onto the high walkway.

I dragged my rope end out after me and went right,

one arm cradled against my chest, one quaking as it supported my weight. By the light of Leo's torch, spilling through the broken windows above me as he reached the top step, I could see my walkway was built of curved iron sections bolted together. Looking through the grille of the thing directly down the side of the lighthouse wall to the clifftop below, and then down into an impossible, fog-filled emptiness beneath that, I nearly dissolved. Ocean roared against rocks somewhere under everything. The weather had stripped the metal of its paint, rendered it raw and harsh. It hurt like hell just to crawl: my left palm, pressed hard against the metal, stung, and the knees of my jeans quickly shredded.

'Tess,' said Leo Bodin. 'I know you're up here.'

My heart hammered through my muscles until my fingers hurt. Even if I'd wanted to reply, my voice was beyond working. There was a ladder somewhere, I remembered, fused to the exterior of the building. Was I heading the right way? It descended at the front, near the date carved into the stone. I needed to circle the tower and reach that ladder.

'Tess,' Leo said again. I could hear the wet sound of his boots in the oil as he circled the lens. He'd surely suspect me of hiding inside it. 'We can make this easy. I need your hard drive, and I need access to this phone. I'm betting you have the passcode. Give me the code and we can come to some arrangement.'

Older phones required four-digit passcodes. I had no idea why Leo thought I might know it, but I had bigger problems. It was only a matter of time before he saw the door that led out to the parapet. Above the noise of the wind, I could still hear the low glug of haemorrhaging oil, and Leo's sloppy footsteps come to a stop. A laugh. 'Playing with oil was foolish enough. But if you're outside, Tess, you're being very stupid indeed. Come back in and let's talk. Once I have the hard drive and the phone code, I'm sure we can come to some arrangement about everything else.'

I held my position, ears aching in the wind, the rusty walkway stinging my knees. The parapet doorway was already hidden beyond the curve of the building and the rapid currents of fog, but I heard him emerge, the metal singing with his presence as he took a couple of steps outwards. Mike had said it would never hold two people.

When Leo spoke again, his voice was closer, raised over the noise of the wind. 'I imagine a certain amount of money will be enough to buy your silence,' he called, and waited for this miserable blow to land. I closed my eyes at the force of it, waiting as it thrummed through me. 'After all,' he said, 'it's worked in the past, hasn't it, Tess?'

Somehow, Leo Bodin knew my most shameful secret.

There was a part of my story I hadn't told Alex earlier – hadn't told anyone ever – and it was surely the reason Leo had hired me. The haste with which I'd been contacted, the ease with which the deal had been struck, it all made sense now. He hadn't wanted me because of my previous work or professional pedigree.

He'd wanted me because he knew I could be bought.

47

After the meeting with the minister's aide – after Gretchen and I had left the back of that car having turned down huge amounts of money in return for stopping our investigation – I didn't see my partner again for a couple of weeks.

I went back to my flat in Hackney and spent the following days planning the final section of *Spill*. Those sessions were haunted by an uncomfortable tension: part alarm, since this was the phase of the investigation the MP didn't want to happen; part weary despair with the whole project. Once each day's work was done and my mind released its hold on the material, I found myself brooding about the money we'd just turned down.

With autumn arriving, I'd reached a milestone – a year since graduation; a year since Channel 4 had picked up *Spill*, and a whole year working with Gretchen Harris. My peers from university were mostly in jobs. Back then, we were all still on Facebook, and that autumn, as pay cheques rolled in, the bars and restaurants they chose for meet-ups became increasingly expensive. After my lucky break at the graduate show I'm not sure how welcome I'd have been, but I couldn't have gone even if courage had allowed. I was broke. I'd extended my overdraft in order to repay Dad, and delayed my latest rent instalment; I'd borrowed from Gretchen to cover expenses and Christmas was on the horizon.

I guess the minister's advisor must have known all that. It didn't take a genius: one glance at the two of us side by side in the back of that car would have been sufficient to tell him who was the weaker link.

So when he'd got in touch next, it was just with me, and it was by phone.

This time he introduced himself with his first name as if we were firm friends. 'Listen, Tess,' he said. 'Let's be frank. This is your project. Think of all the hours you've put into this; all the time you invested on your own before they even brought Miss Harris on board.' He paused and then, unintentionally echoing Gretchen's words, went on. 'It's your name on the title screen, so let's not forget who's making the decisions here, OK? I have an improved offer.'

My flat was cold and I was pacing in my coat to warm up. 'Improved?'

'That's right. But there are caveats. I'm afraid whatever footage you do collect in Saltfleet – yes, we know that's where you're going – will be so heavily redacted as to be basically unusable. However, unrelated footage, perhaps with a voiceover we approve, will work perfectly well to conclude your investigation. You'll lose less than five minutes of film, the rest stays intact, and you receive a generous settlement.'

He mentioned a figure close to twice the size of the first.

Head swimming, I held it together long enough to tell him I'd have an answer when he next called. That night I went over my accounts, checking every credit card and overdraft. The calculations were unequivocal. I'd clear everything with plenty of money to spare. Enough to start a little production company of my own. *Spill* would still be a powerful piece of journalism, I told myself, a film that still held Chase to account. And the money would allow me to pursue malpractice elsewhere, bring down other companies. Wasn't accepting this deal – which didn't actually compromise the main section of the investigation – the right thing to do for my future career as well as my present self?

When he called again the next day, I was ready.

'I'm still going out there,' I told him. 'I have to finish this.'

'But?' he asked, quietly hopeful.

'But I'm not going to use any film I collect.'

There was a pause in which I heard him exhale. 'That's a very wise decision, Miss Macfarlane,' he said, calculating. 'Stay where you are. A courier will arrive with a document for you to sign. You should receive a transfer before close of play.'

I don't remember how I responded. I was probably breathless.

'Miss Macfarlane,' he finished, 'I assume you have no plans to let your partner know anything of this?'

I closed my eyes. 'No,' I said. 'No, I don't.'

I'd be going to Saltfleet with Gretchen, and I'd be feigning the collection of footage. There wasn't a chance in hell I'd ever be admitting to that. Or so I thought.

★

I backed slowly along the parapet, heading for the ladder, reversing on two knees and one palm, the stone of the tower to my left, a drifting grey void to my right.

I'd betrayed Gretchen Harris. She'd been killed collecting footage I'd already agreed was never going to be used.

Vibrating metal told me Leo was following, placing each foot carefully. Another sound too: metal upon metal. It sounded a lot like the blade of a knife, I realised, tapped against the fencing as he moved forwards.

'Tess. Come inside,' he called. 'You don't need to make this film. It's not worth the effort.'

'Clay worked it out,' I shouted, moving backwards, praying the balcony would hold and the ladder would appear. 'You're smuggling gold, using the island to transfer cargo and refuel. Not the kind of story I can stay quiet about.'

He laughed at this. I deserved it. 'I'm sure you can stay quiet about anything if the money's right,' he called back. *Tac, tac, tac.* Blade against balustrade.

'Is that the knife you killed Clay with?'

'And his partner,' he replied, chillingly offhand.

313

Fear and confusion clouded my blood – *his partner?* – but before I could conjure a response, the parapet shifted. Swallowing back a scream that nearly suffocated me, I froze, white-knuckled and dissolving as the walkway dropped, a little downward jolt.

Metalwork screeched.

I checked the wall, saw a rivet had worked its way free from the stone, leaving a bracket dangling. The walkway seam beneath me was loosening as the moving section shifted. Tears came in unruly floods as I steadied myself, pressing my back against the lighthouse wall, one arm throbbing in my lap. I wiped my face with a forearm, wondering how close the downward ladder was. It felt nearby, but I couldn't see it in the fog. Had to get there before the whole balcony came down.

Through hazy clouds of pain, an idea asserted itself. I felt it move slowly upward, heading for the light like a surfacing seal. It might work. Leo had me trapped out here. I wasn't going to make it back to Madeira, or onto my flight home. I'd be disappointing DCI Rafiq. I was as good as dead. Which legitimised the plan: if I tried it, at least there'd be lots of light. At the very least, I'd draw rescue for Alex.

I only needed two things to make it work and one was tied to my waist, its loose end gathered between my feet. The deck rope. Braided polyester, filthy white flecked with yellow, thin but strong. Slowly and quietly, I turned and checked the windows above me. Glass blown clear long ago; nothing but jagged teeth trapped in their iron frames.

Leo must have taken another step, because the grille of the walkway tipped outwards, screeching as it tore. I had to press my boots against the fencing. Behind me, long metal pins were detaching themselves from the stone, slithering outwards, pulled by the movement.

I heard Leo swear. 'No one's going to watch your film, Tess. I'll give you double what it's going to earn you right now. No need to even do the work.'

The last time I'd been bought off, it had seemed an easy route out of a difficult situation. My entire debt wiped by a deal struck over the phone in my freezing flat. But that was ten years ago. I thought I knew better now – but I found my certainty flicker.

'I'm backing up,' Leo said. 'We're both falling if we stay here much longer.'

'You pushed Vinny,' I called.

'Vinny and Steven got too close. They knew the danger but they kept digging. You're different, Tess, much more sensible. Come back inside. Hand over the hard drive, give me the phone code, and all of this goes away.'

I'd be safe inside, solid flagstones beneath my feet. I might not have the code he was after but I could strike a deal, get myself off this crumbling death trap. 'Hang on,' I called. 'Give me a second.'

I fed the loose end of my rope around the back of the window-frame strut and pulled it out the opposite side until I had sufficient to work with. Buntline hitch, Tess. Over to the left, under to the right, over both and pinch, twist through the gap. Easy in theory, but terror made

315

a simple process impossible. My shoulder beat a steady pulse across my body. My good wrist felt weirdly man- acled and my fingers were stiff with adrenaline. Over to the left, under to the right – then what? Kept missing my through, couldn't find sufficient strength to pull it tight. Eventually I made something approximating a knot but it looked wrong. I abandoned the job, considering the loops of rope that now lashed me to the window. Would it hold? Even in the heat? Any miscalculations and I'd be dashed to the rocks like Vinny.

Nothing more I could do, no time for further preparation.

Tac, tac, tac. 'Tess, last chance. This thing is going to fall if we don't get inside.'

I pulled the orange flare gun from beneath my belt. No mystery about this device: chunky plastic, safety catch deactivated by a thumb, flare already inserted, trigger waiting to be pulled.

I turned to face the building, a perilously slow process I had to execute in stages, each likely to send the walk- way plunging down to the clifftop rocks. Finally I was kneeling, my good shoulder against the stone, my head ducked down beneath the open window. Inside, I could hear oil sluicing downstairs in viscous sheets.

I didn't have much time. Leo was backing off, surely heading back to the safety of the tower before the bal- cony detached itself and fell.

'Tess,' Leo called, further away now.

I readied the flare gun, raised my head, took aim, and fired through the window.

48

I had two seconds of cowering foolishly, hearing the fizz of the flare strike the floor; just long enough to wonder if I'd made some horrendous miscalculation.

Then the room above me erupted. There was a ghostly whoop, a big lung dragging in oxygen before exhaling a screaming wall of fire. The walkway vanished from beneath me and I fell – probably the only thing that saved me, looking back – and I pendulumed into the lighthouse wall, my lifeline twanging and shuddering as I swung and bounced. My shoulder began to roar and moments later whiplash bruises joined the chorus. The rope bit my middle like a glass edge. I raised an arm over my head as a storm of smashed debris rained down. Something struck my temple and I felt warm blood in my eyes. I swung and spun wildly, impact-sounds stuttering like machine-gun fire as blasted building struck the rock below.

The ladder loomed, appearing against the stonework then retreating again as I swung away. I swung back, missed it again. Above me, something else ignited and blew, a great fountain of flame sending waves of glass raining. The lens had exploded. I missed the ladder a third time, flurries of glass in the air like hot snow. Got it on the fourth, clung to that ladder like a shipwrecked sailor. Shortly after I'd wrapped the crook of my good arm beneath its rungs, my rope went slack and its upward end fell past me, swirling downwards, aflame like a snaking wick.

I descended, hot palms slipping on the rust. Down past the lighthouse's carved date of construction. Down to where the ladder ran out. I didn't have long before the boat diesel went the same way as the whale oil. I dropped to the roof of the outbuilding, tiles cracking and slipping beneath my feet. Crashed onto my backside, slithered downwards, and despite the blood in my eyes, managed an ungainly jump to the rocks below.

Thank God Leo had fallen the way he had; away from the edge, smashed into the rocks amongst the bird bones face down and, something I only realised as I started searching him, still breathing. I patted his pockets, ran my one good hand down his sides until I felt the telltale shape of Clay's phone. Plucked and pocketed it. Above me, the lighthouse was headless and blazing wildly, and all around the fog was thickened by gouts of stinking smoke.

I gave Leo a one-armed tug and succeeded in pulling him twenty metres further from the blaze.

A desperate glance at the building, still thinking about the boat diesel. As soon as the middle floor collapsed – and by the look of the flames, it wouldn't be long – we'd have another eruption to deal with.

I got my breath back, swaying dizzily and watching the shell of the place, its skeletal windows and ragged stonework wobbling in the haze of a white-hot column of climbing heat. 1857 read the stone inscription. If that was its date of construction, tonight marked its complete destruction. I watched the numbers blacken. 1857, I thought.

1 8 5 7.

Tucking Clay's phone against my breast, back to the wind, I found Leo had charged it. He'd powered it up, and had been trying to gain access. I typed the numbers in.

It worked.

Between the moisture condensing on the screen, the thick clots of smoke and the blood in my eyes, I couldn't assess much of what I'd found. Besides, I needed to make an escape. Bodin was far enough from the building not to be incinerated, so I left him there. A few moments later, the boat diesel went up with a blast so spectacular, the thrown heat and energy carved a temporary hole in the fog. For a few seconds I could follow the path down the mountain, red rocks burnished a bouncing orange by walls of flame. Then the grey snaked back in, re-blanketing me. I wondered how far Alex had got by now.

Wiping the phone screen against my top, I investigated again as I walked. It was an impersonal object; no colourful pictures as backdrops to the app-swatches and no screen-saver; a burner, I guessed, used specifically for the collection of Seawild evidence. I skipped the unread messages – there were close to a hundred – and instead selected the camera app and checked the photos. It was hard to study them in detail because of the blood. My forehead was gushing, and the stuff was drying stickily, threatening to glue my eyelids. I wiped it away with the arm of my top, saw with alarm how much came away on my clothes. Distracting myself, I went back to the screen. There was just enough battery left for me to scroll Clay's collection of pictures: screenshots from Google maps that looked as if they captured the exact position of the gold mines; dozens of carefully photographed documents followed which, though impenetrable to me, would doubtless prove something crucial about the movement of the contraband. Clay had shots of trucks all taken idling at desert-road checkpoints and featuring security teams scanning documentation. A number seemed to have been taken solely to capture handshakes; Lukas Larsen's work, I guessed, sent secretly. There were pictures of the sort of equipment I'd seen back in the locked lighthouse room, including a video which explained the ripple-based tray which, when powered up, shook particulates free from water samples, testing for the presence of gold. There were close-ups of different boat-hulls capturing the watercraft registrations painted on them; there were pictures of dockhands loading, and of sailors captured with the slack, unrehearsed expressions of those oblivious to a camera's presence. I saw the jumble of images with a film-maker's eye. This stuff was an interconnected data trail.

I knew I'd get a lot of professional satisfaction from piecing together the story these pictures told, and exposing Leo Bodin's corruption.

The torch was waiting patiently for me, propped against a rock, its column of light illuminating a shifting soup of bad-smelling smog. I continued my unsteady descent, illuminating the way with my newly acquired flashlight. It wasn't until I'd reached the *faja* forty minutes later that I realised what a statement the lighthouse made. Looking up the mountain, I could clearly see, even through darkness and gauzy cloud, the flicker of the tower-top and its pulsing banks of black smoke.

A light that would carry for miles.

It would draw eyes first; those of taxi drivers, shift-workers and late-night revellers. And then, slowly and one by one, it would draw bodies from beds, coats onto backs and boots onto feet before, eventually, boats onto the water between there and here.

49

I was on my second night in the Hospital Centro do Funchal when my doctors finally relented, and allowed me a walk.

I knew where I was headed. Beyond my window was a little garden fringing an ambulance turning circle. I'd been staring enviously at the benches down there for hour after empty hour, waiting for Clay's phone to charge again and imagining the sounds and smells of the city.

I'd come off monitoring that morning after a raft of readings, only some of which involved my dislocated shoulder and head wound, seemed to please medical staff. Despite my exhaustion, sleep had been hard to come by since the night at the lighthouse. Each time I closed my eyes, flickering footage of Vinny's distorted shape replayed itself, or images of Leo falling from the cupola, or Clay's skull, salt-preserved tendons pulled tight across its lower jaw, or the toughened leather of his innards and the key that had been stowed inside.

My increasingly shallow breathing woke me, and I lay sweating in bed, trying to regain some composure as panic thrashed and pulled. If it wasn't the anxiety, it was my arm throbbing in its too-tight sling, or the stitches flaring in my eyebrow, or the pain that inexplicably coursed through my legs when I lay still for too long.

Alex had been with me for the afternoon; gifted me a charging cable, fresh bananas, orange juice and a melting strawberry ice cream. And she'd brought me up to date with what she knew, starting with Mike, who was under police surveillance in a private hospital, she said. 'He's got an armed guard, the officer told me. He's almost fully recovered. They'll be transferring him to a cell tomorrow.'

'What about Leo?'

Her forehead creased at that. 'They won't say. I got the impression . . . ' she faltered.

'What?'

She shrugged, removed her glasses to breathe on the lenses. 'Got a sense that they didn't have him in custody.'

'He was alive,' I said, 'when I left him on the rocks up there.'

'Like I say, just an impression, but if I had to guess, I'd say they haven't found him yet.'

Alex left when visiting hours were over, and I returned to Clay's phone, sifting his photos for further clues. Once I'd forwarded what I could to my own number, I took the device with me and walked my wheeled drip along bleached corridors towards the lifts, wearing a pair of white slippers and pyjamas under a backless polyester smock, seeking my first fresh air for fifty hours. At ground-floor reception, I accidentally caught myself reflected in the glass of the patient café windows and nearly fell. I looked unrecognisable; cowed and staggering, some sort of lunatic scarecrow.

Outside, three concrete benches sat empty in the evening sun beneath a row of ornamental palms. I settled myself, drank the air, and returned my attention to Clay's phone, this time finally opening the hundred or so unread messages to see whether I might find further leads among them.

And I saw something that made my blood chill.

Towards the top of the unread list was a three-word message from an unknown number.

Two of those words were my name.

It said: Tess Macfarlane, remember?

I stared. My mind, still foggy with shock and medication, couldn't find purchase. Had Clay been discussing me with someone? Impossible, I'd never heard of him until a few days ago. The message was the second of two. Fingers trembling, I checked the other.

It said: call me when you've got a min

I gawped into the evening light, my mind reaching hopelessly for something beyond its grasp.

These were my two short messages to Lukas. Steven Clay had been carrying Lukas Larsen's phone.

Across from me, glittering with the afternoon's rain, deep beds of foliage hung heavy with orange flowers, and on the street beyond the ambulance entrance – I must have passed semi-conscious through those gates, I guessed, two nights ago – noisy tourists made their way down the hill into town. Short-sleeved shirts, pale legs and open-toed sandals, sunburnt noses, summer dresses.

I was sitting there, cradling Clay's phone in stunned silence, when my last visitor arrived.

The bearded man with the camera crossed the asphalt towards my seat. The man whose presence had marked the start of all this – the one who'd followed me on the bus and sought me out on the station platform at Poplar. No camera this time, but the same guy. Which meant he'd been the one I'd seen outside the market the morning we'd sailed on the *Auk*. He'd followed me out here from London.

I had nothing left in me. Every sinew had been strained to breaking since I'd last seen him. All I could do was tighten inside as the fear and confusion rose. Operating on muscle-memory alone, I hit record on the phone's voice memo function and looked for cameras. A brief hope that the hospital's CCTV was working buoyed me, but my visitor chose the next bench along, the one out of range. Clever. I got a good look at him. Cream chinos, white socks and deck shoes, a pale-blue shirt and a thick, greying beard. He was tall and slim, lithe with quickly moving brown eyes.

'Tess Macfarlane?'

It was the first time I'd heard him talk. He had a dry, measured voice. British cop, I guessed. He was smarter and leaner than I'd first thought; a lively intelligence in his posture and expression.

I saw no point in lying so I nodded confirmation, still

stunned, and turned the phone towards him. A few moments of silence passed. Two taxis drifted by, windows down, music playing. In the end I said, 'And you are?'

He took a deep and deliberate breath, gaze measuring the space around us, and said, 'I'm Steven Clay.'

50

I felt my thoughts physically shudder against the obstacle of his presence.

When I eventually got my voice working again, I managed a feeble 'No, you're not,' through a cracked throat. He waited, silently assessing me as my mental gears shifted. 'So if – who ... '

He checked the camera perched over the automatic doors to our backs, nothing more than a dart of the eyes, then he cleared his throat and spoke downwards into his beard. Even if we were caught on film, it'd be nothing more than a grainy shot of his back. There'd be no evidence we'd conversed. I followed suit and we talked quietly, looking for all the world as if we were ignoring each other. 'The dead man out on Navigaceo,' he said, 'is my friend. Lukas Larsen.'

Lukas hadn't gone off-grid. Though – perhaps he had; dead on a beach five hundred kilometres from Africa was certainly that. I scratched at my stitches. 'I don't understand.'

'I met him back when I was working in Tunisia. Lukas had been out there shooting material for some mad documentary or other. Crazy guy, difficult to like, but against my better judgement, a friendship developed. I'm glad it did. I ended up sharing my suspicions about Seawild. Asked if he was interested in helping.'

'And he was.'

Clay nodded. 'So Lukas started investigating.'

'Mineral smuggling,' I said. He'd been in Morocco before the Seawild trip, not after. 'Gold ore coming through the Ilhas to Madeira.'

He threw a glance my way. 'Impressive,' he said, and gave me a sad smile. 'If you know about it, you won't be safe, you know. Lukas is dead and I've had to vanish.'

He'd done a fine job of leaving his life behind, I thought. 'Leo tried to buy me,' I told him. 'Did the same happen to you, that night on Deserta Grande?'

Clay fell silent for a moment, preparing his words with the care of a man who'd waited two years to tell his story. 'I talked Vinny into lending me his card. Must be nearly three years ago now, I managed to access Bodin's offices in Paris, found the paperwork relating to the Ilhas activity: the shipping route, collection and transfer arrangements and a money trail. I stole his lighthouse key,' he said. 'Then, when the Ilhas expedition came up, I took it. Good opportunity to get closer to Navigaceo and find out more. I recommended Lukas to them. But with his key gone, I knew Leo would be coming for me. Each night Lukas and I waited up for him. We had a hidden camera ready to capture the meeting, and a

Covid cover story. Lukas did his disappearing act, then slept rough on the island, waiting for Bodin. The night he eventually came, I'd given Lukas all the material he'd need in case anything went wrong; Vinny's ID card, the key – typical Lukas, the madman wanted to swallow it to be double sure it wasn't recovered – and he had access to my files, everything to finish the investigation. And we'd figured out a plan. If Bodin took me elsewhere, Lukas was to follow at a distance and film the encounter.' Clay pushed thin fingers through a tangle of beard. 'So we were ready when Bodin came to make whatever offer he had in mind. He took me out to a Seawild boat in the bay. Lukas followed at a distance, rowing after us. Bodin led me up to the cockpit. He began talking money.'

I knew that particular speech, or a variation on it. 'Then what?'

'I guess Lukas messed up. Not the lightest on his feet. He slipped on the ladder. Bodin heard, went crashing out of the cockpit door, furious. The two of them fought and Lukas fell from a height, smashed his head hard on the lower deck as he landed.' Clay pinched the bridge of his nose, wincing at the force of the memories. 'Lots of blood. Bodin was raging. I've never been so scared, he had this steel crew-knife with a folding blade and he drove it into Lukas's chest. Just rolled him into the water. I tried to escape, but he got me too.'

He paused, ran a hand self-consciously along his lower left side. I waited, rewatching the images, vivid and chaotic, in my mind. Leo Bodin's words made sense now. Up at the lighthouse I'd asked him if he'd used the knife to kill Clay. He'd replied, *and his partner*. I'd been so shot through with terror since, I hadn't stopped to think about that reply.

'I don't remember much after that,' Clay continued. 'I knew my wound was deep, I was in shock and I went overboard. I'm still not sure whether I fell or pretended to. Desperate moments, thrashing around. I managed to disappear in the darkness. I thought at first the cold water would help with the bleeding ...' he nodded to himself, chewing his lower lip, drawing a lungful of air through his nose. 'That time in the water, Jesus.'

'But you were rescued?'

'Totally by chance. A fishing boat caught a circling shark and some bright spark wondered what had attracted its attention. They pulled me from the water. So,' he said, raising his chin to indicate the building behind us, 'I was here for a couple of days, maybe more, mostly unconscious. They stitched me up. Soon as I could, I escaped. Just walked right out of these doors and started a new life. I've been terrified Bodin might find out and come after me,' he said, rolling his shoulders, 'so I've made sure to keep my staff access to the Seawild servers. The minute anything goes online, I know about it.'

'You saw the job advert and my invitation to interview.'

He nodded. 'And there was a press release announcing your company. I was in the UK. I tracked you down.'

'Photographed me in Canning Town.'

'You'd think I might be better at sneaking around after two years of practice.'

'I have Lukas's phone,' I said, holding it up. 'It's packed with evidence. If you let me interview you — anonymously, of course, we can disguise your voice — I can try and expose this whole thing.' I broke off, slowing my breathing to quell the tightness in my chest.

Clay gave a grim smile. 'I've been looking for someone who can help tell the story. Someone with enough ... I don't know, guile, determination. Someone with integrity.'

Integrity. The word made me curdle. 'Not me, then.'

Clay raised his eyebrows, mildly taken aback. 'What makes you say that? I think you'd be perfect.'

Back on the ward, I found my own phone had fully recharged.

I stowed the contact number Steven Clay had given me so we could arrange to meet, then I recorded a voice memo. Four minutes, direct and honest, phone close to my chin and voice low.

Ten years of carrying my shame everywhere I went. It needed to end. It was all there in the Reddit threads anyway — combine the correct items of dark speculation and you'd arrive at the truth, just like Leo Bodin had. When his boss had insisted on a filmmaker following the site visit, he must have been furious. Once he'd recovered, though, Leo had begun looking for someone he could easily buy. Someone guilty. Someone responsible for the death of their former collaborator.

It was time to set down the burden.

'DCI Rafiq,' I said into my voice memo, 'this is Tess Macfarlane. I'm in hospital in Madeira. I'm sorry I've missed our interview. But there's something I want to tell you in advance of a rescheduled meeting.'

And with that, I took a shaky breath and I admitted everything.

I was washed out and weary afterwards. Forcing myself onwards, I attached the file to an email and sent it through to DCI Rafiq. The audio you have here includes details I didn't go into when I was first spoken to ten years ago, I wrote. I was ashamed. I know now that I should have been more honest with investigating officers, but I was young and frightened. I can speak more about this when I return to the UK.

The politician was no longer in the cabinet or indeed the public eye. I wondered whether this made things easier or harder. I watched the message go until it was out of drafts and into sent. No going back now.

I might have imagined it, but for a moment or two, the pain eased slightly.

Epilogue

Brixton, an early October day.

I'd been at the police station, a concrete block at an intersection opposite a concert venue, for three hours.

DCI Rafiq turned out to be a small woman with piercing eyes who conducted herself with smiling efficiency. I knew when she laid her belongings out on the table – a notebook and pen, tissues, cherry menthol chewing gum – and then adjusted them to ensure neatness, that I was dealing with a woman for whom orderly precision was paramount. She wore her hair in a bob so severe she recalled a thirties flapper girl, and liberally applied hand sanitiser each time she had cause to touch the table. This laser-focused rigour had been applied to everything I'd told her. She'd stop me with a smile, glistening index finger raised to the ceiling, each time she wanted further clarity. 'Question,' she'd say, halting me in my tracks.

I'd gone over the incident with the minister's special advisor. ('Question,' she'd said, before demanding a full description of the man and woman, as well as the precise location of the restaurant.) I'd taken her through the second meeting and the exchange of money – 'Question' – and we'd gone over the night in Saltfleet four times. 'If you don't mind, Ms Macfarlane,' she'd say each time I concluded my story, 'I'd like to – ah – rewind.' And each time she'd give herself a little smile, pleased at her capacity for pun.

Eventually, she was satisfied. Rafiq collected together her items singly, replacing them in the same pockets from which they'd emerged, then sanitised her hands, delicate fingers intertwining with the neat speed of a doctor's. I was desperate just to lay my head on the pillow of my crossed arms and catch up on sleep, but my left was in a sling and my stitched-up eyebrow itched fiercely.

Besides, I wasn't done. 'I've something else I'd like to discuss with you,' I said, seizing my chance. 'An unrelated matter.'

DCI Rafiq didn't bother herself with the ritual of the tissues and chewing gum this time. She perched on the edge of her chair and checked her watch – a tiny gold thing with twelve polished stones, one at each hour – before gathering her hands together in her lap. 'OK,' she said. 'Go on.'

This was the moment of truth; as important as any pitch event or job interview. If I got this right, I could follow the subsequent police investigation, strengthen credibility, deepen drama and deliver justice. 'I've just come back from Madeira,' I said. 'I was out there filming for an environmental foundation called Seawild.'

Rafiq nodded at my arm. 'And things got messy?'

'They did,' I said. 'I'm making a documentary about it.' I cleared my throat. 'I want to alert you to some discoveries we've made in the course of putting it together.'

Rafiq shifted in her chair, moved back from the edge. Less perching now, and more sitting, she offered me gum.

I accepted and we chewed together, companionably silent for a moment, before I said, 'You might want to write this down.'

Rafiq produced her notebook, snapped the elastic, and uncapped a gold pen. 'Shoot.'

A relief bordering on weightlessness was fizzing in me. 'OK,' I said, feeling unburdened – clean and free again, charged with curious energy. 'Have you ever heard the name Steven Clay?'

Acknowledgements

Big thanks to Cal Kenny, whose insightful advice and generous suggestions have been completely invaluable. My story is so much better for it, Cal. To agent-extraordinaire Kate Shaw, tireless enthusiast, cheerleader, connoisseur of all things narrative and canny spotter of implausibilities – again, this book has benefited immeasurably from your wise eye. Huge thanks go to Zoe Caroll and Donna Hillyer for their close reading and helpful feedback. Many thanks and much appreciation to two documentary filmmakers who generously gave their time to answer my questions: Chris Chapman and Mat Heywood. Both coped effortlessly with even my most ridiculous queries. I took a lot of notes. Once we hung up, fictionalising the filming process was my job; any errors in the story are of course mine and mine alone. Many thanks go to Ben Burville and Oscar Gudayol, research scientists and marine biology experts whose insights and descriptions of research trips were crucial, and to Stuart Humphries for putting me in touch. We talked boats, camping, food, communication protocols, team dynamics, data-gathering, booze ... again I hold my hands up; any subsequent errors in the text are mine. Thanks to Arnaldo who, alongside the other crew on the *Santa Maria*, took myself and family out onto the waters around Madeira. We watched wildlife, ate cake, jumped from the deck into the ocean to swim and, on the way back to Funchal, got badly seasick. Arnaldo's stories of his expeditions to the Ilhas Desertas were just the tonic we needed as we tried to keep the cake down. Arnaldo – you made it into these pages! Many thanks to Eugenia Correia Pires for checking – and let's face it, more often than not completely overhauling – my Portuguese, and to Emilio Fox Castiñeiras for his help. A shout-out to the artists – they have no idea they've helped but I'm indebted nevertheless – who soundtracked the world of this story, speeding my return visits. All I had to do was put a pair of headphones on, press play, and I was there. The Navigaceo chapters: Paul Leonard Morgan's score for *The Boston Strangler*, Amine Bouhafa's *Animalia*, and for when it got darker, Steph Copeland's scores for *Outpost* and *The Oak Room*. The California Chapters: Stuart Earl's music for *Gold Digger* and Lesley Barber's *The Moth Diaries*. Thanks to all the booksellers, bloggers and readers who've enthused about my previous novel, *The Second Stranger*. And, closer to home, thanks and love as always to Mum and Dad for bringing up three boys in a house full of paperbacks, and to my wonderful family and friends. Most of all, thanks to Jo and Aggie, for making all the work worth it. 3 29 50 Adventure awaits.

A final word on the setting. The Ilhas Desertas are real – Chao, Deserta Grande and Bugio exist and can be visited. However, if you're intent on seeing Navigaceo, I'm afraid you'll be disappointed. Upon completion of this book, it mysteriously sank beneath the ocean waves, taking the lighthouse with it, never to be seen again.

HAVE YOU READ

Remie Yorke has one shift left at the Mackinnon
Hotel in the remote Scottish Highlands before
she leaves for good. Then Storm Ezra hits.

As temperatures plummet and phone lines go down,
an injured man stumbles inside. PC Don Gaines was
in a terrible accident on the mountain road. The only
other survivor: the prisoner his team was transporting.

When a second stranger arrives, Remie reluctantly lets
him in from the blizzard. He, too, is hurt. He claims
to be a police officer. His name is also Don Gaines.

Someone is lying and, with no means of escape,
Remie must work out who. If the cold doesn't kill
her, one of these men will get there first . . .

'If there is a finer crime debut this year, it
will be a surprise' *DAILY MAIL*

'Clever and bold' **LISA GARDNER**

1

Since the night was going to be a milestone for me, I poured a plastic cup of wine and took a moment to watch the storm.

It was a quarter to seven, I'd handed my notice in twenty-eight days before and I was about to begin my final ever night shift. Leaning against the snow-covered balustrade of my balcony, I was dreaming of the following morning; of packing my meagre belongings, driving my Nissan into Aberdeen, and dropping it off with its eBay buyer. Car sold and cash in my purse, I'd be at the airport for my 11 a.m. flight. A hop to Heathrow, on to Madrid for my connection, and then heading out to Santiago, Chile, by tomorrow evening. *Tomorrow evening.*

The wild possibility of this unburdening, an escape I'd dreamt about for fifteen years, made me dizzy. I sipped the wine. Thinking like this felt something close to lunacy. *My final night at the Mackinnon.* It was a chance to say goodbye to my old self; to escape abroad a new person. I might not have box-ticked the other expectations associated with one's early thirties – I had no career any more, no permanent home, no children and, after tonight, no job – but my final shift felt like it was the start of something. Live-in staff all got attic rooms with balconies, but the remainder of my colleagues had started their leave so I was the third floor's only occupant. It seemed somehow appropriate, given the course of my life so far, that I was marking this special occasion alone, a woman in a winter jacket and beanie hugging herself against the snow.

The wine was the cheap stuff that came in minibar bottles, but it tasted good enough as I cast my eyes across the Mackinnon's grounds for what might be the final time. On summer days my quarters had a beautiful view, but early February was different. Loch Alder was frozen over the colour of Lakeland slate, a silent presence between our two mountains: Bray Crag on its far shore, snow-covered and wild, and, rising above the hotel on this side of the water, the peak of Farigaig. Tonight it was nothing but a silhouette on tracing paper, though the tangle of its steeply forested flanks came all the way down to the hotel's perimeter fence. The sight of the loch, the mountains and the distant prison had become my life this last eighteen months. Most of HMP Porterfell was hidden by the pine plantations of Farigaig's foothills, but the lights of the exercise yard were bright points haloed by driven snow, and the north watchtower was visible. I raised my cup in its direction in a final silent toast to Cameron and sipped, relishing the warmth of the alcohol.

I was still staring at the place when I heard the klaxon's wail.

The sound was a familiar one. When trouble flared at Porterfell, as it often did, overcrowded and outmoded as it was, the first signs were always barking sirens and strobing lights. I felt a sudden rush of memory. I had to set my cup down and steady my pulse with big, deep breaths. A year ago, a Porterfell riot had killed my brother. The same wail of sirens had marked its beginning. Back then there'd been the flicker of fire against distant brickwork, a windborne roar of crowd noise and a night punctuated by the droning engines of security vehicles going back and forth along the mountain road. I hadn't known Cameron was dead at first. Next of kin weren't informed until later. In a fifty-five-inmate brawl, it's apparently impossible to finger the murderer of a particular individual and, because unlawful killing was hard to prove, Cameron's passing was recorded as misadventure. So now my brother was gone, his death remained unpunished and I'd been stranded here, a thirty-three-year-old woman working night shift at a highland hotel, studying the place that had penned him in.

I watched the distant buildings, listening to the moan of the siren. Through curtains of snowfall across the loch, I could see the intermittent flicker of lights. The prison gates were open now. Three distant vehicles were pulling out; a car either side of a van that looked like a high-security transport. That might explain the disturbance. An inmate leaving, violence erupting as desperate scores were settled. The siren continued its looping moan and I watched the convoy turn left towards us, setting off along the mountain road in our direction. I thought about the drivers, thought about my two-hour drive tomorrow. I'd have the advantage of daylight, but we'd had plenty of snow in the last week and plunging temperatures had hardened the drifts into sculptured pack. The wind had changed direction, polar air from Siberia triggering red weather warnings, and Storm Ezra had arrived, bringing new snow and turning the old into ice. Driving on a night like this was surely an act of desperation.

By morning it would be clearer, though. It would be. Everything ended in twelve hours. At 7 a.m., Mitchell, my colleague on the day shift, would park his Fiat 500 outside reception and trot across the tarmac in his brogues and hotel livery. In the course of a fifteen-minute handover I'd bring him up to date for the last time, put my bags in the boot of my car and go.

I retreated back into my room, shutting the noise out and warming myself at the electric heater before shucking off my coat and dressing for work. I tugged a vest on beneath my blouse for extra warmth, pulled on my trouser-suit and buttoned my jacket before removing my badge. *Remie Yorke*, it said. Underneath, the gold plastic was embossed with, *How can I help?* The Mackinnon's last two guests knew me by name so I left the badge on my bedside table next to the few items I hadn't yet packed: my pro-turf hockey ball, my Eyewitness guide to Chile and Easter Island, my Spanish phrasebook. Locking my door behind me, I followed the third-floor corridor past empty rooms to the old service stairs. The prison sirens must have stopped; the only sound as I descended was the old hotel creaking in the rising wind.

The Mackinnon is sixteen guest rooms in a grand Victorian lodge tucked into a dell at the bottom of Farigaig, steep-roofed, with turret windows and two spires rising above squat chimneys. Guests adore the conical clocktower, the formal gardens and the wisteria across the entrance. When I'd arrived to take up the post of night manager eighteen months ago, all I'd needed was somewhere to work that was driving-distance from my brother Cameron's prison cell. To find instead this loch-side curio had been a sliver of good news in a world of bad. At first, I'd cherished the hope I might actually fall in love with the place – my flat in Leith had always felt temporary and, even though I didn't visit often, I'd felt cast adrift when Mum and Dad split up and the Northumberland family home was sold – and those first few months at the Mackinnon really had seemed like they might be a fresh start. I'd almost allowed myself to relax. Once or twice, I'd even woken in the morning refreshed. Then there'd been the violence at the prison and Cameron's death. After that, I'd been forced to return to my previous existence of permanent, exhausted vigilance. But those days were nearly over now. In sixteen hours, I'd be on a plane.